SECRETS OF THE TOMBS

THE
PHOENIX
CODE

Helen Moss

Illustrated by Leo Hartas

Orion
Children's Books

First published in Great Britain in 2014
by Orion Children's Books
a division of the Orion Publishing Group Ltd
Orion House
5 Upper St Martin's Lane
London WC2H 9EA
An Hachette UK company

1 3 5 7 9 10 8 6 4 2

The Orion Publishing Group's policy is to use papers that are natural,
renewable and recyclable products and made from wood grown in sustainable
forests. The logging and manufacturing processes are expected to conform to
the environmental regulations of the country of origin.

A catalogue record for this book is
available from the British Library.

ISBN 978 1 4440 1039 8

Printed in Great Britain by Clays Ltd, St Ives plc

www.orionbooks.co.uk

SECRETS OF THE TOMBS

THE
PHOENIX
CODE

For Mac

TOMB

AS RYAN FLINT craned to see past the crush of archaeologists and workmen crammed into the narrow tunnel, he could barely breathe for excitement.

It wasn't every day you got to look inside a chamber that had not been entered by a single soul for more than three thousand years.

At least, not by a *living* soul.

For this was the final resting place of Pharaoh Smenkhkare.

The tomb, hewn deep into a remote crevasse in the limestone cliffs of the Valley of the Kings, had been discovered only a few months earlier. Stone by stone, rock by rock, the rubble had been cleared from the ancient complex of burial chambers.

So far there'd been no sign of the magnificent treasures that would surely have been buried with the pharaoh.

But everyone was certain that in *this* chamber they would finally hit the jackpot.

And now Dr Pete McNeil was about to slide back the huge boulder that blocked the entrance.

Spotlights flooded the scene with glaring white light, as though they were on a film set. Ryan tried to ignore the sweat sticking his T-shirt to his back. Here, deep inside the cliff, the tunnel was hotter than the Sahara in a heat wave. The rattling fan rigged up in the corner barely stirred the stewed air.

He felt a nudge in his side and looked down to see his mother bouncing up and down to get a better view, waving her voice recorder in the air, her short blonde hair hedgehog-spiked by dust and sweat.

'This is history in the making,' Mum whispered, grinning like a kid about to see Father Christmas coming down the chimney. 'It'll be the biggest discovery since the tomb of Tutankhamun. Bigger, even,' she added, 'if we find the Benben Stone!' She lowered her voice a few notches and sort of *breathed* the words *Benben Stone*.

Ryan had noticed that everyone did that.

Yes, he thought. *It's all about the Benben!*

He'd hardly heard about anything else since Mum had landed the job of reporting on the story. Every day he'd come home from school to their end-of-terrace house in Manchester to find her sitting at the kitchen table with her laptop, a pile of library books and a pot of coffee. The Benben, she told him, was one of the most important relics of all time, up there with the Ark of the Covenant and the Holy Grail. According to Ancient Egyptian myths, it was the Stone of Creation, a mysterious pyramid-shaped mound that had emerged from the primordial ocean at the dawn of time.

It was so sacred that the pyramids were built in its image.

But the Benben Stone had been lost from history thousands of years ago. Some said it was smuggled to a secret location in France by the Knights Templar, others that the Queen of Sheba's son took it to Ethiopia. There was even a theory that aliens had transported it to a far-off galaxy.

Many had searched, but it had never been found.

Until now, it seemed!

A single roll of papyrus had been discovered, tucked inside Smenkhkare's coffin. It claimed that the long-lost Benben Stone had lain hidden *right here in this very tomb* for thousands of years.

All at once, the boulder teetered and rolled to one side with a sound of rock grating over rock. Everyone jostled and surged forwards. Professor Lydia McNeil, the excavation leader, turned round and held up a hand to the team. 'Steady! We need to record everything exactly as we find it . . .' She gestured to a barrel-shaped man who was jugwgling an oversized camera and flashlights. 'No one is to touch anything until Max has taken all the photographs we need.'

The local Egyptian diggers had all backed away, as if unwilling to witness what lay inside, and had been swallowed up by the black shadows beyond the reach of the spotlights. Ryan found himself near the front of the group, so close to the entrance that he could feel the stale, clammy air exuding from the chamber like the breath of a sleeping animal.

Despite the heat in the tunnel, a feverish chill made the hairs on his arms stand on end. Legend had it that the Benben

Stone possessed certain *powers*. It could grant eternal life and the knowledge of secret magic. It could also be deployed as a terrible weapon, mightier than any nuclear bomb, toppling mountains and triggering earthquakes, floods and volcanic eruptions.

Ryan had even read stories on the internet that Hitler and the Nazis had searched for the Benben during World War Two, eager to harness its destructive force against their enemies. *No wonder this excavation is all so hush-hush,* he thought. Security guards were posted outside the tomb and down in the valley. Adolf Hitler might be long gone, but there were plenty of others out there who would stop at nothing to get their hands on an object of such mythical power . . .

One of the spotlights flickered off and then on again.

'Er, aren't we meant to recite special rituals to protect us from all the curses that guard the stone?' Ryan muttered nervously to nobody in particular.

'My parents do know what they're doing!'

Ryan looked down. The voice came from the McNeils' teenage daughter, who was kneeling near his feet, busily scraping fragments of rock away from the entrance with a trowel.

Ryan wasn't so sure. Hadn't any of these people heard about the death and misfortune that had befallen Howard Carter and his team after they'd opened Tutankhamun's tomb? The Mummy's Curse, it had been called. And that was *without* a mountain-toppling weapons-grade artefact in the mix. *Surely there are more than enough earthquakes and weapons of mass destruction in the world already*, he thought. *Maybe we should leave the Benben Stone in peace. Wedge that boulder back in place and walk away . . .*

Before he could stop himself, Ryan lunged forward, propelled by a sudden urge to grab Professor McNeil and pull her back from the chamber.

He was blocked by the bulky figure of Dr Rachel Meadows, one of the senior archaeologists. 'Watch your step!' she said sharply, gripping Ryan by the elbow. Then she smiled and patted his arm. 'Do be careful, dear. It can be very uneven underfoot in these tunnels.'

As he was swept along into the chamber, Ryan reached up and felt for the tiny St Christopher pendant that hung from a chain under his T-shirt.

He didn't realize he'd squeezed his eyes closed until he forced them open.

Blinking in the dim light, he saw shadowy wall paintings shrouded by a thick layer of dust. He saw a rubble-strewn floor and a low ceiling that had been washed a beautiful midnight blue and studded with gold five-pointed stars.

But there were no magnificent treasures.

No mystical stone.

The chamber was empty.

2

OFFERING

RYAN LEFT THE others in the tunnel to argue over their next move and trudged back up the passageway to the main burial chamber.

He took a bottle of water from the icebox and perched on the edge of the sarcophagus in the centre of the room. He probably wouldn't have sat on it if Pharaoh Smenkhkare had still been inside – it would have felt disrespectful somehow – but the mummy had been removed and shipped off to Cairo for scientific tests.

Ryan took a deep breath. The air was a little fresher up here. The crowded tunnel had been smellier than the school changing room after rugby practice. There was some natural light too. Sunlight sliced in through the entrance and splashed a long diamond shape across the stone floor.

Picking up his pencil and sketchbook, Ryan turned to the copy of the wall painting he'd been working on earlier. The scene, which covered most of the north wall, showed Pharaoh Smenkhkare kneeling, making an offering to Osiris, Lord of the Underworld. Jackal-headed Anubis rested a hand on Smenkhkare's shoulder, while falcon-headed Horus, and Hathor – with her headdress of cow horns – looked on from either side. The colours sang out as if they'd been painted yesterday; bright white, brick red, coal black and sky blue against the pale ochre background.

But it was the object on Smenkhkare's offering tray that really commanded attention: a gleaming black pyramid, its peak gilded with gold, and beams of golden light radiating from it in all directions. It was an image of the Benben Stone, of course.

Ryan dragged his eyes away and tried to focus on drawing Anubis's long pointed ears, but they kept going wrong. They were starting to look more like devil's horns.

He groaned and rubbed out the troublesome ears again.

He felt a bit embarrassed about getting so spooked down in the tunnel. He hoped nobody had noticed. *It was just my imagination playing tricks*, he told himself. *That's what happens when you hang around in old tombs all day*. Or maybe it was jetlag. He and Mum had only flown out to Egypt to join the dig two days ago, and his brain still hadn't quite caught up with his body.

After all, he told himself, the Benben was only a *stone*.

A black, triangular stone.

In fact, if you ignored the rays of light shooting out of it, it looked as if Smenkhkare were offering Osiris a giant triangle of dark chocolate Toblerone, with a scrap of its foil wrapper still sticking to the top. The Lord of the Underworld was eyeing it suspiciously. Ryan flicked to a new page and quickly sketched a comic-book version of the scene, adding captions. *Not for me, thanks, Smenkers, old chap!* Osiris was saying. *I'm allergic to chocolate*. Ryan was so absorbed in adding a speech bubble for Anubis (*This way to the afterlife, Sir. Have you made a reservation?*) that he jumped when he heard voices behind him. The team were coming up from the tunnel, plucking at their sticky shirts and wiping their foreheads with the backs of their arms.

Dr Rachel Meadows sank her wide khaki-trousered bottom into a folding chair and blew her springy brown curls off her face with a handheld fan. 'I just don't get it,' she sighed into the whir of the blades. 'I thought you said the stone would be in the third chamber along the passage.'

Professor McNeil ground the heels of her hands into her temples, smearing streaks of dust over her dark skin like war paint.

'We'll find it, love,' Pete McNeil said, patting his wife's shoulder.

Dr Meadows smiled at them both. 'Yes, Pete's right. Of course we will.'

Ryan stopped listening as he noticed the McNeils' daughter sit down cross-legged on the floor and lean against the side of the sarcophagus.

It was, he thought, difficult *not* to notice Cleo McNeil. Although it wasn't for her fashion sense! She was sporting a shapeless green T-shirt that looked like it belonged to her dad (*Glasgow University Table Tennis Team, 1992*), a pair of beige hiking shorts with zip-off legs and an old leather belt with a bum bag containing her own personal trowel.

Who, he wondered, *has their own personal trowel?*

But somehow she still managed to look stunning. Her glossy black hair was tied in a loose plait that reached almost to the hem of her T-shirt. Her fringe fell across wide-set green eyes. Ryan could almost hear his friends at school: *She's way out of your league, mate!*

They'd be right, of course. If she ditched the bum bag, stood sideways and wore a long white dress – and possibly a set of cow horns on her head – Cleo could have stepped straight out of the wall painting: the reincarnation of the goddess Hathor. Not that she was doing anything very goddess-y right now. She was scowling at a bundle of photocopied papers by the light of her head torch, muttering to herself like someone you'd move to avoid if they sat down next to you on a bus.

'Hey, Mum!' she called. 'Dad! I think I know . . .'

But Lydia McNeil was still locked in a debate with Rachel Meadows, and Pete McNeil was trying to calm Max, the photographer, who was complaining about the spotlights, which were all starting to flicker alarmingly.

'I can't work like this!' Max grumbled in a gruff Yorkshire accent. 'Is this a dig or a disco?'

Ryan slid down from the sarcophagus. 'What's the problem?' he asked.

Cleo glanced up at him with a doubtful look. They'd only spoken once before but Ryan could tell she'd already filed him under *Hopeless Halfwit.* It wasn't really his fault. When they'd met at the welcome dinner the McNeils had organized at their apartment, and she'd introduced herself as Cleopatra, he'd naturally assumed she was joking. 'Good one!' he'd laughed. 'And I'm Tutankhamun!'

She'd stared at him with those ridiculously green eyes.

'You know? Cleopatra, Queen of the Nile, had a thing with Julius Caesar? I'm King Tut . . . the boy pharaoh . . .' Ryan had ploughed on, even though he knew that the second you started *explaining* a joke you might as well tattoo L for Loser on your forehead and go home.

She hadn't even blinked.

Ryan had suddenly clapped his hand over his mouth. 'Oh, no! Don't tell me your name really *is* Cleopatra?'

'Cleo for short,' she'd said stiffly, before turning away to discuss the finer points of Ancient Egyptian funerary texts with someone who wasn't a total idiot.

And she was staring at him again now, blinding him with her head torch.

Ryan reached out to switch it off but he missed and jabbed her between the eyes instead.

Cleo flinched, but finally she spoke.

'I think I know where the Benben Stone is hidden,' she said.

3

CONFESSION

CLEO SUSPECTED THAT the tall, gangly boy with the disorganized sand-coloured hair was making fun of her again.

All she knew about him was that he was the son of Julie Flint. Julie was the only journalist allowed on the dig, because she was working for the Danny Farr Foundation which was funding the project. On the one occasion they'd met, he'd laughed at her name. And now he'd nearly taken her eye out. But if she didn't get *someone* to listen to her theory she was going to explode.

'We've been looking for the Benben Stone in the wrong place,' she said.

The boy raked his floppy fringe off his forehead and twitched one eyebrow. 'How do you make that out?' He looked as if he were about to burst out laughing at her again.

I should have kept quiet, Cleo thought. *He might actually be psychologically unstable.* But she'd started now . . .

'Do you know what the Smenkhkare Confession is?' she asked.

'Du-uh!' the boy groaned, rolling his eyes, even though, as far as Cleo could see, it was a perfectly reasonable question. 'Of course!' he said. 'It's why we're all here. Here, in this tomb, I mean, not like why we're all here on the planet and what's the meaning of life and stuff.' He grinned, as if expecting her to say something, but Cleo didn't know what he was talking about so she just waited. 'It's the papyrus document that was found in the sarcophagus,' the boy said eventually. 'The one where Smenkhkare 'fesses up to stealing the Benben Stone.'

Cleo nodded. At last the boy was making some sense! 'That's right. Smenkhkare admitted that he stole the Benben Stone from the Mansion of the Phoenix in the Great Sun Temple of Heliopolis and installed it in his tomb as an offering to Osiris. He hoped it would gain him passage to the afterlife. He must have needed something extremely impressive to make up for the fact that he had committed, in the words of his Confession, a *double abomination.*'

The boy frowned. 'A double abomination?'

'It means a terrible crime,' Cleo explained.

'I know what *abomination* means!' the boy laughed. 'But what on earth did Old Smenkers do that was so bad?'

Old Smenkers? Cleo thought. It was hardly the way to talk about a pharaoh, but she let it go. 'We don't know. The

Confession doesn't give any details. It just says this double abomination was *so terrible that it would never be spoken of in the Two Lands*. That means Upper and Lower Egypt,' she added.

'So it's a mystery,' the boy said.

'*Everything* about Smenkhkare is a mystery,' Cleo agreed. 'We think he reigned for a short time just before Tutankhamun came to power but that's not certain. One theory even says he was Queen Nefertiti in disguise. That reminds me,' she interrupted herself. 'What *is* your name? I'm guessing it's not *really* Tutankhamun?'

The boy shrugged and pulled a face. 'Yeah, sorry, that was my lame attempt at a joke. I'm Ryan.'

Cleo held out her hand. Ryan stared at it as if he'd never come across this form of social greeting before, before giving it an over-hearty shake.

'Anyway, that's why this tomb is so important,' Cleo said, getting back to the point. 'As well as the Benben Stone and the other grave goods we should find here, we hope for all sorts of clues about Smenkhkare's life. Then we can fill in a missing chapter of history.'

'The Abominable Pharaoh and his Secret Life of Crime,' Ryan said. 'Wow! That would make quite a headline.' He grinned. 'And *you're* the one who discovered the tomb in the first place, aren't you? Mum told me the story: how you nosedived in through the roof and landed on this thing.' He slapped his palms on the sarcophagus they were leaning against. 'Solid granite. That must've hurt a bit.'

Cleo winced at the memory. 'More than a *bit,* actually!'

'I heard you broke your ankle?'

'It wasn't a break,' Cleo corrected. 'It was a complex

bimalleolar fracture. Plus significant ligament damage, obviously.'

'*Obviously!*' Ryan repeated. For some reason he seemed to think this was funny. 'This may be a silly question,' he said, 'but how come you were wandering around in the Valley of the Kings by yourself in the first place?'

It was, Cleo thought, a perfectly logical question. 'I'd been helping Mum and Dad excavate a small mortuary temple in the valley. I went out for a walk along the ridge to get some air and I ended up going farther than I meant to . . .'

'You mean you got lost?'

'Of course not!' Cleo protested, although she *had* strayed a little way from the path and got her bearings *slightly* muddled. Her voice tailed off as she remembered how the earth had given way beneath her feet. Eyes screwed tight, hands clamped over her head, she'd hurtled headlong down a landslide of loose rock, rolling and tumbling until, at last, her feet slammed into a hard surface . . .

'And you crash-landed right into this tomb?' the boy prompted.

Cleo nodded. 'I didn't know where I was at first. I couldn't see through the clouds of dust. My ankle was in agony. I tried to sit up. Some rubble fell away from the stone block I was lying on and suddenly I was looking at two cartouches carved into the surface. That's when I knew it was no ordinary stone block!' Cleo stood up, reached across the smooth dark granite of the sarcophagus lid and traced the sequences of hieroglyphs enclosed within their oval frames with her finger. 'I knew straight away, of course, that the mummy inside this sarcophagus had to be a pharaoh!'

'How?' Ryan asked scrambling to his feet.

'These oval cartouches were only used to frame the names of royalty,' Cleo explained. She pointed to the top one. 'This is the throne name. The sedge and the bee symbols mean *King of Upper and Lower Egypt.* The lower one, with the duck and the sun symbols, is the birth name: Smenkhkare-Djeserkheperu.'

Cleo repeated the names under her breath, reliving the incredible moment she'd first set eyes on them. The pain in her ankle had vanished; the excitement had been stronger than any anaesthetic. She'd always dreamed of making a Highly Significant Discovery – and they didn't get any more significant than this!

Ryan waved a hand in front of her face. 'Hello! Earth calling Cleo!'

Cleo snapped back to the present. 'After I was rescued we opened the sarcophagus. The mummified body was clutching a scroll of papyrus . . .'

'The Confession!' Ryan whistled. 'That's so cool!'

Cleo pulled a printout from her folder and opened it, using the sarcophagus as a table. 'This is a photograph of the original.' The unfurled papyrus looked like a large strip of bark, the fibres dark brown with age and ragged along one edge. She ran her eyes over the neat, close-packed lines of hieroglyphs. 'I've been going through this again and . . .'

'Whoa!' Ryan laughed, throwing up his hands as if a runaway horse had just charged into the tomb. 'Let me just stop you there. You mean you can read *hieroglyphics?*'

'You mean you *can't?*'

'Er, no-o!' Ryan laughed. 'I must have been off school that day!'

'It'd take more than a day to . . .' Cleo began. Then she realized that Ryan was joking. Now she thought about it, they probably didn't study ancient writing systems in ordinary schools. Not that she'd ever been to school herself. She'd always travelled the world with her parents, and they were her teachers too. If an extra subject took her interest – like Russian philosophy or nanotechnology – there were always online university courses she could sign up for. 'Sorry,' she said. 'I spend a lot of time around Egyptologists. I suppose we're not exactly . . .'

'Normal?' Ryan interrupted with a grin.

'I was going to say *typical*.' Cleo glanced across at her mum, who was pacing up and down talking to herself, mostly in Ancient Egyptian, and her dad, who was dangling from a stepladder trying to fix the spotlight, his red hair glowing like copper wire under its faltering beam, while at the same time happily discussing infectious skin diseases in mummies with his graduate student, Alex Shawcross.

Maybe Ryan has a point, Cleo thought. But she had to correct him on one thing. 'It's hiero*glyphs*, not hiero*glyphics*,' she explained. '*Hieroglyphic* is the adjective, not the noun.'

Ryan slapped himself on the forehead. 'Of *course*! I feel such a *fool*!'

Cleo smiled, pleased to have been of help.

'So,' Ryan said, offering her his bottle of water, 'where do you think Old Smenkers really hid this magic stone then?'

Cleo untied her old cotton scarf, tipped water onto it and dabbed the back of her neck. 'We all thought that the Benben Stone would be in the third chamber because Smenkhkare says *it resides in the third house on the journey to the realm of Osiris*. The realm of Osiris was the Underworld, of course, which the Egyptians believed to be in the west, where the sun sets.'

Ryan nodded. 'And the main passage runs due west . . .'

'Which means the Benben *should* be in the third "house" along it.' Cleo pointed to a symbol on the papyrus. It was composed of three small lines. 'This is the sign for *third*. But if you look carefully, there's a crease mark that could be obscuring another faint line . . .'

'Using my razor-sharp powers of deduction,' Ryan cut in, leaning over her shoulder and squinting at the symbol, 'if *three* little lines means *third,* then *four* little lines must mean *fourth*?'

'Exactly!' Talking to Ryan hadn't been such a bad idea after all, Cleo thought. He was a good listener. And she was starting to realize that he wasn't really laughing at her *all* the time; his mouth just naturally turned up at one corner as if he'd thought of something amusing. 'So that's my theory,' she said. 'I think Smenkhkare's telling us the Benben is in the *fourth* chamber along.'

'Just one teeny-tiny problem,' Ryan said, pinching a centimetre of air between his thumb and forefinger. 'The passageway comes to a dead end right after that third chamber. It's solid rock.'

'A-ha! What if it's a false wall?' Cleo's words came out much louder than she'd intended, but she was so excited to be getting to the crux of her theory at last that she couldn't help it. 'It could have been built to fool tomb robbers.'

Ryan nodded slowly. 'That makes sense!'

Cleo beamed at him. 'It does, doesn't it?' But her excitement suddenly evaporated. It was one thing to convince a newcomer like Ryan, but how was she going to get anyone else to take her idea seriously? 'The trouble is,' she sighed, 'my parents are certain the passage stops in a dead end because that's what it shows on the builder's plan for Nakhti's tomb . . .'

'Hang on!' Ryan laughed, holding his head in his hands. 'I was keeping up when it was just a case of counting to four. But you've lost me now. Who's Nakhti?'

Cleo shook out her scarf and knotted it back around her neck as she began to explain. 'This tomb was *recycled*. It wasn't originally built for Smenkhkare.' She ran her fingers over the cartouches on the sarcophagus again. 'You can see the damage where the name of the original owner has been hacked away and Smenkhkare's names have been carved over the top.'

Cleo passed Ryan another sheet of paper from her folder. 'This is a copy of the plan for the tomb of a high official called Nakhti. It was found on an ostracon – a flat shard of limestone – in a tomb-builders' workshop not far from here. It's in the British Museum in London now. When Mum saw it, she was convinced that it was the plan for *this* tomb. The dates were right and the layout matched – a main burial chamber and a steep passage heading west with *three* small chambers off to the side. Then a dead end.' Cleo tucked a lock of hair behind her ear and looked up at Ryan. 'But what if this *isn't* Nakhti's tomb and it wasn't built to this plan . . .'

'In that case there *could* be a fourth chamber . . .' Suddenly Ryan broke off. He stabbed his finger at the heading on the tomb plan.

'Do those hieroglyphs say *Nakhti*?'

Cleo nodded. 'Yes. It means *Strong One*.'

'That's not all it means,' Ryan said. 'It also means your theory's right. This definitely *wasn't* Nakhti's tomb.'

4

DEAD END

'**HOW COULD YOU** possibly *know* this isn't Nakhti's tomb?' Cleo demanded, her dark eyebrows bunching up as if she suspected this might be another joke she didn't get.

But Ryan *wasn't* joking this time. 'From this,' he said, pointing up at the offering scene on the wall. 'I've been staring at it most of the morning.' He picked up his sketchbook from the sarcophagus and held it out to show Cleo.

She flipped over the pages. 'Did *you* do these?' she asked. 'They're brilliant!'

Ryan was so surprised at the compliment he almost blushed. Cleo didn't strike him as the kind of girl who gave them out free with boxes of cereal. She was smiling at him too – another rare sight! But when she *did* smile, her face was suddenly hijacked by an astonishingly wide grin that showed a gap in her front teeth and transformed her from regal goddess to ordinary-if-stunningly-beautiful girl.

Well, *almost* ordinary!

But the heart-warming moment didn't last long. Cleo had already turned the page and was glowering at his comic-book sketch complete with speech bubbles. '*Not for me, thanks, Smenkers, old chap! I'm allergic to chocolate*,' she read out loud. She frowned again. 'That *obviously* can't be what Osiris is saying. Chocolate wasn't even known outside South America before the fifteenth century AD. You're thousands of years out!'

'Oh, is that a fact?' Ryan asked innocently, as if he'd really believed that the Ancient Egyptians went around scoffing Cadbury's Creme Eggs and Mars Bars. He took his sketchbook back. 'The point is,' he said, 'the original painting has been altered. The Benben Stone has been painted over the top of a pile of fruit and meat on that offering tray. And that cobra on Smenkhkare's forehead has been added later too; the pigments are a slightly different shade.'

Cleo nodded. 'The cobra is called the *uraeus*. It's a symbol of royalty. It's been added to make the original owner look like a pharaoh, but that doesn't prove it wasn't Nakhti.'

'No, but *this* does.' Ryan pointed up at the two cartouches above the pharaoh's head. 'The original name has been painted out and Smenkhkare's written over it just like on the sarcophagus. But they've not made a very good job of it. You can still see the old lettering through the paint.' He paused to enjoy the look of surprise on Cleo's face. 'I've no idea what it says but it's not the same as the name on your tomb plan.'

'Let me see!' Cleo stretched up on tiptoe but it was no use. The cartouches were way above her head.

Ryan grinned. Since his fifteenth birthday his body had embarked on a record-breaking growth spurt. Being almost six foot tall all of a sudden was weird. He saw a lot of dandruff and bald patches these days, and low doorways were a constant hazard, but it did have its advantages. 'Piggy back?' he offered, scooping Cleo up before she had time to say no.

'You're right!' she gasped somewhere near his left ear. 'This says Nakht*min* not Nakh*ti*. I can't believe no one noticed this before.'

'Who's Nakhtmin?' Ryan groaned, bracing himself for another lecture on Ancient Egyptian tomb building.

'Never heard of him!' Cleo laughed. 'But it doesn't matter. If it's not Nakhti's tomb, we're definitely working off the wrong plan, which means my theory could be right – there *could* be a fourth chamber beyond that wall! I've got to show this to Mum and Dad.'

Ryan wheeled round. Most of the team were gathered at the other end of the chamber but the McNeils, it appeared, had gone outside with some of the workmen to sort out the problem with the generator that powered the spotlights.

'They could be ages,' Cleo groaned. 'We'll have to wait . . .'

Ryan had a better idea. 'Why don't we just check out that dead end ourselves?'

Cleo shook her head. 'I have to discuss it with Mum and Dad first . . .'

Ryan laughed. 'We're only going to *look at a wall*. Surely you don't need parental permission for that?'

'It's not because they're my *parents*,' Cleo said. 'It's because they're the excavation leaders. *Everyone* has to clear their activities on the site with them. There are certain procedures and protocols that archaeologists follow, you know. It's not all just running around and grabbing treasure like in those Indiana Jones movies!'

Ryan shrugged, bouncing Cleo up and down in the process. 'Suit yourself!'

There was a pause as they both gazed at the Nakhtmin cartouches. 'Oh, well, never mind!' Ryan said at last. 'We can always just wait until tomorrow. Good thing we're not *that* bothered about investigating your brilliant theory . . .'

Cleo made a sort of strangled noise. 'It's no good! I *can't* wait! I'm sure a quick look won't hurt.'

Ryan grinned. Maybe Cleopatra McNeil wasn't quite as uptight as she made out! He felt a tap on his shoulder. 'Just one thing,' Cleo said. 'Can you put me down now?'

As he stooped to let Cleo slide to the ground Ryan suddenly hesitated, remembering his near-freak-out in the tunnel. What was he doing helping Cleo to find the Benben? Hadn't he decided it would be better if the dangerous stone *stayed* lost and out of trouble? But Cleo was already heading off down the tunnel. He couldn't back out now; she'd definitely write him off as a total no-hoper! And anyway, she was right – surely a quick look at a wall couldn't hurt . . .

Ryan and Cleo stood side by side staring at the wall at the end of the tunnel.

The spotlights hanging from the ceiling cast long shadow-puppet shadows across the ancient stonework. It must once have been covered in painted scenes. Now only a few flaking patches of coloured plaster remained. It looked, Ryan thought, like a map of an unknown world, with pink and green marbled islands floating in an ochre sea of limestone. He glanced over at Cleo who was crouching down, directing her head torch into the corner. She was running her fingers over the stone and poking and prodding at it. 'I thought we were just *looking*,' he said.

Cleo carried on without turning round.

Well, in that case . . . Ryan thought.

He began knocking on the wall, and listening to the sound, the way he'd seen people do on TV when they were searching for secret passages. Nothing happened – unless you counted skinning his knuckles. 'Maybe it really is a dead end,' he said at last.

Cleo sighed. 'It *can't* be . . .'

Her words were cut off by an electrical fizzle and a pop, followed by total darkness and the bitter smell of burned wire.

'Spotlight must have fused,' Ryan muttered. 'Hang on.' He fished his torch out of his jeans pocket, clicked it on and turned it towards Cleo.

But Cleo wasn't there.

Even the light of her head torch had vanished.

Ryan felt his way along the wall. As he reached the spot where Cleo had been standing, his hand suddenly slid off the solid stone and met nothing but air.

A small doorway had opened up in the stone.

Cleo's theory was right. The wall *wasn't* a dead end!

Ryan ducked through the gap. His heart pounding against his ribcage, he swept his torch shakily from side to side, looking

23

for Cleo. He seemed to have entered a long passageway. He was about to take another step when he staggered backwards, his legs suddenly as weak as pâpier maché. Strange figures were lunging at him out of the darkness, part-human, part-animal: serpents, crocodiles, vultures, baboons, unknown things with horns and tails . . .

I knew disturbing the Benben Stone wasn't a good idea!

Then he heard Cleo scream for help.

What have they done with her? Ryan forced himself to peer into the gloom, and laughed out loud with relief. The freakish figures weren't real! It was just the torch beam moving over the wall paintings that'd made them come to life and appear to leap out at him.

This is some serious jetlag! he thought as he took another step.

'No! Stop!' Cleo yelled.

Ryan's heart almost jumped out of his mouth again.

Cleo's voice was coming from somewhere near his feet.

He looked down at the ground. Or, rather, where the ground *should* have been. A large square hole extended almost the full width of the passage. His torch beam picked out arms and legs and a face with wide, terrified green eyes. Cleo was wedged only about a metre down. She must have toppled in backwards and somehow managed to brace her hands and feet against the sides of the shaft to arrest her fall.

'I thought you were about to pitch in on top of me,' Cleo gulped, 'and then we'd both end up at the bottom of this pit.'

Ryan inched back from the hole. 'It's OK,' he said, doing his best to sound in control. 'Just don't move.'

'I wasn't planning to!' Cleo snapped.

'I'll go for help.'

'*No!* Don't go!' Raw panic pulsed through Cleo's voice. 'I'm starting to slip.'

Ryan knelt and peered over the edge. He couldn't see the bottom but maybe the hole was just for show and wasn't really all that deep. He felt around for a loose stone and dropped it over the side. It plummeted past Cleo's left foot and disappeared. There was a bone-chillingly long silence before a dull thud sounded from the depths.

'Two and a half seconds,' Cleo said in a tiny voice. 'That's thirty metres.'

Ryan wished he'd left the stone where it was.

'Not accounting for the time it takes for the sound to travel back up from the bottom, obviously,' Cleo added.

'Yeah, *obviously*!' Ryan muttered sarcastically. Mathematical precision wasn't exactly their number-one problem right now.

'I'm not sure . . . I can hold on . . . much longer,' Cleo panted.

5

CURSES

RYAN KNEW HE had to act fast.

He crawled round the ledge that surrounded the hole, then dropped to his knees and positioned his torch on the ground so that it shone down into the void. Then he lay flat on his stomach and wormed forward until his head and shoulders were hanging over the edge. He wiped his palms down the sides of his T-shirt and reached down towards Cleo's hand. Her fingers were splayed out on the rock, her knuckles white with strain. He took a deep breath and clenched his teeth.

Not letting himself think about what would happen if he got this wrong, Ryan clamped his hand around Cleo's wrist, moving so fast she didn't have time to react and lose her fragile hold.

Yes! He'd got her!

Ryan puffed out his cheeks with relief. 'OK?' he asked.

'OK,' Cleo whispered. But suddenly her legs slumped downwards. 'My feet are slipping!' she screamed.

Ryan snatched at Cleo's left wrist, just as her feet slid down the wall. His shoulders wrenched in their sockets as he took all her weight. 'I've got you,' he muttered through clenched teeth to the top of her head. Cleo was hanging straight down now, with only Ryan's grip on her wrists between her and thirty metres of gravity.

Ryan tried to pull Cleo up. His muscles screamed for mercy. There was no way he could lift her all the way out at this angle. He tried a different approach: lowering her a little, then jerking her upwards, letting go of her wrist with his right hand and sliding his hand down to her elbow. He repeated the process with his left hand. At last Cleo was able to clasp his forearms, doubling the strength of the hold.

'I should be able to swing my legs up and get my feet braced on the wall again now,' she gasped. 'Are you ready?'

This must be how it feels to be a trapeze artist, Ryan thought. The only difference was that circuses provided safety nets . . . 'Ready,' he said, tensing to take the strain again.

Cleo arched her back and kicked out, pushing off from the wall with one foot then the other, as if running up it in a crazy parkour move. Ryan heaved with every gram of strength he had left. Just when he thought they'd lost it, he forced himself to let go with one hand, grabbed Cleo under the armpit and flipped her round to face him so she could get her elbows over the edge of the hole. With a flurry of frantic scrambling and hauling, she was over the side at last. They both flopped down on the cold stone, gulping for air like a pair of landed fish.

'Are you all right?' Ryan gasped at last.

Cleo sat up. She flexed her feet and stretched her arms. 'Bruised coccyx, grazed elbows, minor contusions to the knees,' she listed, like a paramedic reporting a patient's injuries. 'I thought you'd dislocated my shoulder but it seems to have re-engaged.' She looked back at the false wall, shaking her head in disbelief. 'I must have released a hidden catch of some kind. The door just sprang open and I fell through. I was turning back to call you when I lost my footing and stumbled backwards into the hole.' She removed her head torch, which had broken during the fall, and wound the strap around her fingers for a few moments. 'Thanks for getting me out of there.'

'Don't mention it,' Ryan said, although his heart was still galloping. 'All in a day's work.'

Cleo smiled. 'No, I mean it. You were great. Much better than I . . .' She broke off and pressed her lips together.

'. . . better than you thought I'd be?' Ryan said, finishing the sentence for her. He grinned. 'Thanks for the vote of confidence!' He held out a hand and pulled Cleo to her feet. 'We'll soon get back up top. Hang on to me if you're feeling wobbly.'

But Cleo shrugged his hand away. 'We can't stop now! This is brilliant. The false wall, the secret door, the deadfall . . .'

'Deadfall?' Ryan asked.

Cleo nodded. 'Some tombs had a ceremonial well, but this hole *has* to be a booby trap. Why else would it be placed right behind the wall where you can't see it until it's too late?' Her green eyes sparkled in Ryan's torch beam. 'I knew my theory was right! There's definitely *something* worth protecting down here.'

She scrambled to her feet, grabbed Ryan's torch and headed off down the passage. 'These wall paintings are superb, aren't they?' she said over her shoulder. 'They're scenes from the *Book of Amduat*. They show the sun god Ra's journey through the Underworld during the twelve hours of the night . . .'

Ryan followed. He didn't have much choice since Cleo had taken his torch. And she was clearly a girl on a mission. A girl with a theory, in fact! But he checked very carefully before every step. He'd watched enough action films to know all about booby traps: spikes shooting up from the ground, vats of boiling oil, avalanches of flesh-eating beetles . . .

Cleo stopped so suddenly he barrelled into her.

'Curses!' she cried.

'Sorry, but if you will stop without any warning . . .'

'It's not that! I meant there are curses written here.' Cleo directed the torch at the wall. 'Actually,' she said, 'the correct term is *threat formulae*, not *curses*.'

She ran her finger along lines of hieroglyphs, the paint faded to the rusty brown of dried blood. '*He who dares violate the resting place of the sacred stone shall have no heir,*' she translated. '*His name shall be forgotten in the Two Lands. Ra shall smite him. He shall be devoured by the lion, the crocodile, the serpent, the scorpion and the hippopotamus.*' She looked up and smiled. 'Oh, yes, this is all perfect!'

Ryan leaned down for a closer look. The writing was surrounded by a horde of ferocious-looking beasts. He eyed the gnashing teeth and tearing claws and dripping fangs. For once he was lost for words. What could you say to a girl whose idea of perfect was being devoured by an assortment of wild animals?

'We must be close to the fourth chamber,' Cleo breathed. 'Keep looking.'

Ryan wasn't really sure what he was looking for, or even if he wanted to find it, but he tried to be helpful by running his hand over the wall. Almost immediately his fingertips caught on a groove in the stone, inside the gaping jaws of a fat crocodile with a malicious gleam in its eye. He curled his fingers and tugged. The stone gave a little. He laughed in amazement. 'I think there's some kind of sunken handle here!'

But Cleo snatched his hand away. 'We can't just *open* it!'

Ryan couldn't believe he'd almost made such a stupid mistake. 'No, of course not!' he said, shrinking back from the wall. 'It's probably booby-trapped.'

Cleo peered down as if expecting another hole to open up under her feet. Then she looked along the wall and up at the roof of the passage. 'Yes, that's possible, but I can't see anything.'

'And,' Ryan went on, still a little nervous, 'don't we need to say a load of spells to ward off all those dire curses?'

Cleo rolled her eyes. 'I'm not worried about the *curses*. They're just irrational beliefs with no basis in a scientific framework of cause and effect . . .'

Ryan wished he could be so sure. The curses gave him the major creeps. But he didn't want to look *irrational*. 'So what's the problem then?'

'We can't just go barging into an unopened chamber. Like

I said, there are procedures and protocols. It's all got to be recorded properly.' Cleo hesitated, tugging at her bottom lip with her teeth. 'Actually, we've already broken loads of rules by coming through the wall ... I think I got a bit carried away.'

Ryan grinned. 'Yeah, and falling down holes without requesting permission in advance is *definitely* not correct procedure.'

'Cleo? Ryan? Are you two down there?'

They both whipped around at the sound of Professor McNeil's voice echoing down the tunnel. It was followed by footsteps and more voices.

'We're down here!' Cleo yelled back. 'Watch out for the deadfall!'

Ryan hadn't *meant* to squeeze the hidden handle, but Professor McNeil's shout had made him jump and grip the wall. He stared in wonder as a jagged crack formed in the rock, zigzagging through the throng of painted beasts. Slowly, it began to creak open.

Without a word, Cleo shone the torch through the widening gap.

A tower-shaped plinth, richly decorated with bands of blue and red and gold, stood in the centre of the chamber. As if in a trance, Ryan stepped inside. Slowly, he raised his eyes to the jewel-encrusted platform on the top of the plinth. Despite his fears, he couldn't wait to see the mystical Benben Stone ...

He heard Rachel Meadows' voice booming outside in the tunnel. 'Have you found something?'

But Ryan could only shake his head in dismay.

It was Cleo who spoke first. 'It's gone!' she murmured.

6

SECRETS

CLEO CLIMBED THE steps from Smenkhkare's tomb.

Shading her eyes against the midday sun, she stood and gazed out over the parched limestone crags and valleys below, glowing bronze and gold beneath a sky of deepest blue.

The Valley of the Kings – the great Necropolis, or City of the Dead, where generations of New Kingdom pharaohs lay buried – was one of her favourite places in the world. The rock was honeycombed with tombs – the *Houses of Millions of Years*, as the Ancient Egyptians had called them – bursting with timeless secrets waiting to be discovered. But today the stark landscape felt as hostile as the scorched surface of a planet that orbited too close to the sun to support human life.

Today the City of the Dead was refusing to give up its secrets.

Cleo sighed. She'd been so sure the Benben Stone would be in the fourth chamber, and the jewelled platform had clearly been designed to hold a sacred relic – yet it had been empty.

Where was the Benben Stone?

And it wasn't just the Benben that was missing, of course. New Kingdom pharaohs equipped their tombs with precious goods to meet their every need in the afterlife: gilded thrones, jewelled collars, rare perfumes, chariots, shrines, carved *shabti* figurines of servants who would come to life and carry on their work in the Underworld.

And yet they'd found nothing in Smenkhkare's tomb.

Not even a single canopic jar.

Cleo stared down into the mouth of the big blue plastic chute that began near her feet and snaked down the cliff. The rubble, extracted from the tomb and passed up in buckets along a chain of workers, was tipped into the chute to collect in a huge spoil pile at the bottom.

Rubble! she thought despairingly. *That's all we've found.*

Smenkhkare's life and death remained as much a mystery as ever. Stirring herself at last, Cleo trailed after the rest of the team as they picked their way down the steep cliff path in single file, clinging onto the rope handrail pegged to the rock face until they reached the bed of the *wadi,* or valley, and headed for their pick-up trucks parked under a stand of gnarled acacia trees.

There was little else to see except a guards' hut and a flat-roofed concrete building, which served as the storeroom for any artefacts found on the surrounding digs. The steel door glinted in the sunlight as a group of Italian archaeologists checked in box after box of finds with the store guards. They were excavating a complex of workers' tombs beyond the next ridge and had clearly had a successful morning.

Unlike us, Cleo thought, as she helped pack the equipment into the back of the trucks. No one was talking much. But after two false alarms in one morning, Cleo knew they were all starting to think the same thing: had tomb robbers ransacked Smenkhkare's tomb and taken everything?

Everything – including the Benben Stone.

They were almost ready to leave when the gloomy silence was broken by Rashid, one of the drivers, cursing loudly at his truck as he kicked the tyre. 'Flat! Again!' he yelled in Arabic.

While Cleo's dad and Ryan helped change the wheel, her mum set up a camp stool and sat, hunch-shouldered, recording notes in her excavation log. Not that there was much to write up. She managed a weak smile as Rachel passed her a cup of tea from her flask. Julie Flint looked on, muttering into her voice recorder.

Cleo drifted away and sat down in the ribbon of shade cast by a crumbling mud brick wall. She could hear Dad whistling *Always Look on the Bright Side of Life* as he worked. It didn't help. Dad always saved the cheeriest tunes for the worst situations. *If he starts on* Oh, What a Beautiful Morning, she thought, *then we're really in trouble.* Little bursts of light sparked in front of her eyes. *Low blood pressure,* she diagnosed. *Must be delayed shock from the deadfall.* She rested her forehead on her knees and watched a procession of ants marching past.

Almost dozing off, Cleo's head snapped up at the sound of a door slamming. A young man climbed down from an old blue van parked nearby. He opened the back and hoisted out a crate of bottled water. *Must be a delivery for the guards,* she thought. But, to her surprise, the man put down the crate and strode across the sandy track towards her. 'You with the McNeils?' he asked, lounging against the wall and pushing his mirrored sunglasses up onto his head. His white shirt was spotless, his chinos crisply pressed. A lemony smell of aftershave wafted around him.

Cleo was suddenly aware that the sweat patches under her arms weren't doing her any favours. She clamped her elbows to her sides. 'I'm their daughter, actually.'

'So you're the famous Cleopatra, the one who . . .' the water-delivery man hooked his fingers into air quotes, '*stumbled on* Smenkhkare's tomb.'

Cleo frowned up at him, wondering how he knew so much about her.

He smiled. His teeth were even whiter than his shirt. 'I'm afraid I'm rather obsessed with Ancient Egypt.' He swept his arms wide. 'The tombs, the temples, the history . . . it's just magnificent. Sorry. I haven't introduced myself. Nathan Quirke.'

Cleo let him shake her hand.

'I'm a big fan of your parents' work . . .' Quirke paused as one of the tomb guards walked by and eyed the blue van. 'Water delivery!' Quirke shouted, pointing at the crate. 'I'll bring it over in a minute, mate!' Then he turned back to Cleo. 'Security's a bit tight, isn't it?'

Cleo nodded. 'It's to keep the media out.'

Quirke raised his eyebrows. 'A lot of interest, is there?'

'It's one of the conditions of our funding,' Cleo said, not wanting to give too much away. 'Our sponsors' own reporter has exclusive rights to cover the dig.'

'Fair enough,' Quirke said. 'Mind if I sit down in the shade here for a minute?' He settled down before Cleo could reply. 'Hey, is that a genuine, pre-war William Hunt and Sons trowel you've got there?'

Cleo smiled as she took the trowel from its leather holster and turned it over in her palm. It was her most treasured possession. The wooden handle was worn smooth and felt as if it had been made for her hand. She showed Quirke the initials stamped into the steel: *E. M. B.* 'It belonged to my grandmother,' she explained. 'Eveline May Bell. She was famous for her excavations in China.'

'Awesome! May I look?' Quirke ran his thumb along the honed blade of the trowel. 'Actually, my main interest is the Egyptian creation myths,' he said. 'Particularly the Bennu Bird. *It skimmed over the primordial waters,*' he intoned in a dramatic voice, '*until it alighted upon the Benben Stone at the dawn of time and let out a cry that told of what would be and what would not be.* Did you know the Bennu Bird is the origin of the phoenix legend?'

'Of course,' Cleo said, sliding the trowel back into its holster. 'The Bennu Bird started out as a humble wagtail in earlier Pyramid Texts but by the New Kingdom it's usually shown as a grey heron with a crest of two long feathers. Then the Ancient Greeks wove it into their legend of the fiery phoenix, the fabled bird that lives for hundreds of years and is reborn from its own ashes.'

'Many others cultures have a similar mythical bird,' Quirke said. He began counting them on his fingers. 'There's the Chinese fenghuang, the Russian firebird, the Persian simurg . . .'

'Don't forget the Native American thunderbird,' Cleo

put in. She was about to come up with some more examples when she broke off, distracted by an explosion of laughter from near the pick-up trucks. She looked across to see the diggers and drivers all sitting in a circle under the acacia trees with Ryan. At first she thought they were playing a game, but then she saw his sketchbook open on his lap. Ryan was drawing their portraits. Nearby Dad was plastering on factor thirty suncream; his pale freckled skin had been designed for the cloudy skies of Aberdeen, not the blazing Egyptian sun.

'Talking of the Benben Stone,' Quirke said, 'have you found it yet?'

Cleo snapped back to the conversation. 'Not yet,' she sighed. 'Worst luck!'

'A-ha!' Quirke made a gun of his fingers and mimed shooting from his hip. 'So you confirm that you *are* searching for the Benben Stone in Smenkhkare's tomb?'

'No!' Cleo spluttered. 'No! I didn't say we're actually *looking* for it.' Her heart went into freefall. Like everyone else involved in the dig, she'd signed an agreement not to reveal that the Smenkhkare Confession had even *mentioned* the Benben Stone. If word got out, they'd be swamped by reporters from all over the world and crowds of people clamouring to see the famous Benben with its fabulous mystical powers.

Cleo tried her best to backtrack. 'I just meant it *would* be a lucky find . . . if we *were* looking for it . . . which we're not.'

Quirke got to his feet. 'Well, nice talking to you, Cleopatra,' he said, brushing dust from his trousers. 'Most informative.'

Maybe it's not so bad, Cleo told herself. *He probably won't tell anyone . . .*

'That's quite a scoop you've given me!'

'Scoop?' Cleo echoed. 'What do you mean?'

Quirke gestured towards the water van. 'I'm afraid I may have used a *tiny* bit of subterfuge. Lucky for me, the driver was happy to take a break for a couple of hours while I borrowed his van.' He winked and rubbed his thumb and fingers together to hint that a bribe had been involved. Then he whisked a card from his shirt pocket and flashed it in Cleo's direction.

NATHAN QUIRKE, THE MYSTICAL TIMES, Cleo read. She had to close her eyes and wait for a lurch of nausea to pass. This was like plummeting backwards into the deadfall again. Only much, much worse. 'You're a *journalist*?' she stammered.

Quirke raised his hands as if in surrender. 'Afraid so!'

Cleo clenched her fists so tightly her nails dug into her palms.

She'd walked right into Quirke's trap!

Quirke flipped his sunglasses back over his eyes and slid the card back into his pocket. 'Just one more question . . .'

'No comment!' Cleo snapped.

Cleo didn't say a word on the journey home.

She stared out of the window as Dad drove the pick-up down the winding road. The rocky foothills, scattered with ancient ruins, slowly gave way to neat fields of sugar cane and wheat, and dark groves of mango and orange as they drew closer to the River Nile. As they approached the village of Gezira, the traffic increased: donkey carts, motorbikes and tourist coaches all competed for space. Plush concrete villas and hotels stood side by side with mud-brick houses. The bright pinks and yellows of bougainvillea and mimosa scrambled over elegant verandas and ramshackle lean-tos alike.

As soon as the truck pulled up outside the small old-fashioned apartment building where they were renting a flat on the second floor, Cleo jumped out and hurried inside. She called a quick greeting of *salaam alaikum* to Mr Mansour, the caretaker, who was watching a cowboy film with his grandson in his room on the ground floor, scooted across the tiled hall and ran up the elegant curved staircase.

She shut her bedroom door and slumped against it.

Nathan Quirke was probably sitting at his computer already, typing up his article: DAUGHTER REVEALS MCNEIL TEAM IN TOP-SECRET SEARCH FOR MAGIC STONE. How long would it be, she wondered, before crowds of reporters and tourists started swarming onto the site?

She tugged off her tool belt and threw herself down on her bed.

How could she have been so foolish? She'd studied degree-level courses in logical philosophy and neuropsychology, and yet she'd been hoodwinked by a smooth-talking journalist with a toothpaste-advert smile. Her brain functions must have been impaired by low blood pressure. But that was no excuse . . .

She pulled *Advanced Mathematics* from the bookshelf and tried to take her mind off her mistake by getting her teeth into a really complicated equation. But it was no good; she just couldn't focus. She threw the book down onto the handwoven rug next to the bed.

Through the paper-thin wall she could hear her parents arguing in the kitchen.

Mum's words were punctuated by the banging of pots and slamming of drawers as she prepared lunch. 'What if the Benben' – *smash!* – 'isn't in Smenkhkare's tomb?' *Crash!* 'If it turns out it's *not* here, I'll be a public laughing stock.'

'Don't worry. Hardly anyone knows we're even looking for the stone, remember,' Dad said reasonably. 'That's the advantage of the media blackout.' Cleo's entire body burned with guilt. She clamped her pillow over her head, trying to drown out the voices, but Mum was too loud. 'Thank goodness! After what happened in Peru' – *bash!* – 'I don't think my professional reputation could stand another disaster.'

Cleo couldn't bear it another moment. She darted out of her room and across the kitchen.

'Do you want some salad?' Mum called after her.

Dad was whistling *Here Comes the Sun* as he set the table.

'Not hungry!' Cleo mumbled as she headed for the stairs.

She was dashing out onto the street when a football whizzed towards her head. Instinctively she reached up and caught it.

'Hand baaaaaaall!' came a yell from somewhere behind a parked minibus.

Cleo dropped the ball as a pack of small Egyptian boys hurtled towards her. One of them kicked the ball to an older fair-haired boy. Cleo did a double take. It was Ryan! He headed the ball neatly between a eucalyptus tree and a No Entry sign.

'Gooooooaaaal!' shouted the little boys, mobbing him with high fives before running off after the ball.

Ryan laughed and turned to Cleo. 'I came to see if you wanted to go for a Coke or something. You looked like you needed cheering up.'

Cleo was about to say a polite *no thank you* – she definitely wasn't in the mood for being cheered up – when she heard herself saying, 'Thanks, that sounds like a good idea.'

Maybe she *was* in the mood for being cheered up after all.

7

CATASTROPHE

RYAN BOUGHT TWO cans of Coke at the counter inside the El-Masry Café at the end of the street and took them out to the table where Cleo was sitting under the chequered shade of a canopy of woven rushes.

He sank onto a dusty plastic chair and popped open his can. He took a swig. Pain shot across his forehead. He gasped. Then he grinned. 'I think there might be something in all those curses round that chamber. I stepped in a massive pile of donkey pooh on the way here and now I've got brain freeze!'

Cleo shook her head. 'They're *threat formulae*, not curses!' But then she smiled. 'I don't remember seeing that one though. *He shall be smitten by the mighty brain freeze of Ra!'*

Ryan laughed. A lot. In fact, he guffawed. OK, it wasn't *that* funny, but this was Cleo, and she'd actually made a joke. And she'd looked so tragic since the moment they'd clapped eyes on that empty plinth, this had to count as a major breakthrough. Still laughing, he felt something brush against his ankle. He looked down to see a little white cat. It mewed at him, showing off its needle-like teeth. Ryan shrank back in mock terror. *'He shall be devoured by the lion,'* he said. 'Yep, that threat formula is definitely out to get me!'

Cleo smiled again.

Ryan reached into his backpack, pulled out a crushed shortbread biscuit left over from the plane, and began to feed pieces to the cat. Now that Cleo had lightened up a bit, he couldn't resist teasing her. 'I saw the hunky water-delivery guy chatting you up earlier.'

Cleo stopped smiling. 'He wasn't a water-delivery man.'

Ryan took out the sketchpad and pencil he always carried with him and began to draw the cat, which had finished eating and set about cleaning its ginger-tipped ears. 'Oh, was it one of those Italian archaeologists, then?' He put on an exaggerated accent. *'Ciao, bellissima!'*

Cleo jiggled the straw in her can of Coke. She shook her head.

'What is this, Twenty Questions?' Ryan asked. 'You don't have to tell me if it's a secret love affair or something.'

'It was just some reporter,' she mumbled.

'But reporters aren't allowed—' Ryan began in surprise.

'You think I don't know that?' Cleo snapped.

'So what did he want?'

Cleo kept her eyes fixed on a flock of sparrows twittering over the crumbs of leftover baklava on the next table. 'Oh, nothing.'

Ryan put down his pencil and looked at her. She couldn't hold his gaze. *Cleopatra McNeil might be able to read hieroglyphs and calculate the velocity of a falling stone while hanging upside down in a hole*, he thought. *But she's a useless liar.* 'Nothing?' he asked.

There was a long pause. 'OK. I told him we were looking for the Benben Stone,' Cleo said in a voice that was barely more than a whisper.

Now Ryan got it! No wonder Cleo was so upset. She wasn't just disappointed they'd not found the stone. She'd given away confidential information; she was disappointed in herself too. He grimaced in sympathy. 'Oops!'

'Oops?' Cleo burst out. 'It's more than oops! It's a *catastrophe*!' She sank her chin in her hands. 'He's called Nathan Quirke. He started talking about the Bennu Bird, like he was all interested, and then just casually asked the question and the words slipped out before I realized what I'd said . . .'

'Hey, don't blame yourself,' Ryan said when Cleo finally paused for breath. 'He separated the weakest member of the herd and attacked you while you were down.'

Cleo glowered at him, her face as dark as thunderclouds. 'I am *not* weak and I'm *not* part of a herd.'

'Sorry, it's just a figure of speech,' Ryan laughed. 'And you *were* feeling weak. I saw you sitting by the wall with your head down. It's not surprising after that fall. I was about to come over and see if you were OK when all the workmen started asking me to draw them.' He turned his sketchbook round to show Cleo a page of pencil portraits.

'I wish you had,' Cleo said.

Ryan gulped a mouthful of Coke. 'I bet the sleazeball buttered you up with loads of compliments too?'

Cleo gave a grim nod. 'Yes, he did. He said my trowel was awesome.'

Ryan tried so hard not to laugh that Coke spurted out of his nose. Never mind flattering remarks about her hair or her smile or her eyes! Only Cleo could be bowled over by trowel talk. He had to hand it to Quirke – the man was a genius!

'It's not funny!' Cleo said. 'If he spreads the word, there'll be busloads of people wanting the Benben to do magic tricks. It'll be a circus, like when people used to buy tickets to mummy-unwrapping shows in Victorian times. And then if it turns out the Benben isn't even here, we'll look even more ridiculous . . .'

'I'm sure the fuss would soon die down,' Ryan said, wiping his face with a paper napkin. 'And there'll be loads of other digs.'

Cleo sighed. 'It's not that simple. After what happened in Peru . . .'

Ryan stopped mopping. 'Peru?'

'It's a long story.'

Ryan shrugged. 'I'm in no hurry. There's not much on Egyptian TV this afternoon anyway.'

Cleo spent a long time bending her straw into a tiny concertina. 'It was last summer,' she said at last. 'Mum was in charge of a major dig of a Mayan pyramid tomb in Peru. It's Mum who's the lead archaeologist really. My dad's a palaeopathologist. He's just interested in ancient diseases. Anyway, we found a hugely important artefact – a gold ceremonial cup for drinking the blood from human sacrifices.

It was taken straight to the local museum and locked in a safe.'
Cleo looked up from twisting the straw. 'But it disappeared.'

'Disappeared?' Ryan echoed. 'How?'

Cleo sighed. 'I don't know. There was an investigation. It seems there was a break-in at the museum. My parents were cleared of having anything to do with it, of course, but the media went into overdrive. They made out it could have been an inside job, or that we'd only *pretended* to find the Bloodthirsty Grail, as they called it, for the publicity. Mum lost her temper and told them where to go, which didn't help. They hounded her even more. That's why this dig is so important. It's a chance for Mum to prove herself again.'

Ryan had been about to get another drink but he changed his mind. The thought of a cup of human blood had put him off. 'What happened to the Bloodthirsty Grail?'

'It never showed up. Mum almost lost her job over it. It was almost impossible to find anyone to put money into this dig because of all the bad publicity from that one. Luckily the people at the Danny Farr Foundation came forward. The trouble is that Mum practically had to *guarantee* that the tomb would be full of treasure *and* the Benben Stone, just to get them to sponsor us. We were convinced the tomb had escaped being looted by tomb robbers.'

'Why were you so sure?' Ryan asked. 'Weren't most of the tombs ransacked years ago?'

Cleo nodded. 'Yes. But there were no signs that Smenkhkare's tomb had been broken into. It's hidden away in the cleft right at the top of the cliff, and the seal on the entrance, bearing the official symbol of the Guards of the Necropolis, was still perfectly intact.'

Ryan stroked the little cat, which had jumped up onto

his lap and fallen asleep. 'Maybe it was an inside job?' he suggested. 'One of the guards, who would have been able to reseal the entrance?'

'It did happen sometimes,' Cleo agreed.

'So the Benben Stone is probably long gone?' Ryan couldn't help thinking it might not be such a bad thing; at least it meant that no mystical fanatics or crazed tyrants would be able to get their hands on it, hoping it would grant them eternal life or blow up their enemies.

'I'm not sure . . .' Cleo murmured. 'It just doesn't look like the tomb's been ransacked. Tomb robbers usually only made off with the items of greatest value. They'd leave behind a trail of shattered pots and broken furniture. But Smenkhkare's tomb is completely bare . . .'

'Maybe they were just tidy looters?' Ryan suggested. Then he remembered something. 'Oh, but they did miss one thing.' He fished in his pocket and pulled out a small oval beetle fashioned from blue-green stone. About the size of a large egg, it felt smooth and cool in his palm as he held it out to show Cleo. 'I found this on the floor in the fourth chamber. My foot knocked into it. I stuck it in my pocket and forgot all about it when the others all came piling in behind us.'

Cleo took the beetle from his hand. 'It's a scarab amulet,' she said. 'A dung beetle.' She ran her finger across the wing cases. 'There's a little hole at the head end. The owner must have worn it on a lace round their neck. They were believed to protect the heart.'

'Could it have belonged to Smenkhkare?' Ryan asked.

'It's a bit plain for royalty. Maybe one of the funeral attendants . . .' Cleo turned the scarab over. 'They usually have an inscription on the base. Yes, here it is. *In honour of the coming to the throne* . . . Oh, it's a commemorative amulet to celebrate the coronation . . .'

'Like a Royal Wedding souvenir mug?' Ryan said. 'I've got one of those!'

'They were quite common . . .' Cleo fell silent. After a long moment she looked up from the scarab.

Ryan could tell from her face it wasn't good news.

'I think we've just *proved* that the tomb was looted in antiquity,' Cleo said. 'This was definitely dropped by one of the robbers.'

'How can you tell?' Ryan asked.

'The inscription says *the coming to the throne of King Usermaatre Setepenre.* That's the throne name of Rameses II.'

There was a pause. Ryan knew that Cleo was telling him something vital, but he had no idea what it was. 'And?' he prompted. 'That's important because . . .'

'Rameses II came to the throne fifty years *after* Smenkhkare died! Whoever dropped this entered the tomb long after it had been sealed up.'

'And they probably made off with the Benben . . .' Ryan broke off and threw his hands up to shield his eyes as a sleek white tourist coach rolled past and a beam of sunlight reflected from its tinted windows. 'Wow, that black glass really dazzles!' he groaned.

He was reaching under the table to retrieve the pencil he'd dropped – trying not to tip the cat off his knees – when Cleo jumped up from her chair.

'That can't be right!' she cried. 'There's no light! The Benben Stone *can't* have been in that fourth chamber.'

8

REVELATION

CLEO SANK BACK into her chair.

An idea was taking shape, her brain a ferment of electrical activity leaping across synapses from one neuron to another. The reflection from the coach windows . . . *that black glass really dazzles . . .*

Ryan emerged from under the table. He was clutching his fingers. 'What are you talking about?'

'Let me see your hand,' Cleo said. 'They can carry rabies, you know.'

Ryan looked blank. 'What?'

'Rabies,' Cleo repeated 'It's a serious zoonotic viral disease transmitted by bites from certain animals.'

Ryan erupted with laughter. 'The cat didn't bite me! You ran over my hand with your chair when you did that *I've-seen-the-light* routine. I don't know what zoonotic means, but I'm sure rabies isn't carried by *chairs*!' He held up his hand and examined the red mark across his knuckles. 'Maybe it's another of Smenkhkare's curses. *His right hand shall be crushed by the mighty chair leg of Cleopatra . . .* Lucky I'm left-handed!'

'I'm really sorry. It's just . . .'

'You've had one of your theories, haven't you?' Ryan cut in. 'I can tell. You've got that look in your eye!'

Cleo was flattered. 'Inspired, you mean?'

Ryan drained the last of his Coke. 'I was going to say *deranged*, actually . . .'

Cleo couldn't help grinning. She supposed she did tend to get a bit carried away when she had an idea. 'It was when that coach went by and the light off the windows got in your eyes.'

'Yeah, I've still got red squares stamped on the backs of my eyeballs.' Ryan blinked and rubbed his eyes. Cleo noticed for the first time that they were an unusual greyish blue, tiger-striped with amber.

Your retinas, not your eyeballs, she thought, but she decided to let it go. She had something more important to explain. 'You said *That black glass really dazzles.* That's what made me think of it. The Benben Stone would have dazzled too. It was made of gleaming black rock, possibly from a meteorite. And its tip was gilded with electrum . . .'

'Electrum?' Ryan asked. 'I thought it was gold.'

'Electrum's an alloy of silver and gold. It was even more valuable. It was also highly reflective. In ancient times the

Benben Stone was kept in a special open courtyard called the Mansion of the Phoenix in the Great Sun Temple in Heliopolis. It was positioned so that its peak reflected the first rays as the sun rose. It represented the dawn of time . . .'

Cleo waited a moment for Ryan to get her point, but he was absorbed in drawing a picture in his sketchbook of the Benben Stone with a magnificent fiery phoenix rising from the top, so she spelled it out. 'Why would Smenkhkare bury the stone deep underground in a chamber with no windows and no way for the light to get in at all? It would be completely useless.'

Ryan looked up from shading phoenix feathers. 'I get it. It'd be like buying a massive flat-screen TV and then not plugging it in.'

Cleo wasn't sure it was *quite* the same thing, but she was too excited about her new theory to quibble. 'Which means that maybe the stone wasn't really installed in the fourth chamber at all.' Cleo's words tumbled over each other in her haste to explain. 'That empty plinth could just have been a decoy to fool any would-be robbers into thinking the stone had already been stolen, so they'd give up. Perhaps the Benben Stone is really hidden in *another* chamber that does have some way for the light to get in. *A chamber we haven't found yet.*'

Ryan's pencil began to fly over a new page of his sketchbook. 'It would only need to be a very narrow slot to let a sliver of light in,' he muttered as he drew. 'And you'd angle it towards the east, where the sun rises. You'd need a system of shafts and mirrors to channel the light so that it comes out in the right place.' He slid his sketchbook across the table. 'Something like this.'

Cleo studied Ryan's diagram. It showed a cross-section of the cliff containing the tomb with its passage and chambers. A shaft or pipe zigzagged its way down from the surface to end in the roof of the fourth chamber. She checked the positions and angles of the mirrors Ryan had marked and made a few corrections.

'Yes, this shows that the builders *could* have fed light into the chamber,' she agreed at last, 'but it doesn't disprove my theory. We were there yesterday. We didn't see any slots to let the light in, did we?'

Ryan shrugged. 'We could easily have missed them. Remember, it was late morning and they would be designed to let the sun in at dawn.'

But Cleo was already getting up from her chair. She couldn't wait to tell her parents what they'd figured out. If the fourth chamber was a decoy, it meant the *real* hiding place might be somewhere else in the tomb *with the Benben Stone still in it*! But then she hesitated. What if Ryan were right and they'd missed the light slots in the fourth chamber? She'd already got everyone's hopes up once by finding the fourth chamber, which had turned out to be empty. Another false alarm would be unbearable . . . Mum might actually have a nervous breakdown.

Ryan seemed to read her thoughts. 'It might be best to check it out ourselves before we say anything.'

Cleo frowned and sat back down. 'How?'

Ryan pushed his diagram towards Cleo again. He'd added two stick figures – one boy, one girl – climbing up the ridge towards the tomb entrance as the sun rose behind them, its rays radiating to every corner of the page.

'We sneak into the tomb at dawn?' Cleo spluttered.

Ryan laughed. 'You look like I just suggested breaking into Buckingham Palace and stealing the Crown Jewels! But this is the only way to be sure. We go to the chamber at sunrise, and see if a ray of light enters and hits the spot where the tip of the stone would be if it were sitting on that plinth. If there's no light then we know you're right and the Benben was probably never in the fourth chamber.'

Before Cleo could respond, she noticed a familiar group settling down at a nearby table. Rachel Meadows, Alex Shawcross and Max Henderson were joined by two of the Italian archaeologists from the nearby dig. Rachel waved and started to make her way towards Cleo and Ryan, doing a little sideways hop to squeeze her stocky frame between the tables and chairs, her bright pink and purple tie-dyed tunic flapping around her.

'Do you think she was a rugby forward in a past life?' Ryan whispered with a wicked grin. 'I wouldn't like to go up against her in a scrum!'

'How's your mum, sweetie?' Rachel asked Cleo. 'Not too upset, I hope. I'm sure we'll find that silly old stone soon!'

'She's OK, thanks,' Cleo mumbled, trying not to giggle at Ryan's rude remark.

'It's nice to see you've found a friend your own age.' Rachel ruffled Ryan's hair. Then she held up a finger to the waiter. 'Two ice creams for this table. Put them on my bill, please.'

'Rachel's one of Mum's best friends,' Cleo explained to Ryan, once Dr Meadows had side-shimmied her way back to her own table. 'She was there on that dig in Peru I told you about. I don't know what Mum would've done if Rachel hadn't taken care of everything. She doesn't have any family of her own, so she treats us all like she's a mother hen and we're her chicks! She still thinks I'm about six!'

'I don't mind being six if it means free ice creams!' Ryan laughed as they headed to the freezer cabinet to choose. 'Now, let's get planning for tomorrow morning,' he said, as soon as they were sitting down again.

'Planning?' Cleo nearly choked on her white chocolate Magnum. 'I don't remember agreeing to anything!'

'Oh, come on,' Ryan coaxed. 'We're a great team. We found the fourth chamber together, didn't we?' He grinned. 'And since I rescued you from that hole and saved your life, you're officially in my debt forever and have to do anything I say. It's an old Chinese tradition.'

Cleo was about to point out that there was no genuine basis for the life-debt concept in Chinese culture, or any other culture for that matter, but Ryan had disappeared inside the café. When he came back he handed her a paper napkin.

Cleo read the numbers scribbled on it in biro. 'What's five point five-eight?'

'The time of sunrise tomorrow,' Ryan said, licking the last of the strawberry sauce from the Cornetto wrapper. 'Two minutes to six. I just looked it up on Yusuf's computer.'

Cleo was perplexed. 'Who's Yusuf?'

'The guy at the counter,' Ryan explained. 'I helped him download a football app when I went in to get the Cokes earlier. All the error messages were in English.'

'But how would we even get to the tomb?' Cleo asked. 'Not that I'm saying I'm doing it,' she added swiftly.

'Didn't I see some bikes outside your apartment building?'

'They belong to the Mansours.'

Ryan grinned. 'I'm sure we could borrow them. I'll ask Ali.'

'Ali?' Cleo echoed.

'The Mansours' grandson. He was one of the kids playing football.'

Cleo shook her head. Ryan had only been in Egypt for forty-eight hours and he was already best friends with half the population! She tried another tack. 'How would we get in? There's a padlock on the tomb.'

'Your parents must have a key.'

Cleo pictured the small metal key. She'd seen Dad hang it on the hook by the kitchen door. He wouldn't notice if she returned it by breakfast time . . .

But wait! What was she thinking? Entering a locked tomb at night without permission was definitely *not* approved archaeological practice. *It would be totally unprofessional,* she thought.

And yet, if I can prove that the Benben Stone could *be hidden somewhere else in the tomb, it might just make up for the fact that I let on to Quirke we were looking for the stone in the first place . . .*

9

SUNRISE

RYAN SHIVERED AND zipped his hoodie up to his chin.

I thought Egypt was meant to be a hot country!

He checked his watch again: 4.15 a.m. He scanned the dark façade of the McNeils' apartment block. There was no glimmer of light, no stir of sound.

Now he thought about it, Cleo hadn't *technically* agreed to join him on this mission. He stuffed his hands in his pockets and crossed his fingers.

At last the door opened.

A slight figure in black jeans and a shapeless black jumper at least six sizes too big for her slipped out.

Ryan stepped out of the shadows and greeted her with a

brisk nod as if he'd never doubted for a moment that she'd come. 'Have you got the key?' he whispered. His breath puffed into a white cloud that hovered between them.

Cleo patted her pocket. 'I put the little key from an old cash box in its place on the hook in case Dad gets up early and sees it.'

'I bet you stuffed pillows under your sheets too?'

'Of course,' Cleo said seriously.

Ryan was impressed. For all her reluctance, Cleo was a natural at stealth manoeuvres! He climbed aboard Mr Mansour's ancient sit-up bicycle, as black and solid as a London taxi. Cleo looked doubtfully at Ali's mountain bike – customized with a red and white Manchester United paint job – but she got on without a word.

They pedalled past the sleeping houses and up the twisting road into the hills, all greys and blacks like a charcoal sketch in the ghostly light of a half-moon. The squeak of pedals and crunch of tyres seemed deafeningly loud in the silence. Ryan jumped as a donkey stamped and snorted in its sleep at the side of the road.

The pre-dawn prayer call skirled from the minaret in the village below.

A dog howled in the distance.

It was a long, steep climb, but at last they made it to the *wadi*. They leaned the bikes against the old acacia trees and crept past the hut where the night watchman sprawled in his chair, feet up on his desk, a thick anorak over his long blue *galabaya*. Discarded cigarette ends formed a white tidemark around his chair. He snored loudly, almost waking himself up, then settled back down with a grunt.

They padded past the hut and picked their way up the cliff

path, clinging to the guide rope, not daring to switch on a torch in case the light gave them away. Ryan was first to reach the cleft at the top. He turned and pulled Cleo safely over the last narrow section to the mouth of Smenkhkare's tomb. A sturdy new wooden door had been fitted and secured with a padlock. Cleo's hands trembled as she inserted the key.

The door creaked open.

They stepped into deeper darkness. Ryan pulled the heavy door closed behind them. He switched on his torch and flicked it over the wall paintings. The gods were still acting out their timeless rituals.

But *something* in the burial chamber had changed.

Ryan's heart almost burst with fear.

The sarcophagus was open!

The stone lid had been taken off and propped up against the side.

As if compelled by an unseen force, Ryan stepped closer and peered in.

He'd seen mummies before, of course, in films and cartoons, shuffling along zombie-fashion, white bandages flapping like swathes of toilet paper, but the shrivelled form in the coffin was nothing like that. Its arms were crossed high over its chest, the long bones twisted and dark as rusty iron, the knobbled fingers clawing at its ribcage. The rags of linen that curled around the body like shedding skin were stiff and brown, as if crusted with old blood. At least Ryan was spared the face; it was covered with a broad gold mask. Painted eyes with kohl-black rims stared up at him from beneath a wig striped with blue and gold.

'What . . . how . . .' Ryan's mouth was so dry he could barely croak the words.

'It's cartonnage,' Cleo said. 'Strips of linen and papyrus, stiffened with resin. A bit like *papier mâché*. It's been covered in gold leaf. The blue in the wig is probably lapis lazuli.'

Ryan gaped at her in disbelief. 'I wasn't asking for a dissertation on the construction of Ancient Egyptian death masks. I meant, what's the mummy doing in *here*? I thought it was in a lab in Cairo.'

'Oh, Dad and Alex drove up and brought him back last night. The tests were all complete.' Cleo directed her torch beam to a small label attached to a wizened toe. There was an identification number and the words *Pharaoh Smenkhkare: died 1334 BC (estimated)*.

'You might have warned me!' Ryan muttered. 'I'll be having nightmares for weeks.'

'Sorry. I didn't know they were going to leave the sarcophagus open.' Cleo looked up and grinned. 'Or that you were so squeamish.' She turned back to the mummy. 'He's quite well preserved. Dad said you can even see the marks made by the embalmers' hooks when they were extracting the brain through the nose . . .' She reached down but Ryan grabbed her hand and pulled it away before she could remove the mask. He'd seen enough without adding mutilated nostrils. He backed away.

'Come on, it's nearly sunrise.'

They hurried down the passage and through the false wall. The deadfall was now safely covered over with boards and the concealed entrance to the chamber marked with a fluorescent sticker. Ryan slotted his fingers in to the mouth of the crocodile, slid back the stone and they stepped inside.

He checked his watch: 5.55.

Three minutes until sunrise.

While he waited he gazed at the judgement scene from the *Book of the Dead* that covered the back wall, the vivid colours glowing in the torchlight. The wall paintings told a story, just like his favourite comics and graphic novels. Cleo had explained it all to him yesterday: Anubis weighed the heart of the deceased person on the scale of Ma'at in the Hall of Two Truths. If your heart was as light as the feather of truth you were waved on through to the afterlife. If your heart was heavy with its burden of sins . . . well, then things got messy. The lower panel showed Smenkhkare in the process of having his heart ripped out by Ammit, Devourer of the Dead, a fearsome beast with the head of a crocodile, the body of a leopard and the legs of a hippo. The blood dripping from Ammit's jaws gleamed as if freshly spilled.

You didn't have to read hieroglyphs to get the message.

Ryan remembered the words of Smenkhkare's Confession: *a double abomination.* Smenkhkare's heart must have been pretty heavy with all that sin. *No wonder he stole the Benben Stone,* Ryan thought. *He needed a serious bribe to avoid the slavering jaws of Ammit!*

Just what had the man done that was so *abominable*? Ryan wondered. Was it murder . . . corruption . . . betrayal . . .?

Cleo nudged his elbow. 'It's time!'

They turned off their torches and waited.

And waited.

Ryan counted to twenty. Then he counted to one hundred.

It had to be well past 5.58 now. The sun was above the horizon. And yet no shaft of light had found its way into the chamber to pierce the deep blackness and strike the gilded tip of the Benben Stone.

'I was right,' Cleo whispered as she turned her torch back

on. 'This can't be where the Benben Stone was installed. There's no way the first light of dawn can enter. I'll tell Mum and Dad and we can start searching for another chamber today.' She hesitated and looked a little awkward for a moment. 'I think it'll be best if I just tell them the *theory* and don't mention that we came up and actually checked it out. I don't want to worry them any more. You won't say anything, will you?'

Ryan grinned. 'Your secret nocturnal life as a tomb raider is safe with me!'

Cleo smiled. 'Thanks.' Then she looked at her watch. 'It's past six now. Let's get home before anyone notices we're gone.'

They were about to step out into the passageway when the hairs pricked up on the back of Ryan's neck.

Footsteps! Coming down the tunnel!

Ryan's thoughts teemed with images of night-time things that lived deep in underground tombs, scurrying out of sight before the light of day. Ghoulish, mutant things with translucent skin and bulging eyes.

Maybe he'd imagined it . . .

No, there they were again. The footsteps were heavier now. They seemed to be coming from the main burial chamber.

Cleo had clearly heard them too. They both flicked their torches off. They stood side by side in the dark, not daring to breathe.

'The night watchman must have seen us and come up to investigate,' Cleo whispered at last. She poked her head out into the passage and listened. 'I think he's gone . . .'

Her words were obliterated by a sudden boom. The walls of the tunnel shook. Ryan felt the sound resonate deep inside his bones like a massive rocket at a firework display. Cleo clutched his arm.

'What was that?' he gasped. 'Dynamite?'

'I don't know.' Cleo pointed towards the burial chamber. 'But it came from up there!' Without another word, their hands clammy and shaking, they felt their way back along the passage in total darkness. When they reached the burial chamber they stood for a long moment, not daring to enter. But the room was empty and silent, apart from the boom still ringing in Ryan's ears, as if he were standing inside a church bell. Finally he took a deep breath and switched his torch on.

His legs almost gave way beneath him.

The lid of the sarcophagus had moved. It was no longer propped against the side of the coffin. Now it was lying on the ground.

'*That's* what made the noise,' Cleo murmured. 'It just toppled over.'

'Just toppled over!' Ryan echoed. 'It's a ten-tonne slab of granite, not a domino. It can't have *just toppled over*.' Suddenly a rollercoaster lurch of fear gripped his stomach. If there was no one else in the chamber, there was only one possible explanation for the footsteps and the fallen lid: *Smenkhkare must have woken from the dead and climbed out of his coffin to wreak revenge on us for breaking into his tomb!* Ryan whisked round, half expecting to see the mummy looming behind him, wrappings trailing from its withered limbs . . .

'Look!'

Ryan turned back to see Cleo leaning over the side of the open sarcophagus, waving her hand for him to join her. He forced his feet to carry him closer and made himself look down.

He closed his eyes for a moment, dizzy with relief. Smenkhkare was lying there just as before. *Of course,* Ryan told himself, *mummies don't really come back to life. You've been watching too many films!* But when he opened his eyes, a new wave of horror crashed over him. Smenkhkare *wasn't* just as before.

His death mask had been moved.

Ryan was looking straight into his face.

Strips of earth-coloured linen were stretched tight over the skull and the open mouth was twisted in what looked like a scream of unimaginable terror.

'It must have slipped off with the vibrations when the lid crashed down,' Cleo said, reaching in to the coffin and picking up the death mask, which was lying next to the head. Respectfully she placed it back over the staring face.

Ryan nodded slowly. He really needed to get out of here!

He hurried towards the mouth of the tomb and pulled open the heavy door – just in time to catch a glimpse of a figure hurrying down the cliff path.

Ryan blinked, but by the time his eyes had adjusted to the bright dawn light that painted the crags and ridges in fiery shades of ruby, coral and gold, the figure had disappeared behind an outcrop of rock.

Ryan looked back to Cleo, who had joined him at the door.

He could tell from her face she'd seen the figure too.

No shred of doubt remained.

Someone had followed them into the tomb.

10

ETERNAL SUN

CLEO LEANED ALI'S bike against the wall of the apartment block.

She climbed the wide steps that led up to the front door. She turned back for a moment and watched Ryan hurrying off down the street. It was light now and the village was already beginning to stir. A boy zipped past on a motorbike, balancing a plastic tray of bread rolls on his head. He pulled up outside the El-Masry Café on the corner where the owner was pushing up the shutters. The little white cat stalked past him and pounced on a leaf. A light was on in the Mansours' apartment. Mrs Mansour was silhouetted in the kitchen window, grinding coffee for breakfast.

It was all so *normal.* Cleo could hardly believe that only half an hour ago she'd been looking into Smenkhkare's coffin.

She shivered – but it wasn't the hollow-eyed face of the mummified pharaoh that was haunting her. It was the thought of someone following them into the tomb. Someone who was in such a hurry to get away without being seen that they'd knocked over the lid of the sarcophagus as they'd left.

That didn't sound like any kind of night watchman or guard. *A guard would have yelled at us or bundled us off to the police station, not spied on us and then scurried back down the cliff path.*

Cleo checked her watch. She'd have to be quick to get back into her room before her parents woke. She reached for the door handle.

That's when she felt a tap on her shoulder.

She whipped round, her heart fluttering like a trapped bird.

It was the lemony aftershave smell she recognized first. Then the spotless white shirt and the designer stubble.

Nathan Quirke!

He was standing behind her, but three steps down, so she was looking him straight in the eye.

Of course, she thought. *It was Quirke who followed us to the tomb!* Now she thought about it, there *had* been a faint scent lingering in the air when they'd returned to the burial chamber.

'Are you spying on me?' she demanded.

Quirke smiled and climbed another step. 'No need to be unfriendly! Actually, it's your mother I've come to see. I wanted to catch her before she leaves for the dig. I know you archaeologists like to start early.' He shot her a knowing glance. 'What are you doing out at this time anyway? Meeting your boyfriend?'

'None of your business!' Cleo snapped. Quirke had moved so close that his aftershave was going right up her nose. But at least it meant that she could now tell it *wasn't* the same as the smell in the tomb. That had been soapier, more medicinal, somehow – it could have been suncream, perhaps, or hair gel or insect spray . . .

'I thought I'd just drop by,' Quirke was saying, 'and see if Professor McNeil would like to comment on how the search for the Benben Stone is progressing – now that you've confirmed that you *are* looking for it.'

Cleo shrank back against the door. 'No, please don't do that!'

A sly grin spread across Quirke's face. 'Well, maybe if you can answer a couple of questions for me I *might* not need to bother her . . .'

'All right,' Cleo said. *Anything to stop him telling Mum I let slip that we're searching for the Benben* . . . And she had to get rid of him and get inside *fast*. Mum and Dad would be up any second.

'Can you confirm that the Danny Farr Foundation is providing the funding for this dig?'

Cleo almost laughed with relief at such a harmless question. It was public knowledge. 'Yes, of course!' she said.

Quirke rubbed a palm over his stubble. 'And you don't think it's a bit fishy?'

Cleo frowned. 'Fishy? Why?' she asked. 'They're a big charity. They fund all sorts of projects.' Although Cleo had never heard his music, she knew that Danny Farr had made a fortune as one of the biggest rock stars of the 1980s. He'd invested some of his millions in setting up a foundation to do good works. 'And they've agreed to build a visitor centre here when the dig is complete,' she added.

Quirke shook his head as if he felt sorry for her. 'So you haven't heard the rumours?'

'What rumours?' Cleo asked.

'That Danny Farr is a member of the Ancient Order of the Eternal Sun. In fact, some sources say he's their High Priest.'

Cleo was so surprised she couldn't help snorting with laughter. 'The Eternal Sun? You mean that weird occult group who are always predicting the end of the world?'

'They prefer,' Quirke said, 'to call themselves a *Learned Society.*'

'Whatever they call themselves, it's all nonsense!' Cleo said, starting to push the door open. 'They believe in alien visitations and people coming back from the dead and—'

'And the Return of the Phoenix,' Quirke cut in.

Cleo let the door bang shut. 'What do you mean?'

Quirke's grin twisted into a smirk. 'Oh, I'm sure you know the legend. The phoenix – or should we say the *Bennu Bird* – returns to land once more upon the Benben Stone every five hundred years. That's why the High Priests of the Eternal Sun have been searching for the Benben for centuries. They've always wanted it for their own temple so that they can witness the Return of the Phoenix.' He paused and looked Cleo in the eye. 'So, the big question is, is the Benben Stone safe from Danny Farr?'

Cleo turned away, let herself in and shut the door in Quirke's leering face.

She was still in shock and only halfway across the kitchen when the door of her parents' bedroom opened. Dad emerged in his pyjamas, looping his glasses over his ears. Cleo had just enough time to kick off her shoes and pull open the fridge door before he could see her clearly.

'Couldn't sleep!' she said, taking out a carton of yoghurt.

Well, she told herself. *It's not a complete lie. I couldn't sleep because I was in Smenkhkare's tomb.* 'I kept thinking about the Benben Stone not being in the fourth chamber,' she added.

'Don't remind me!' Mum groaned, joining them at the table.

Cleo explained her theory that the fourth chamber was a decoy to fool tomb robbers because there was no way for the light to enter. She left out the fact that she'd just been to the tomb and proved that point in person.

Mum looked up from pouring honey over her fruit and yoghurt, the wide smile that Cleo hadn't seen for days firmly back in place. 'Of course!' she said, so excited she drizzled honey across the tablecloth. 'The *real* chamber could be hidden farther down the tunnel.'

'There might even be another fake wall to get past,' Cleo pointed out.

'We'll start looking this morning,' Dad said, already heading off to get dressed. Cleo could tell he was delighted too; he was whistling a mournful version of *Cry Me a River* through a mouthful of toast crumbs as he went.

Cleo yawned. 'I'm really tired. Do you mind if I stay at home this morning?'

Mum placed her palm on Cleo's forehead. It wasn't like her to miss out on a dig. 'Perhaps I should call a doctor?'

'No, it's OK,' Cleo said quickly. 'I just need to go back to bed for a bit.'

And she did.

For all of seven minutes.

As soon as she'd heard her parents leave she ran to her desk and switched on her computer. She rested her head on her arms while she waited for the hard disk to chug into action. Nathan Quirke's words were spinning round and round in her head like test tubes in a centrifuge: *the Return of the Phoenix, the Ancient Order of the Eternal Sun, Danny Farr* . . .

If Quirke were right, she thought, and Danny Farr were secretly a member of the Ancient Order of the Eternal Sun, it would make sense that he was funding the excavation of Smenkhkare's tomb for one reason and one reason only: so that he could get his hands on the Benben Stone for his group's strange magic rituals. He wouldn't do it himself, of course. Danny Farr was famous. He'd be far too recognizable. He would send someone in – another member of the sect, perhaps – to do the dirty work.

Cleo suddenly sat up straight as a horrible idea exploded into her mind: perhaps he already *had* done!

Could someone be spying on the excavation already?

The 'someone' who'd followed them into the tomb that morning?

Just when it seemed that the stone might not have been stolen from Smenkhkare's tomb by ancient looters, after all, and that it could still be down there in another hidden chamber they'd not yet found, it turned out someone might be trying to steal it! It would be unbearable to find the Benben Stone, only for it to be stolen from under their noses by a retired rock star and his bizarre secret society!

Or am I just getting carried away? Cleo wondered, as the computer screen finally lit up. *Maybe Quirke made up the whole story just to rattle me. He's obviously a skilled liar!*

There were so many questions.

Cleo was determined to find the answers.

She opened a search box and typed in ANCIENT ORDER OF THE ETERNAL SUN.

She clicked on what looked like the group's official website. A plain black page opened up, edged with flickering flames. A chorus of low, sinister voices chanted in Ancient Egyptian, reciting verses that Cleo recognized as spells from the *Book of the Dead*.

Suddenly a three-headed serpent flashed up in the centre of the screen. It seemed to lunge right out of the computer, making Cleo shrink back in her chair. Her heart was still pounding as two Ancient Egyptian ankh symbols, circled by a fiery sun in a black border, popped up in its place. Then the words *Access Denied* zoomed across the screen and the web page disappeared.

Cleo took a deep breath and continued her search, reading every article she could find about the Ancient Order. It was soon clear that the Eternal Sun was much more than a 'learned society'. Its members weren't just interested in studying the magic of Ancient Egypt: they wanted to *practise* it. They believed that occult rituals would reveal lost knowledge recorded in the legendary *Book of Thoth*: astral travel, scrying, alchemy . . . There were stories of summoning spirits from beyond the grave, of dark forces and terrible curses, of people driven mad by fear.

At last Cleo came across a piece about the Return of the Phoenix, a blog post by someone who claimed to be an ex-member of the Eternal Sun. Not surprisingly, they were too afraid to give their name.

Many will have heard of the myth of the Return of the Phoenix,

Cleo read. *But to members of the Ancient Order of the Eternal Sun, it is no myth. It is a very real event that takes place every five hundred years. They believe that the phoenix, or Bennu Bird, returns to the mighty Benben Stone to lay a new egg and be reborn in flames. For them, the phoenix embodies the soul of the Sun God, Ra. Anyone who witnesses the Return, and hears the cry of the phoenix, will be granted powerful magic and control of the untold powers of the Benben Stone. The soul or* ka *of Atum-Ra may even enter their body . . .*

Cleo gazed at the words. If they believed all that, no wonder the Ancient Order of the Eternal Sun wanted to get hold of the Benben Stone.

But was Danny Farr really a member?

Did *he* believe this stuff?

Of course, there was no handy membership list. Initiates of the Ancient Order of the Eternal Sun were sworn to utmost secrecy. They vowed never to reveal their identity, even to their closest family and friends. But the internet swarmed with rumours of a shadowy network that included people from all walks of life: politicians and police chiefs, business leaders and bankers, gangsters and celebrities . . .

Celebrities like millionaire rock star, Danny Farr! His name came up more than once.

Cleo got up from her desk, threw open the French windows and stood on the tiny balcony gazing out across the jumble of flat rooftops, where bunches of dates were laid out to dry in the sun among the TV aerials and satellite dishes. The air shimmered in the heat. The muezzin struck up his call to prayer from the mosque. One by one, the call was echoed from distant prayer towers in the villages strung along the banks of the Nile.

A chill slithered down her spine as she thought over all she'd read about the Ancient Order.

She didn't believe any of it, of course. It was just the secrecy that gave her the creeps.

She watched a group of schoolgirls in matching yellow headscarves walk along the street. Two men sat at a small table outside an open front door, drinking coffee and playing cards. A taxi driver was leaning against his car, reading a newspaper.

Any one of them could be a member.

She turned back to her room and saw the copy of *Advanced Mathematics* still lying on her rug. If only life were as simple as a mathematical equation! She picked it up and flicked through the pages. *Find the value of the unknown variable, x, in the following equation . . .*

The members of the Eternal Sun were unknown variables. But, unlike an equation, there was no logical way to solve the problem.

She sat back down at the desk and entered the name DANNY FARR into the search box. Within seconds she'd found a video clip of a recent interview about a school his foundation was building in Africa. Farr looked relaxed, lounging on a sofa, one ankle resting across his knee. He was wearing white jeans and a studded jacket, his bleached hair pulled back from a high forehead and tied in a ponytail. His face was as leathery and tanned as an old briefcase.

'Yeah, yeah,' he said, his accent halfway between London and a Hollywood celebrity drawl. 'It's, like, so important to me to give something back, y'know?'

Cleo tried another clip. A much younger Danny Farr was standing in an artificial snowstorm on a 1980s programme called *Top of the Pops*. He was playing a star-shaped electric guitar and crooning a soppy love song called *My Christmas Valentine*.

Cleo jumped as she heard the door of the flat open. Mum and Dad were home. It must be lunchtime already. *Should I tell them about Danny Farr?* she wondered. But was there any point in worrying them? After all, there was no real evidence that Farr was a member of the Eternal Sun, only rumour and speculation.

Dad put his head round the door from the kitchen.

'*My Christmas Valentine?*' he laughed. 'That's a blast from the past! I didn't know you were a Danny Farr fan!'

'I'm not,' Cleo mumbled. 'I was just looking for something else.'

'Do you remember this one, Lydia?' Dad called over his shoulder.

Mum groaned. 'How could I forget?'

Dad grabbed Mum and they began to waltz around the kitchen. 'You know,' Dad puffed as he whirled Mum around, 'I've always thought the foundation is Farr's way of making up for all the cheesy Christmas number ones he inflicted on the world in the 1980s!'

Cleo needed to get out of the flat, and it wasn't just the sight of her parents dancing that was sending her into a spin.

She found her phone and sent off a text.

Meet me at El-Masry. Urgent!

It's peculiar, she thought, as she slipped out of the door. *I've only known Ryan two days. What did I do before I had him to talk to?*

11

SCARAB

RYAN TEXTED STRAIGHT back.

He was, it seemed, already at the café.

When Cleo arrived she found him sitting at an outside table eating pizza with a man she recognized as Josh Jennings. Josh – or J.J. as he was always known – was an American graduate student who worked with Cleo's mum at London University. He'd joined the dig late because he'd been at a conference. He'd only flown into Egypt last night, but it seemed that he and Ryan were best buddies already.

J.J. was sprawling in his chair, his long legs sticking out onto the pavement. He was wearing a sleeveless vest, baggy shorts and high-top trainers. 'We've been down at the park shooting some hoops,' he explained as Cleo sat down and ordered a drink from the waiter.

Ryan looked up from feeding pizza crust to the little white cat. 'Yeah, did you know J.J. had a basketball scholarship all the way through college in Arizona?'

Cleo had to admit that she didn't. Even though she'd known J.J. for over two years, they'd mostly discussed New Kingdom temple architecture, which was the topic of his research. Basketball had never come up in conversation.

'So what's up?' Ryan asked.

'Oh, nothing,' Cleo mumbled into her mango juice.

J.J. laughed. 'Hey, looks like that's my cue to leave you two kids to hang out together.' He and Ryan conducted a complicated high five and handshake routine. 'Laters!' J.J. said, saluting to Cleo.

'I had another visit from Nathan Quirke this morning,' Cleo whispered, once J.J. was out of earshot.

Ryan's eyes widened. 'What did Old Smooth Moves want this time? You didn't give away any more state secrets, did you?'

'Of course not!' Cleo looked over her shoulder to make sure no one could overhear, before recounting Quirke's disturbing claims. 'But he says Danny Farr is a member of the Ancient Order of the Eternal Sun and that they want to steal the Benben Stone in time for the Return of the Phoenix.'

Ryan took a long time brushing pizza crumbs off the table into his hand. 'Don't believe everything you read on the internet,' he said at last. 'There are loads of mad conspiracy theories about celebrities who are aliens in disguise or part of some evil mind-warping cult. Quirke works for the *Mystical Times*, remember, so he probably loves all that stuff.'

'I know that,' Cleo cut in, slightly disappointed that Ryan didn't seem more worried by her news, 'but it does all fit. The Danny Farr Foundation was very keen to fund this project when no other agencies would get involved because of Mum's bad publicity. And it would explain why Danny Farr didn't want any other journalists around. With just your mum here, Farr is the only one who'll get a full report if and when we find the stone. Then he can send in his henchmen to whisk it away to one of their temples before anyone else even knows it's been found!' Cleo's voice trailed off as she suddenly thought of something. She stared at Ryan. 'How long has your mum worked for the Danny Farr Foundation?'

'She *doesn't* work for them,' Ryan said, offering another handful of crumbs to the cat. 'She's a freelance reporter. She met some of Farr's publicity people when she was doing an article about celebrity charities. They asked if she'd be interested in covering the Smenkhkare tomb dig.' He shrugged and brushed the last of the crumbs from his palms. 'She thought it sounded fun. And it's good money.'

Cleo was relieved. For one moment she'd thought that Julie Flint could have been the 'someone' who was working with Danny Farr to help him steal the Benben Stone. 'So, your mum's never mentioned any rumours about Danny Farr being in a strange occult group?' she asked.

Ryan shook his head and leaned down to tickle the cat's ginger ears. 'I've named her Snowball,' he said. Then he reached into his pocket and pulled out a handful of coins. 'Do you want an ice cream? I think I've got enough here.'

Cleo watched Ryan make his way through the tables to the café. Was she imagining it, or had he deliberately changed the subject? He'd reached up to touch the St Christopher that hung round his neck too. She'd noticed him do that before, when they were faced with the threat formulae outside the fourth chamber. *Of course,* she thought. *Ryan must be really superstitious. That's why he's so uncomfortable talking about the Ancient Order of the Eternal Sun and their black magic.* She would have to set him straight.

'There's no way all that Eternal Sun magic stuff can actually work, you know,' she said when Ryan returned, holding out a white chocolate Magnum. 'It's all nonsense.'

Ryan pulled a shocked face. 'You mean I can't *really* live forever and blow up all my sworn enemies with the Benben Stone?'

'No, of course you can't!' Suddenly Cleo realized Ryan was teasing her. 'Well,' she said a little crossly. 'You can't deny that *someone* followed us into the tomb this morning. *Someone* wanted to know what we were looking for.'

'Yeah, that's true.' Ryan looked up from licking drips of ice cream from the side of his Cornetto. 'I nearly died of fright when that sarcophagus lid fell off.'

'Perhaps that was the point,' Cleo said, suddenly realizing that the crash of the stone lid might not have been an accident after all. 'Maybe they did it to try to scare us off. Perhaps they're not even planning to wait for the dig team to find the Benben for them. Maybe they're going to sneak into the tomb and search for it themselves and they don't want anyone around to see what they're up to. Either way,' she added, 'we've got to find the Benben first and make sure it's under lock and key as soon as possible. If the Eternal Sun *are* trying to get hold of it for the Return of the Phoenix ceremony, they're not going to hang about . . .'

Ryan looked at his watch and jumped up. 'That reminds

me! I can't hang about either. I promised Ali Mansour I'd go into school and do some drawing with his class. They want to make Batman comics. I'll call you later.'

'. . . because,' Cleo continued, now addressing her words to an empty chair and a cat called Snowball, 'the next Return of the Phoenix is predicted to take place on the spring equinox this year – and that's only ten days away.'

Snowball showed little interest. She flicked her tail and stalked away.

Cleo sighed and looked around the café. She noticed a familiar face. Dad's student, Alex Shawcross, had sat down at a nearby table. She looked like an old-fashioned film star, wearing a white nipped-in vintage blouse and stylish beige shorts, her wavy fair hair tied up in a red scarf in the style of a 1940s war effort poster. Cleo waved, but Alex didn't notice; she was too busy reading *Dental Disease in Ancient Egypt* while tucking into a large ice-cream sundae.

Cleo got up to leave and was searching in the leather purse on her tool belt for some change for a tip, when she felt something smooth and solid at the bottom: the scarab amulet! It had been in there since Ryan had showed it to her yesterday. She took it out and looked it over again. It was beautifully crafted in steatite, or soapstone, the domed wing cases glazed with lustrous blue-green faience. The flat underside had been left unglazed, so that hieroglyphs could be carved into the stone. Cleo read the inscription again.

To celebrate the coming to the throne of Usermaatre Setepenre, Lord of the Two Lands, beloved of Amun . . .

Usermaatre Setepenre – that was the throne name of the pharaoh known to history as the great Rameses II. His coronation had taken place in 1279 BC, which meant that whoever had dropped the scarab in the fourth chamber – presumably a tomb robber – had entered the tomb fifty-four years after the estimated year of Smenkhkare's death.

Cleo tried to picture the raid. The looters must have found their way through the fake dead-end wall, made it past the deadfall and then located the hidden handle to the fourth chamber inside the crocodile's mouth, just as she and Ryan had done. But when they entered the chamber, what had the robbers found? *If our theory is right,* Cleo thought, *and the fourth chamber is a dummy, then they will have found an empty plinth, just as we did. Did the gang go looking for the Benben Stone further along the tunnel?* she wondered. *Did they find any more secret rooms? Or did they cut their losses and leave, taking any other treasures they'd found with them?*

Cleo held up the scarab and gazed at the turquoise wings. 'If only you could talk!' she murmured. 'You could tell me *exactly* what happened.'

Suddenly she was scraping her fringe out of her eyes, trying to get a better look. She hadn't noticed those tiny hieroglyphs near the edge before . . .

In search of more light, Cleo ran out from the shade of the canopy and onto the street, ignoring the shouts of an angry vegetable seller as she stepped in front of his motorbike cart, causing him to swerve towards a crowded minibus. Horn honking wildly, the minibus screeched to a halt, narrowly missing a passing goat. The vegetable cart toppled over and tomatoes, onions and radishes rolled all over the road.

Cleo could hardly believe what she was reading. She took the magnifying glass from her tool belt and squinted at the miniature symbols just to be sure: *The Great Sun Temple at Iunu pledges loyalty to the new Pharaoh.*

Iunu was the Ancient Egyptian name for the city of Heliopolis.

Could it really be a coincidence that one of the tomb robbers had been carrying an amulet from the very temple where the Benben Stone had been kept until Smenkhkare had stolen it? The temple in Iunu or Heliopolis – over four hundred miles north of the Valley of the Kings?

Completely oblivious to the chaos all around her – a fight had broken out between the vegetable seller and the minibus driver, while the goat calmly munched on scattered tomatoes – Cleo examined the scarab again.

It seemed she had missed something else.

This time it was on the glazed side, in the groove where the wing cases met in the middle. Something had been scraped into the hard blue faience. The symbols were shallow and untidy, as if they'd been scratched with a pin or a knife point rather than professionally carved. Cleo tilted the magnifying glass and strained her eyes. At last she made them out: *Rahotep*.

It was a name! The owner of the amulet must have added it himself.

Cleo felt the very first inkling of another theory beginning to bubble up in her mind.

Maybe the scarab hadn't belonged to a tomb robber after all.

Maybe it held a vital clue to where the Benben Stone was hidden.

Still clutching the scarab in her hand, she looked up, wondered for a moment why the street was full of shouting men and squashed vegetables, then ran all the way home.

She sat down at her desk, fired up her computer and entered the words RAHOTEP, PRIEST and HELIOPOLIS into the search engine.

She didn't look up again for three hours.

12

RAHOTEP

MEANWHILE RYAN WAS lounging on his bed working his way through a family-sized pack of Doritos and winning the Monaco Grand Prix on his PSP.

The drawing class with Ali and his school friends had been great fun and he felt he'd more than earned an afternoon off. He was about to cross the finishing line when he heard his mum answer a knock at the door and chat with someone in the hallway for a few moments.

'It's Cleo, love!' Mum shouted. 'I'm just off. I've got to run.' She was late for an appointment to interview an important government official about the plans for the proposed visitor centre to display the contents of Smenkhkare's tomb, and had been whirling around like a mini tornado, make-up, clothes and half-finished notes flying in all directions.

Ryan barely had time to kick yesterday's boxers and his smelly trainers under the bed before Cleo appeared in the doorway of his room. He shoved a pile of clothes off the solitary plastic chair. The lodgings Mum had found to rent were in an old-fashioned guesthouse, and consisted of two small bedrooms, separated by a curtain.

Cleo sat down. To Ryan's relief she didn't seem to notice the mess. Her eyes looked red and bleary. 'Have you been crying?' he asked.

Cleo shot him a look that said *as if!* She obviously wasn't much of a crier. 'I've been looking at the screen all afternoon.'

Ryan knew that feeling. He held up his PSP. 'Me too!'

Cleo shot him the same look again. She obviously wasn't much of a gamer either. 'I've been doing research, actually.'

'Snap!' Ryan said. 'I'm researching racing-themed computer games and tortilla-based Mexican snacks.' He shook the Doritos bag in her direction.

Cleo didn't laugh at his joke. Nor did she take a tortilla chip. Instead she drew a folder from her bag. 'I've found out who the scarab belonged to.'

Ryan was so impressed he dropped the Doritos. 'Wow! Have you found his shoe size and his mobile phone number too?'

Cleo rolled her eyes. 'They didn't have phones . . .' Then she caught on to the joke. 'Oh, yes, very funny!' She took out the amulet and showed Ryan the inscription that proved it came from the Great Sun Temple in Heliopolis – home of the Mansion of the Phoenix and the Benben Stone – and the name of the owner scratched into the surface. '*Rahotep* means *Ra is at peace*,' she explained. 'The Great Sun Temple was dedicated to the worship of Atum-Ra, so I figured that *Rahotep* would be the perfect name for a priest who worked there . . .'

Ryan grinned. 'It's amazing what you can find out from looking at a beetle's bottom!'

'Anyway, I scoured all the Ancient Egypt websites to see if I could find any mention of a priest called Rahotep from during the reign of Rameses II. And, ta da!' Cleo waved a computer printout under Ryan's nose. 'It's a copy of the Heliopolis Papyrus. It's a sort of official history of the Great Sun Temple. It was written hundreds of years later, but it's all we've got because the original archives were destroyed. It mentions a young priest, a scholar of great potential called Rahotep. He was about ten when Rameses II came to the throne.'

Ryan stared at Cleo in amazement. She was like Nancy Drew on fast-forward! 'So this Rahotep guy might have got the amulet as a kid?' he asked.

Cleo nodded. 'He was probably already an apprentice priest by then. They started young.'

'So, what was he doing in Smenkhkare's tomb?' Ryan asked. 'Do you think he left the holy life behind and came to seek his fortune in the Valley of the Kings, where he fell in with a crowd of tomb robbers?'

'I don't know,' Cleo admitted. 'There's no further mention of him in the Heliopolis Papyrus.'

'Perhaps he got caught making off with a bag full of swag from Smenkhkare's tomb.' Ryan mimed a throat-slitting action.

Cleo leaned forward, clutching her folder of papers to her

chest, and fixed him with a serious stare. 'Maybe,' she said slowly, 'but . . .'

Ryan grinned. 'Let me guess! You've got a theory?'

Cleo didn't seem to hear. 'What if Rahotep *wasn't* a tomb robber? What if the High Priests of Heliopolis found out that Smenkhkare had stolen the Benben Stone from the Mansion of the Phoenix and hidden it in his tomb? And what if they sent a team in to get it back?' Cleo leaned back in her chair for a dramatic pause. 'Rahotep could have been one of that team.'

'You mean a crack squad of undercover priests on a top-secret Search And Retrieve Mission? *That. Is. So. Cool!*' Ryan grabbed his sketchbook and began to draw a cartoon scene of Ninja priests. 'D'you think they were armed with highly trained attack phoenixes that burst into flames on contact?'

'One thing puzzles me,' Cleo went on, ignoring Ryan's flight of fancy. 'It doesn't say anything in the Heliopolis Papyrus about the Benben Stone even being stolen, let alone about sending anyone to get it back.'

'Yeah, you'd think that misplacing the most sacred object in their entire religion would have been worth a mention.' Ryan put on a gravelly movie-trailer voice. 'So, was it Mission Accomplished for the intrepid Agent Rahotep and his priestly posse? Or was he caught red-handed and thrown to the crocodiles?' Then he shrugged. 'I guess we'll never know.'

Cleo smiled. She looked, Ryan thought, more than a little pleased with herself. 'That's where you're wrong,' she said. 'It turns out there's a small collection of papyri and writing tablets on display in the Theban Museum. I found it listed on their website. They were discovered a couple of years ago during the excavation of the Avenue of Sphinxes in

Luxor. There's hardly any information about them . . . but, apparently, the name Rahotep crops up!'

Ryan jumped up, showering Cleo with crushed Doritos. 'The Theban Museum? That's just across the Nile from here.'

'I know!' Cleo said, brushing crumbs off her legs. 'And I'm sure those papers will hold a clue to where the Benben Stone is now. Just think! If Rahotep did retrieve it from Smenkhkare's tomb, the priests may have decided it was too risky to take it back to Heliopolis again. Maybe they hid it somewhere else for safekeeping – somewhere top secret – which would explain why it's never been found.'

'And it might still be there!' Ryan held up his hand for a high five. Cleo looked a little uncertain, as if high-fiving were a strange tribal custom she'd not encountered before, but she gave his hand an enthusiastic slap anyway.

'Oh, yeah! Team Ryan and Cleo back on the case!' Ryan laughed. 'To the museum!'

Cleo shook her head. 'It's closed now. We'll have to go in the morning.'

'It's a date!' Ryan said. Then he realized how that sounded. 'I didn't mean a *date date,* of course.'

Cleo gave him a baffled look. 'What's a *date date*?'

Ryan laughed. Sometimes he wondered whether Cleo had grown up on another planet somewhere on the far edge of the solar system! 'It doesn't matter.' He made for the door. 'Wait there. I'll get some Cokes to celebrate. The fridge is miles down the corridor.'

Cleo was flicking through Ryan's sketchbook when she heard a buzzing noise.

'Can you get that?' Ryan called from the corridor. 'My phone's lying around somewhere. It's probably just Mum saying when she'll be back.'

Cleo looked around. The ringing was coming from the room next door. She pushed through a curtain made of ribbons of rainbow-coloured plastic. T-shirts, shorts and flip-flops were scattered on the floor. A make-up bag seemed to have exploded on the dressing table. She tracked the phone to the bed and extracted it from a tangle of mosquito net and damp towel.

'Hello?' she answered.

The voice that replied didn't belong to Julie Flint.

It was a man.

A man speaking in Ancient Egyptian. *'Em hotep nefer.'* Be in great peace.

Cleo was so astonished that all she could do was return the greeting. *'Em heset net Ra,'* she said. *May you be in favour with Ra.*

'Em heset net Ra,' the man said, a transatlantic accent twanging through the vowels of the ancient language. It was a voice Cleo had heard before. She couldn't place it for a moment, then she remembered the man she'd seen giving the video interview: the bleached hair, the leathery skin, the white jeans and the studded jacket. *Could it really be . . .* Then he switched to English and there was no longer any doubt. 'Julie, it's Danny. May the Eternal Sun shine upon you. What's happening out there? A lot of our *shemsu* are getting impatient for news . . .'

Cleo felt the phone slip from her hand.

13

LIES

CLEO FELT AS if she'd stepped out of a plane without a parachute.

She was still shaking when Ryan walked through the curtain holding out a bottle. 'Is Sprite OK?'

Cleo didn't answer. She stared down at the phone, which lay in the middle of a scrumpled pink T-shirt on the floor.

Ryan followed her gaze. He made a low *oh* noise in his throat. 'That's not my . . .' He looked back up at Cleo, then down at the phone again. 'It's my mum's.'

'I know.' Cleo's voice came out cold and brittle. 'I just answered it.'

Ryan picked up the phone and tossed it onto the dressing

table. 'She hardly ever uses that one. It's just a spare.' He backed towards the door curtain. 'Probably a wrong number.'

'It wasn't a wrong number. He said, *Hi Julie*.' Cleo's throat was so tight she had to squeeze the words out. She made herself focus on the strip of red plastic curtain dangling across Ryan's forehead. 'Then he said *Em hotep nefer*.'

'Sounds like a drunk,' Ryan laughed as he moved through to his room. He sat on his bed and leaned against the wall.

Cleo followed but she didn't sit down, even though her legs were buckling beneath her. 'It was Danny Farr.'

Ryan shrugged. 'Well, Mum is writing that article for his foundation. Maybe he wanted an update.'

Cleo couldn't believe Ryan was acting so cool. 'He also said *May the Eternal Sun shine upon you*. Eternal Sun! Sound familiar?'

Ryan spent a long time turning to a new page in his sketchbook and sharpening a pencil.

'Danny Farr *is* a member of the Eternal Sun, isn't he? And so's your mum.' Cleo realized she was shouting. She *never* shouted! She tried to calm down. She tried to marshal her thoughts into a rational order, but rationality was losing out to the simmering cauldron of bitter black fury welling up inside her. 'You knew all along! I asked you about it this morning and you pretended you didn't. You *lied* to me! That's why you kept changing the subject, isn't it?'

Ryan stared down at his sketchbook and shook his head. 'I didn't lie. I just didn't tell you the whole truth. I'm sorry. I *wanted* to tell you, but I couldn't. Mum's sworn to secrecy. Even *I'm* not meant to know she's a member.'

But Cleo wasn't listening. 'Now I understand,' she said.

'The Eternal Sun *are* planning to steal the Benben Stone, aren't they? That's why Danny Farr is funding the dig! Nathan Quirke was telling the truth. I should have listened to him, not you!' Her voice grew louder and more hysterical with every word. 'So, is your mum planning to steal the stone herself, or is she just the spy who reports back as soon as we're near to finding it so that Danny Farr's henchmen can move in and snatch it?' She paused for breath. 'Where are they planning to take it? One of the Eternal Sun's secret temples? There's one in Arizona, isn't there?'

'It's nothing like that, honest!' Ryan began to draw, but he was pressing so hard that the paper rucked and tore. 'She's not even in the Inner Circle or anything.'

Cleo wanted to smash the pencil out of his hand. 'Then why's Danny Farr phoning her in person?' she demanded.

'And she's not part of any evil master plan to steal the stone either.'

'I don't believe you!' Cleo shouted. 'It was probably your mum who was sneaking around after us in Smenkhkare's tomb this morning!'

'Think about it!' Ryan fired back. 'If I'd known it was my mum, I'd hardly have been scared, would I? I'm not *that* good an actor. And why would she bother following us, anyway, when she could just ask me what I found when I got home?'

Cleo turned to the wall. She didn't know the answers. She couldn't even bear to look at Ryan. She watched a fly crawl across a crack in the plaster. 'You've been laughing at me the whole time. I thought you liked me, but you were just pretending to be my friend to get information about the Benben Stone for your mum.'

Ryan reached out and placed a hand on Cleo's arm. 'I do like you!'

Cleo shook him away so violently she knocked a bottle of Sprite flying into the corner of the room. She watched the fizz fizzle out of the lemonade bubbles. 'Why should I believe you? Everything you've said to me so far has been a lie.'

Ryan groaned. He flopped back onto his bed and raked his hands through his hair. 'It's not what you think. I wish I could explain, but I can't . . .'

Cleo spun back to face him. 'Try!'

'It's just one of Mum's fads. She's always having them. You name it, she's been into it: wicca, numerology, astrology . . . Neo-druidism was the worst. I never want to see another stone circle again! It's no big deal.'

Suddenly Cleo's anger caved in on itself. She felt scooped out and exhausted. She made for the door. 'It's a big deal to me,' she said in a small voice. 'And it's *definitely* going to be a big deal to my mum and dad.'

Before Cleo knew what was happening, Ryan had launched himself across the room and grabbed her by the elbows. 'No! Don't tell anyone my mum's a member. Please!'

'Why shouldn't I?' Cleo muttered, already turning the doorknob.

'The Eternal Sun are obsessed with secrecy. They can turn nasty if anyone goes public or is uncovered. That's why I didn't want to tell you before. Mum could be in danger.'

Cleo walked out without looking back.

The slam of the door rang in Ryan's ears.

He ground the pencil into the paper until the lead snapped.

If only he could turn the clock back. How could he have been so stupid and let Cleo answer that phone?

But how was he to have known that Mum would leave it behind?

She was meant to keep it with her at all times. It must have fallen out of her bag. It was a special one that she only used for communication with other members of the Eternal Sun. And that Ancient Egyptian greeting was a security check. If the person at the other end didn't answer correctly, they'd know the phone had fallen into the wrong hands and they'd hang up. *Just my luck,* Ryan thought. If anyone else on the planet had answered and heard a strange man saying *Em hotep nefer* they'd have gone, 'You what?' and put the phone down. But Cleopatra McNeil just happened to speak Ancient Egyptian. She'd given the correct reply. Danny Farr had assumed she was Julie and started talking to her.

Ryan thumped his pillow. The Doritos curdled in his stomach.

All he could do now was hope that Cleo didn't tell her parents and blow Mum's cover.

Out of the corner of his eye he noticed the scarab amulet lying on the floor where it had fallen when Cleo stormed out. He picked it up and ran his thumb over the wing cases. 'I thought you were meant to bring good luck,' he muttered. 'I hope you did a better job for Rahotep.' He sighed. Cleo may have failed to get about ninety per cent of his jokes. She may have crushed his fingers with her chair leg. She may have called him a liar.

But she was smart and brave and honest and kind, and when she had one of her Theory Moments, nothing could stop her. She was even funny sometimes, although she'd probably deny it.

And he really did like her.

Cleo marched.

She didn't stop marching until she came to a park, which was little more than a patch of dried-out grass dotted with scrubby oleander bushes with clusters of anaemic pink flowers that drooped among drab grey leaves.

She sank down on a rickety bench.

She picked at the peeling paint. By the time she became aware of a creaking sound she'd flayed almost half the armrest.

A group of small children were playing on a rusty old seesaw.

Up and down, up and down, creak, creak, creak . . .

Just like her thoughts.

Up: one minute Ryan said it was no big deal. So, his mum belonged to a kooky occult group who just happened to believe that a magic phoenix was going to fly in and share some spells with them. It was harmless.

Down: the next minute he was begging her not to tell anyone because his mum's life could be in danger. That didn't sound harmless!

Up: maybe, just maybe, Ryan was telling the truth when he said Julie *wasn't* spying on them for the Eternal Sun. And maybe, just maybe, the Danny Farr Foundation *wasn't* plotting to steal the stone.

Down: but he'd told her so many lies, how could she believe anything he said?

One thing was certain. She would never, ever talk to Ryan Flint again.

14

SOLO

NEXT MORNING CLEO was woken by the clink of crockery through the wall from the kitchen. Mum and Dad's students had called round for breakfast and were busy complaining about Max Henderson, the photographer.

'Man, what a party pooper!' J.J. was saying in his deep American drawl. 'Where did you dig him up from?'

'I can't work in these conditions!' Alex Shawcross said in a perfect imitation of the grumpy Yorkshireman.

Mum laughed. 'I know Max is difficult, but he's one of the best. I've worked with him before.'

'Julie Flint's rather nice,' Alex said, switching back to her usual cut-glass English accent. 'I had a good chinwag with her yesterday. She's really clued up about the Benben Stone mythology.'

Cleo pulled the sheet over her head and groaned. *Oh, yeah! I bet she is.*

She'd spent most of the night with the big question still seesawing up and down in her head: to tell or not to tell?

She'd come to a decision at last. She wouldn't say anything to her parents about Danny Farr and the Ancient Order of the Eternal Sun, or about Julie Flint's involvement straight away. They had enough to worry about at the moment. And if Ryan was right, there was a chance she'd be putting his mother in serious danger. But she would keep a close watch and if Julie Flint showed even a *hint* of suspicious behaviour, she would think again.

In the meantime, she was going to visit the Theban Museum and find out what she could about Rahotep. *If* this were the same Rahotep who was mentioned in the Heliopolis Papyrus, and *if* her theory were right and he'd been sent by the High Priests to retrieve the Benben Stone, his papers could contain clues about where he'd hidden it – if he'd ever found it, of course! There were a lot more *ifs* than Cleo would have liked, but with any luck, she would come back from the museum with a plan for where to start looking.

There was no time to lose.

The Benben Stone belonged to the people of Egypt. It deserved to be on display where everyone could see and study it. Cleo knew they had to find it before the Ancient Order of the Eternal Sun got their hands on it and squirreled it away in one of their secret temples for eternity.

And before Nathan Quirke spread the story and half the world's media turned up for a ringside seat.

Cleo scowled into the speckled mirror on the back of the door as she zipped the legs onto her shorts, pulled on a long-sleeved white shirt and wound her favourite long cotton scarf around her neck.

Ryan said we were a great team! And we were, she thought. *It was so much fun working together. Maybe I should give him another chance.*

Then she remembered the lies.

No! Teamwork was over.

This was a solo mission now.

She headed into the kitchen and grabbed a piece of toast. She didn't bother with butter or even with sitting down. She leaned against the fridge. The dry toast crumbled down her front as she bit into it.

'You look terrible, love,' Mum said, pouring her a glass of orange juice.

Thanks a lot, Cleo thought. Then again, Mum didn't look that great herself. There were inky shadows under her dark eyes and her hair was frizzing out at all angles. She'd probably been awake half the night, worrying about finding the stone. Cleo knew she'd had a phone call yesterday from her boss in London, Sir Charles Peacocke, the director of the Department of Museums and Culture, demanding a progress report.

Alex Shawcross, in contrast, looked as neat and pretty as ever in her cream cotton blouse and tailored shorts. She and Dad were poring over his laptop screen.

'You should see this, Cleo,' Dad said, through a mouthful of cornflakes. 'It's the CT scans of Smenkhkare's mummy from the lab.'

Alex looked up from peeling an orange with a small knife.

'So exciting! We knew Smenkhkare's head was detached, but we thought it must have been severed during the embalming process. It was quite common, especially if the body wasn't terribly fresh.' She freed the peel from the orange in one long curl and popped a segment into her mouth. 'But the way bone fragments from the vertebrae have remained in the soft tissue suggests that he was almost certainly decapitated *before* death.'

'It may have been an execution,' Dad added. 'Punishment for that *double abomination* he talks about in the Confession.'

'Or it might have been murder!' J.J. chipped in. He was pivoting on the back two legs of his chair. The bright kitchen light gave his dark brown skin an odd blueish tinge as he snapped forward to reach for the coffee pot. 'Someone obviously didn't like Smenkhkare much! Have you checked out the wall paintings in the fourth chamber? Usually the judgement scene shows the dead person's heart being as light as the feather of truth and Anubis ushering them through to the afterlife, but not poor old Smenkhkare. No afterlife for him! *His* heart is being devoured by Ammit . . .' J.J. clutched his tracksuit top and writhed as if having his heart torn out. 'I wonder who had that gore-fest painted on the wall.'

'It's all very unusual for a royal burial,' Mum agreed. 'No amulets or herbs wound into the mummy wrappings. No grave goods. It's as if whoever buried Smenkhkare didn't *want* him to make it to the afterlife. Never mind telling us more about Smenkhkare, this tomb just seems to *add* to the mystery!' She glanced up at Cleo. 'What do you think, love?'

'Sorry, what?' Cleo hadn't been listening.

'Are you feeling under the weather?' Mum asked. She

turned to the others. 'Perhaps a bit less decapitation and devouring of hearts at the breakfast table would help!'

'It's not that,' Cleo muttered. She wasn't the slightest bit squeamish about the gruesome details of palaeopathology. Dad had been discussing the dismembered bodies and virulent diseases of the ancient world over the dinner table all her life. Normally she was happy to join in, but today it was as if an invisible wall had descended, cutting her off from the rest of the world. 'I thought I'd get the ferry over to Luxor and have a look round the Theban Museum this morning,' she said.

Dad took a sip of his coffee and cleared his throat. 'Sorry, not on your own.'

'I'm perfectly capable!' Cleo spluttered. 'I've been going around by myself for years. All over the world!'

Dad wiped steam from his glasses with a corner of the tablecloth. 'I know, but you're fourteen now. A young woman.'

Mum nodded. 'You might get unwanted attention in the city.'

'But I'm all covered up!' Cleo gestured down at her attire. 'I've put my legs on specially. And I can deal with anyone who hassles me.'

'And what if you get lost?' Dad asked.

'When have I ever got lost?' Cleo snapped.

Dad raised an eyebrow at Mum. 'What about that time in Athens?'

'And Samarkand?' Mum said. 'And remember when you wandered off in Damascus . . .'

'That wasn't my fault. I was looking for the remains of the Roman city wall using a medieval map . . .'

'I'll go with you next week if you like,' Alex offered. 'There's a lovely new display of preserved entrails at the Mummification Museum I've been dying to see.'

Before Cleo could protest further, there was a knock at the door and the small kitchen was suddenly full of Rachel Meadows and her voluminous orange Hawaiian-patterned tunic. 'I just bought these *basbousas* at the baker's stall,' she announced, plonking a large box of sticky almond-topped sponge cakes on the table. 'To die for! Ooh, and look who I found lurking in the hallway. Come on in, don't be shy, dear!'

Within seconds Dad had pulled out another chair and Mum had set up a glass of juice and a plate.

Oh, this day just keeps getting better, Cleo thought bitterly as Ryan stepped in.

'Er, I just came to bring your notes back,' Ryan mumbled, holding out Cleo's folder. 'You left them behind yesterday. I was going to leave them with Mr Mansour for you, but . . .'

'I scooped him under my wing!' Rachel laughed, shaking the pastry box under his nose.

'Thanks,' Cleo muttered, grabbing her folder without looking up.

Rachel beamed at them both. 'Notes, eh? So what are you two youngsters cooking up?'

'Nothing,' they muttered in tight-lipped unison.

'Well, it's great to have you along on the dig, Ryan,' Dad said, completely failing to notice the toxic atmosphere. 'It's a rare treat for Cleo to have a friend her own age around.' He suddenly slapped his forehead. 'Brainwave! Ryan, how d'you fancy a trip to the Theban Museum this morning?'

'I *don't* need a bodyguard!' Cleo seethed through clenched teeth.

'It'd be much more fun to go together,' Mum said. 'And you'd be safe with Ryan.'

Safe? Cleo thought. *I'd be safer with Apep, Evil Serpent of the Underworld.* But it seemed this was the only way she'd get to see the Rahotep papers today. It didn't mean she had to *talk* to him, though. He'd only run back and inform on her to his mum and the entire membership of the Ancient Order of the Eternal Sun.

'While you're there, be sure to say hello to an old friend of mine, Leila Badawi . . . ' Mum was saying.

But Cleo was already halfway out of the door.

If she had to have Ryan tagging along she wanted to get it over with as quickly as possible.

15

BODYGUARD

'**LOOK, I'M SORRY,**' Ryan said. 'This wasn't *my* idea.'

Cleo didn't answer. Ryan sighed and kicked out at a pebble. She'd stalked in silence three paces ahead of him, all the way from the village to the riverbank. She hadn't uttered a single word as they'd waited on the dock with the small crowd of tourists and traders, nor as they'd bought their tickets, boarded the ferry and climbed the stairs to the upper deck.

Ryan picked an empty bench near the front of the wide low-slung boat.

Cleo sat two rows behind.

Ryan moved next to her. 'Your dad didn't give me much choice in the matter,' he said.

Cleo got up and moved – *three* rows back this time.

Ryan gave up, and took his pencil and sketchbook from his backpack. *You could never be bored in Egypt*, he thought. There was just so much to draw! A fleet of feluccas scudded along in the distance, tall masts all tilted at the same angle, white sails billowing in the breeze. Motor launches and fishing boats zipped about among the cruise boats that glided by like floating buildings. The Nile was, he noticed, the exact blue-green shade of the scarab amulet in his shorts pocket. He'd been meaning to hand it over to Professor McNeil, but it had slipped his mind when he'd suddenly been press-ganged into being Cleo's official bodyguard.

A grey heron soared past, wings outstretched. *Just like the Bennu Bird at the beginning of the world,* Ryan thought. Only *this* grey heron glided in to land, not on a mythical stone, but on the carcass of a dead cow that was floating downstream.

Behind him Ryan could hear a school party of English children showing off their souvenir T-shirts to each other.

'That says my name in hieroglyphics,' one of the girls boasted, pointing to the cartouche containing a mouth, a foot and a reed symbol. 'It says Ruby.'

'My hieroglyphics are way better,' a stocky boy swaggered as he balanced on the back of a bench. 'My name's got a snake and a basket in it.'

Another girl shrieked with laughter. 'Ha ha, Jack's a basket case!'

Ryan glanced round at Cleo. He could tell from her frown that she was listening too. In fact, now she was standing up and walking towards the group. 'Excuse me, but I must just correct you on something,' she said.

Ryan slid down in his seat and groaned.

'These are hiero*glyphs*.' Cleo gestured to the symbols on the purple T-shirt of the loudest of the girls. Then she pointed to the word *lifejackets* on the safety sign on the back of a seat. 'Calling them *hieroglyphics* is like saying this is a *wordy* instead of a *word*. You're mixing up nouns and adjectives.'

'What are you?' the girl called Ruby demanded. 'The Word Police or something?'

The kids all screeched with laughter.

'And only royalty would have their names in a cartouche like that,' Cleo went on.

'Who says I'm *not* royalty?' Ruby challenged. 'Maybe I'm a princess!'

Cleo took no notice. 'And anyway, these glyphs are backwards. That says *Eeb-Ru*, not Ruby. If you look carefully you'll observe that . . .'

Ryan couldn't believe Cleo was still ploughing on with her lecture. The kids were laughing at her so loudly they were starting to attract a crowd.

'Mr Barnes!' one of the boys yelled. 'This weirdo girl's bothering us!'

A fed-up looking teacher glanced up from the pile of timetables and tickets he was sorting on his lap. Cleo began to explain the issue with the T-shirt hieroglyphs again. Mr Barnes frowned at his watch as if checking how much longer he had to survive this ordeal. Sweat dripped from his sun-reddened forehead even though the morning heat was only just beginning to build.

'If we wanted your opinion we'd ask for it, young lady!' he said. 'Now, kindly leave these children alone. They're hyped up enough as it is.'

The kids all cheered and hooted.

Serves her right for being such a know-it-all! Ryan thought. But all of a sudden he caught a glimpse of Cleo's hurt expression and he couldn't bear to watch her being jeered at any more. He was going to have to rescue her – even if she *had* been acting like he didn't exist all morning! He hurried over.

'She knows what she's talking about, actually!' he told Mr Barnes firmly, dragging Cleo away by the arm. 'I don't think they're all that interested in the finer points of Ancient Egyptian writing systems,' he whispered.

'But they'd got it *wrong.*' Cleo snatched her arm back but she followed Ryan and sat down. 'I was only trying to help,' she muttered.

Ryan shook his head, amazed, yet again, at the things Cleo *didn't* know – like, the more wrong people are, the less they enjoy other people pointing it out to them, especially in front of their friends. He decided it probably wasn't the best time to share this wisdom. And, anyway, the screech and beep of the Luxor traffic was growing louder by the second. They were already drawing close to the east bank.

Ryan followed Cleo onto the dock. They elbowed through the press of street traders trying to sell them Tutankhamun-themed fridge magnets, postcards and key rings, and along the busy Corniche-el-Nil street. A short walk past hotels, shops and banks brought them to the museum building. They bought tickets at the kiosk and entered the hushed interior. With its air conditioning on high and lighting on low to preserve the ancient artefacts, it was like stepping into a different world after the bright bustle of the city morning.

Cleo consulted the floor plan. After several wrong turns through galleries of statues and pots, she stopped in front of a cabinet of papyrus scrolls. Ryan let her get on with it while he browsed a display of writing and painting implements, fascinated by the pens and brushes made from reeds and the tools for grinding ochre, charcoal, malachite and ivory to make paints.

He sneaked a glance at Cleo's reflection in the smoked glass cabinet. A frown was crimping her elegant eyebrows into a deep V.

'The documents are missing,' she muttered.

16

TRUST

THERE ARE PLENTY *of perfectly ordinary reasons why the Rahotep documents could have been taken off display,* Cleo told herself.

They could have been lent to another museum, or sent away for restoration work, but she couldn't help listening to the small voice whispering in her ear: *what if someone else has figured out that those documents hold a clue to the whereabouts of the Benben Stone and they've beaten you to it? It could be someone from the Eternal Sun who wants to steal the stone in time for the spring equinox . . .*

Cleo drifted through the galleries, wishing she had a plan and trying to ignore Ryan lurking behind her. She stopped for a moment, realizing that she'd lost her bearings and had somehow wandered away from the public galleries into a maze of corridors leading to storerooms and offices. She doubled back, came to a dead end, and was searching for another way out when a memory flashed into her mind: she was standing over Smenkhkare's coffin, looking down into the unseeing eyes of the mummified skull. *Why,* she wondered, *has that come back to me now?* She wrinkled her nose. *Ah, yes, it's that smell! It's the same smell that was in the burial chamber just after we heard the footsteps . . .*

As if conjured by her thoughts, she heard footsteps now. This time they were behind her . . .

She whipped round. Visitors were almost certainly not allowed in this part of the museum and she'd noticed some serious-looking black-uniformed guards on patrol. She wasn't sure whether they were carrying guns, but she started to put her hands up just in case.

Then she hurriedly let them drop. She groaned, feeling half relieved, half annoyed.

It was Ryan again!

He was certainly taking his bodyguard duties seriously. If a guard *had* pulled a gun on her, Cleo thought, he'd probably have dived to take the bullet. And, for some reason, he was now doing an exaggerated pointing action at the door she'd just passed. She took a step back and looked. The black plastic nameplate read *Dr Leila Badawi, Assistant Museum Director (BSc PhD, AMA)*.

Leila Badawi? Cleo had heard that name somewhere . . . But before she had time to give it any more thought, Ryan had reached over her shoulder and knocked on the door.

'Come in!' came a voice from the other side.

Ryan opened the door and pushed Cleo into a large office, cluttered with packing boxes, headless statues, trays of potsherds, fragments of ancient stonework and a purple plastic ride-on hippo.

'Can I help you?' Peeping out from behind the mountains of papers on the desk was a face as round and polished as an old-fashioned porcelain doll, framed by a cream-coloured *hijab*.

Cleo scoured her memory but she was sure she didn't recognize the small, plump woman in the pale pink silk shirt and black trousers. She was about to apologize and back out of the door when Dr Badawi scooted round the desk and kissed her on both cheeks. 'Lydia McNeil's daughter!' she exclaimed in Arabic. 'You were just a little girl when I last saw you!'

Of course! This was the old friend Mum mentioned this morning. Cleo had been so furious about Dad appointing Ryan as her chaperone that she'd hardly been listening. Ryan must have heard the name and remembered it.

'Beautiful, just like your mother!' Dr Badawi went on. 'Wait. I'll ring for some tea. And who is this shy young man?' she added, switching to English and directing a smile past Cleo's elbow.

Cleo stifled a groan. Her annoying, boy-shaped shadow was hovering in the doorway.

'Ryan Flint. He's a, er, *friend* . . .' the word stuck in Cleo's throat as if she were swallowing sawdust, '. . . *of my parents,*' she added pointedly.

Dr Badawi smiled at him. 'It's a present for my granddaughter,' she explained, as she moved the purple hippo aside and found them all chairs. Soon they were drinking glasses of sweet black tea and nibbling walnut biscuits.

'How old is your granddaughter?' Ryan asked politely.

Cleo almost screamed out loud as Dr Badawi took out her phone and started showing them pictures of a cute but dribbly toddler. They were wasting valuable time.

'Do you know what happened to the collection of writings that mention someone called Rahotep?' Cleo asked.

'Ah, yes, the Bennu Bundle, as we call it,' Dr Badawi said. 'An odd assortment, but there's a lovely little drawing of the Bennu Bird on one of the papyri.'

Cleo almost dropped her glass of tea. This was it! It *was* the right Rahotep! The Bennu Bird was *always* connected with the Benben Stone. 'Where is it?' she asked.

'Down in the stores.' Dr Badawi directed a last fond smile at the screen before dropping her phone back into her handbag. 'We took it off display to make room for some more interesting items. I haven't got round to updating the website yet. We're only a small museum and we're very understaffed. In fact, we may have to close next year if we don't attract some major funding . . .'

Ryan was nodding sympathetically but Cleo thought she might burst with impatience.

'The Bennu Bundle's not much to look at,' Dr Badawi continued. 'Nobody's been able to make any sense of the contents, apart from a few standard wisdom texts.'

'Wisdom texts?' Ryan asked.

Dr Badawi smiled at him. 'The sort of thing an apprentice scribe would copy out as writing practice. Mostly rather dull stuff about how to be wise and good.'

'Rahotep wasn't a priest, then?' Ryan asked.

Cleo shot him a dark look. This was *her* interview.

Dr Badawi blew steam from her tea. 'Oh, yes, he could well have been a priest. They would have learned to write too.'

'Can we see the bundle?' Cleo interrupted, before her boy-shadow could beat her to it.

'Yes, of course.' Dr Badawi disappeared behind her desk and began typing at the keyboard. 'I'll send a request down to the stores.'

At last, Cleo thought, her day was starting to look up!

Dr Badawi ushered Ryan and Cleo into a room that doubled up as a spare office, stationery cupboard and storeroom. 'You can work in here,' she said, issuing them with white cotton gloves for handling the artefacts. She placed a large wooden drawer on the table and left them to it.

Cleo gazed at the contents of the drawer, each housed in its own little compartment. There were scrolls and fragments of earthy-brown papyrus, and writing tablets – rectangular wooden blocks covered with canvas and then coated with stucco, so that they could be wiped clean and used over again. She began to lift them out as carefully as a surgeon conducting a delicate transplant operation.

It wasn't long before she recognized a passage on one of the writing tablets, advising against cheating or stealing from the poor or disabled. Just as Dr Badawi had explained, it came from one of the famous wisdom texts, the *Instructions of Amenemope*. Cleo examined several more of the tablets. They all contained standard verses, obviously copied out as writing exercises. Cleo sighed. This wasn't going to help them find the Benben Stone. Then she caught sight of something that changed her mind.

'Yes!' she cried, turning to Ryan, who'd sat down next to her. 'There's a name and the date!' But suddenly she clamped her mouth shut. She'd forgotten she wasn't talking to Ryan.

'That says *Rahotep,* doesn't it?' Ryan asked, peering at the hieroglyphs on the tablet. 'I recognize it from the scarab.'

Ryan was right – it did say *Rahotep* – but Cleo turned away, shielding the writing tablet with her arm. She heard Ryan bang his hands down on the table and sigh. The hieroglyphs began to blur as her eyes filled with tears of frustration. She longed to share the exciting information on the writing tablet with Ryan, but how could she? *His mother's spying for the Ancient Order of the Eternal Sun and he lied to me about it. I'm working alone now . . .*

Ryan grabbed his hair in both hands. 'I don't blame you for being angry,' he said, staring down at the table. 'I'm sorry I lied. There's something I wish I could tell you, but it's not my secret to tell. It's Mum's, and I've already said too much.'

Cleo clenched her teeth. She was *not* going to be won over.

Ryan didn't give up. 'But I promise you, Mum's not trying to steal the stone.' He waited as a woman cloaked in a black *niqab* veil and long *abaya* came in to collect a box of computer paper. 'All I can do is ask you to trust me and I'll explain when I can. Cleo, please, look at me.'

Cleo turned her head an almost imperceptible fraction and looked at him out of the corner of her eye. The big grin had gone. His jaw was tense, his forehead furrowed. His skin was pale beneath the sprinkle of freckles that had been brought out by the Egyptian sun. She had to admit Ryan looked as if he meant every word. And if it *was* his mum's secret he was protecting, she could hardly blame him for that. *It's more than I managed to do*, she thought, with a familiar stab of regret as she remembered how she'd accidentally confirmed to Quirke that they were looking for the Benben Stone.

Maybe it wouldn't hurt to talk to Ryan just a little bit. It didn't mean she was going to tell him *everything*. She pushed the writing tablet along the table. 'The date on here is the twentieth day of *Peret* – that's the winter season – in the sixth year of the reign of Rameses II. If this is the same Rahotep as mentioned in the Heliopolis Papyrus, that would make him sixteen years old when he wrote this.'

Ryan punched the air. 'I knew it! This *has* to be our guy!'

Cleo smiled. It turned into a much bigger grin than she'd intended. It felt so good to let go of the big vat of rage she'd been lugging around with her, corroding everything it touched like sulphuric acid. But she still wasn't completely sure she could trust Ryan, so she quickly cancelled the smile.

'Does it say anything about going to Smenkhkare's tomb?' Ryan asked. 'Did he find the Benben Stone and take it back to the High Priests?'

Cleo shook her head.

Ryan's face fell. 'So even though you're talking to me you're still refusing to tell me anything?'

'No, it's not that,' Cleo explained. 'I mean, I haven't found any more information yet. These writing tablets over here are just more wisdom texts.' She picked one and read out a line at random, a stern warning not to trample on other people's furrows or move the boundary markers in their fields.

'I'll bear that in mind,' Ryan said.

'These papyri scrolls might contain something more

113

interesting,' Cleo went on, picking up the one with the drawing of the Bennu Bird. 'The problem is I can't read them. It's weird. I recognize the glyphs but they don't go together to make words . . .' She paused and sniffed the air.

Ryan stood and fetched her a box of tissues from the shelf by the photocopier. 'Are you getting a cold or something?'

'It's just that odd smell again,' Cleo mumbled. 'I'm sure I'm not imagining it.'

Ryan pretended to smell his T-shirt as he sat back down. 'Nope! It's not me. I had a shower this morning.'

Cleo frowned. 'Can *you* smell anything?'

'Dusty old papyrus,' Ryan said, wafting air towards his nose like a wine taster. 'There might be a top note of fly spray. And, yes, I think I'm getting a hint of wood polish.'

Cleo couldn't help laughing. 'I smelled it in the tomb when we were there yesterday. And then outside Dr Badawi's office too. It's sort of soapy and woody.' She glanced over her shoulder.

She thought she'd heard something but the room was empty.

Was she imagining things, or was someone following them?

17

MIRROR

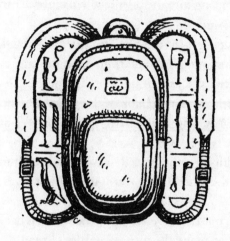

RYAN CHECKED HIS watch yet again.

An hour had crawled by and Cleo was still staring at the papyri, the tip of her tongue sticking out through the gap in her teeth. 'I still can't make sense of these,' she muttered. 'It's as if the symbols have all been jumbled up!'

'Maybe Rahotep was dyslexic,' Ryan suggested.

Cleo sighed. 'He's written out those wisdom texts with no problem.'

'Or writing in code,' Ryan tried, although he wasn't even sure how codes would work in hieroglyphs. He knew from Cleo that many of the symbols stood for individual sounds, but others represented two sounds or even a whole concept.

'If he was sent by the priests of Heliopolis on an undercover mission, maybe these were his top-secret reports.'

'He wasn't James Bond,' Cleo pointed out.

Half an hour later Ryan was wondering whether it was possible to literally die of boredom. He got up and went to the bathroom just for something to do. He was washing his hands and staring into the mirror when the idea came to him. *Could you do mirror writing with hieroglyphs?* He ran back into the storeroom. 'I've got it!' he said, grabbing the front of his T-shirt in both hands and tugging at the fabric.

Cleo looked at him as if he'd totally flipped.

'Remember those school kids on the ferry?' Ryan prompted. 'You said the hieroglyphs on their T-shirts were pointing the wrong way.'

Cleo nodded. 'If they face left, you read the line from left to right. If they face right, you start reading from the right. So what?'

'But you could *deliberately* write the symbols back to front,' Ryan said. 'To make the writing harder to read.'

Cleo didn't look convinced but she pulled a papyrus sheet closer. 'The glyphs all face left. If I start reading from the wrong end, the right, let's see . . .' Suddenly she pushed back from the table, shaking her head in disbelief. 'That's it! You've cracked it!'

Ryan grinned. 'A simple bit of Ancient Egyptian code-breaking? All in a day's work!'

Cleo studied the first line for a few minutes, then read out her translation. '*I have now been studying with the lector priests in the temple of Amun at Karnak for ten days.*' She looked up at Ryan. 'Karnak is a vast complex of many temples and it's right here in Luxor.'

'Result!' Ryan breathed. 'That was probably Rahotep's cover story for coming here. He pretended to be on work experience at the temple so he'd be near to the Valley of the Kings . . .'

'. . . and near to Smenkhkare's tomb,' Cleo agreed. She examined the papyrus again. 'This seems to be some kind of journal. *I hope that my masters will be pleased with my study of the rituals of Amun-Ra . . .*' She broke off, her eyebrows arched as if she'd seen something funny.

Ryan folded his arms and gave her a mock-stern look. 'Come on, share the joke!'

'He says the priests in Luxor are much fatter than in Heliopolis, but the girls are prettier.'

Ryan laughed. 'No wonder Rahotep put this in mirror writing. He wouldn't have wanted the boss priests reading this stuff!'

Just then the door opened.

Ryan and Cleo both spun round, but it was only Dr Badawi.

'I'm sorry,' she said, starting to pack writing tablets back into the box. 'We are closing now.'

'But I thought you were open till nine,' Cleo protested.

'I'm afraid it's a training day.'

Ryan groaned. 'And we were just starting to get somewhere.'

'I have some photographs of the papyri you can take away with you,' Dr Badawi offered, 'but I'm afraid I don't have any pictures of the writing tablets.'

'Could we borrow the tablets?' Cleo asked.

Dr Badawi adjusted her *hijab* under her chin. 'I'm sorry. I can't let them out of the museum.'

'Could I see that picture of your granddaughter again, Dr Badawi?' Ryan ignored Cleo glowering at him as Dr Badawi handed him her phone. He took his sketchbook from his backpack and quickly drew a likeness of the little girl.

Dr Badawi looked over his shoulder. 'Oh, that is wonderful!'

Ryan tore out the page and handed it to her. He'd made the little girl's eyes even bigger and dewier than in the photo.

'It's adorable,' Dr Badawi sighed. 'I will have it framed.'

'We'd be *really* careful with the writing tablets,' Ryan said. 'And we'd return them first thing tomorrow morning.'

'Well, I shouldn't do this really . . .' Dr Badawi said, turning to Cleo, 'but as you are Lydia McNeil's daughter, and these writings are not really of great value, I'll make an exception.'

'Thank you!' Cleo jumped up and hugged her. *'Shukran.'*

'We'll guard them with our lives!' Ryan promised.

Cleo and Ryan found a seat on the return ferry near the front of the top deck.

They were wedged between a young French couple and a very old lady in black buried under a mountain of shopping, which included a sack of rice, two blankets, a power drill and three cartons of cigarettes. Ryan placed his backpack between himself and Cleo on the bench. The writing tablets had been stowed inside, packed into snug foam liners in plastic clip-tight boxes.

The ferry headed for the west bank. The late afternoon sun was already a melting red disc that stained the Theban Hills russet and raspberry pink. As Ryan gazed across the water he thought of all the bodies that lay buried in the Necropolis beneath those rocky crags, the gateway to the realm of Osiris. He patted his backpack, just to check it was still there, and glanced at the crowd standing near the front of the boat. He spotted a familiar face and nudged Cleo. 'Isn't that our friendly neighbourhood photographer?'

There was no mistaking Max Henderson. He had one of those jowly faces that looked as if it were fighting a losing battle with gravity. He was taking photos with a zoom lens. 'I bet he's not happy about having to stand up,' Ryan whispered. 'Call this a ferry?' he said, mimicking Max's voice. 'I can't travel in these conditions!'

'I wonder what he's up to,' Cleo muttered.

Ryan didn't have a chance to reply.

He felt a bump on the bench next to him.

When he looked down, his backpack had vanished!

18

CROCODILE

PANIC JOLTED THROUGH Cleo's body like an electric shock.

She whirled round just in time to glimpse the back of a tall, dark-skinned man in a long blue *galabaya*, with a white *shaal* wrapped turban-style around his head, ploughing his way through the crowd of standing passengers towards the back of the ferry.

Ryan jumped up and opened his mouth to yell after the thief. But Cleo clapped her hand over his mouth before he could raise the alarm. 'No!' she hissed. 'We'll get Dr Badawi into trouble if anyone finds out what we've got in the bag.'

Instead they both chased the man, treading on toes, tripping over bags and ignoring disgruntled cries of protest.

Crouching behind a pile of luggage near the back of the boat, they spotted the thief leaning over the railing, holding the backpack above his head and bouncing it in his hands like a basketball player lining up for a shot.

Then he hurled it over the side.

Cleo ran to the railing but she could only watch as the bag flew through the air, a black smudge against the crimson sky. She heard a cry and looked down to see a man in a tiny blue rowing boat far below. 'I can't catch that!' he yelled in Arabic, as he paddled frantically towards the ferry. 'It's too far!'

The backpack reached the peak of its arc. It seemed to hover for a moment, before plummeting towards the water. Cleo threw her hands over her eyes, unable to watch. The bag would sink to the bottom of the river. The precious wooden writing tablets inside would be soaked. The ancient stucco would dissolve. *Rahotep's secret journals will be lost forever*, she thought. *We'll never learn the true hiding place of the Benben Stone.*

Cleo held her breath and waited for the splash.

It didn't come.

'Look!' Ryan whispered, next to her. Cleo peeped through her fingers. The backpack had come to land on one of the thick mats of bright green weed – a cross between a large raft and a small island – that floated along the Nile. Startled into flight, a pair of white egrets flapped their wings and took off.

The man in the rowing boat dug one oar into the water to swing the boat round, bent his back and pulled hard towards the raft of weeds.

Ryan dropped to his knees and began untying his laces. 'Hold these,' he said, straightening up and pushing his trainers into Cleo's arms.

Cleo gaped as Ryan hauled himself up onto the railing. 'Wh-what are you doing?'

'What do you think I'm doing? Getting the backpack.'

'No! You can't!' Cleo gasped. 'It's too high. And the water's not safe.'

'It can't be that bad!' Ryan nodded his head at a group of small boys jumping into the river from a concrete jetty on the distant bank.

'It's full of—' Cleo began, but Ryan had already jumped over the railing and launched himself into the air in a perfect racing dive. There was hardly a ripple as he entered the water halfway between the raft of weeds and the rowing boat.

'. . . parasitic worms,' Cleo finished her sentence into the empty space in which Ryan had stood just seconds before.

She looked round to see the thief's reaction, but the man in the blue *galabaya* had vanished.

Ryan plunged beneath the surface.

There was a sudden confusion of cold and bubbles and water up his nose and roaring in his ears. Then he popped his head up, spitting and blowing and flicking the hair out of his eyes. He trod water, trying to get his bearings. The river seemed to be on fire in the red glow of the setting sun. Then he heard the splash of an oar behind him. At the same moment he spotted the raft of weeds up ahead.

The race was on.

He sucked down a deep breath. Then he swam as he'd never swum before, even in the last lap of the North-West Schools Regional Freestyle Final.

He swam as if pursued by sharks.

But the rowing boat was gaining on him second by frantic second.

It was so close that when at last the first leafy fronds of the weed raft came into reach he could feel the bow of the boat bumping against his feet. Gulping for oxygen, he hauled his way up through the matted foliage, the slimy tangle of roots and stalks wrapping around his legs as if trying to drag him down into the murky depths. He could see the dark bulk of the backpack now. That's when he realized he hadn't thought this plan through.

Would he be able to outswim the rowing boat again? *Maybe.*

Carrying the backpack clear of the water? *Doubtful.*

All the way to the shore? *No chance.*

But he didn't have any other option.

He lunged for the backpack.

But before he could grab hold, an oar appeared from behind him, hooked under a strap and whisked it away.

'Noooo!' Ryan cried. The man in the boat had beaten him to it. He'd wanted so much to save the writing tablets and prove to Cleo that he wasn't the scheming liar she took him for, but he'd failed. And now, just to complete the disaster, something was buffeting and butting his legs under the water. Something big and solid and alive! Suddenly he remembered the words of Smenkhkare's curse: *he shall be devoured by the crocodile.*

I knew we should never have opened that chamber!

Ryan could almost feel the mighty jaws crushing his thigh, ripping flesh from bone.

A torrent of adrenaline flooded his system. His heart

pumped to bursting point. He kicked his legs. He tore at the weeds. He scrabbled to pull himself up. But it was no good. His arms and legs were already exhausted by swimming. He was slipping back into the water . . .

Then Ryan felt hands grasp him under the arms and haul him roughly over the side of a boat. He lay on his back on the rough wood, eyes closed, waiting for his heart to stop its frenzied thrashing.

He'd been captured by the thieves. Who knew what would happen now?

But it had to be better than being devoured by crocodiles.

He opened one eye. He saw red sky. Then the dark brown fabric of a *galabaya*.

That's odd, he thought. He was sure the man in the boat had been wearing a blue one. He opened the other eye. Was that a red nylon tracksuit?

'Hey! Mr Manchester United!' came a cheeky voice. 'You like swim?'

Ryan sat up and looked round. He was in a rowing boat, but it wasn't the one that had been racing him for the backpack. This one was smaller, the jade-green paint peeling from the weathered hull.

And the occupants were Mr Mansour and his grandson.

Ryan looked back across the water. The thief's accomplice had obviously given up the chase now that they had company and was rowing away into the distance.

Mr Mansour gave the smallest of nods and went back to adjusting his fishing rod, as if scooping drowning swimmers out of the Nile was all part of a normal fishing expedition. '*Salaam alaikum,*' he muttered, the cigarette in the corner of his mouth twitching as he spoke.

'*Wa alaikum salaam,*' Ryan returned, copying the phrase he'd heard Cleo use. Then he held up a hand for a high five with Ali. But as he dropped his hand back his spirits fell. *The backpack!* He groaned as the memory hit home. His backpack had been hooked out of the water by an oar. The thieves had got it.

'You look for this?' Ali asked, his grin showing off his missing front teeth. Ryan stared, hardly able to take in what he was seeing. Ali was holding out his battered old blue backpack. The oar that had snagged it by the strap had belonged to Mr Mansour after all! Ryan took the dripping backpack, pulled off strands of weed and unzipped it. To his huge relief the writing tablets were still dry and unharmed in their plastic boxes.

He leaned back against the edge of the boat and closed his eyes.

Mr Mansour began to paddle for shore. Squinting into the setting sun, Ryan saw that the ferry had already docked and Cleo was running along the riverbank towards them. Ali hopped out into the shallows and guided the boat through the reeds.

Ryan stood up. His legs were streaked with blood and they were starting to sting like crazy.

Cleo helped him out of the boat. 'What happened?' she panted, unwinding her cotton scarf from her neck and handing it to him to dry himself.

'I think it was a crocodile,' Ryan said, 'but I managed to fight it off,' he added, doing his best to sound as if crocodile wrangling was something he engaged in on a fairly regular basis and nothing to make a fuss about.

'A *crocodile*?' Cleo echoed.

She said something to Mr Mansour and Ali. Mr Mansour's wrinkled face split into a huge grin. Ali giggled and hopped around, snapping his arms together like giant jaws.

'What's so funny?' Ryan demanded. 'Next time you lose something, remind me not to bother risking my life to save it.'

Cleo straightened her face. 'Sorry. It's just that there *aren't* any crocodiles in the Nile any more. Not north of the Aswan dam, anyway.'

Mr Mansour reached into the bottom of his boat, hooked two fingers into the gaping mouth of a silver-scaled fish and held it up for all to see. The tail brushed the ground; it was almost a metre long. The old man grinned and rubbed his stomach and chuckled something Ryan didn't understand.

'It's a Nile perch,' Cleo translated. 'That must be what you felt in the water. Mr Mansour says it's delicious.'

Ryan eyed the perch suspiciously. He felt sure it had been thinking the same about *him* just a few moments ago.

'Those scratches on your legs are from the weeds,' Cleo said. 'We should go and get them cleaned up.'

Ryan nodded and handed her the backpack. 'The writing tablets are fine.'

Cleo looked him straight in the eye for a long moment. 'Jumping off that ferry was the most idiotic, dangerous, stupid, mad stunt I've ever seen,' she said. 'But thank you,' she added.

'Don't mention it,' Ryan replied. 'Especially the part about the crocodile attack. Don't *ever* mention that.'

Cleo smiled. 'I promise! Come on. Let's get to the clinic. You'll probably need antibiotics to stop you catching anything from the water.'

Ryan looked down at his slashed shins. 'I'll have to tell my mum I dropped my backpack when we were getting off the ferry and had to wade through the reeds to get it back. She'll go crazy if she finds out how I really ended up in the river. If I'd known being your bodyguard would be so dangerous I'd never have taken the job!' He laughed as he spoke but silently he vowed never to jump into uncharted waters from a moving vehicle again.

And when Cleo wasn't looking he felt for his St Christopher through his sodden T-shirt. Then he slid his other hand into his shorts pocket and closed his fingers around Rahotep's scarab amulet.

Between them they'd just about got him through.

19

JOURNAL

CLEO AND RYAN followed Ali on a shortcut back to the village.

He led them along well-trodden paths through fields of sugar cane. The long green leaves rustled high over their heads on thick bamboo-like stems. The heat was seeping out of the day as dusk gathered and swifts swooped for low-flying insects. Ali skipped ahead, swishing a stick at the eucalyptus and willows that grew along the irrigation channels. Cleo decided not to mention the giant monitor lizards that made their homes in the undergrowth bordering the ditches. Ryan had had enough close encounters with the local wildlife for one day.

And she had a feeling that they had something more

sinister than monitor lizards to worry about anyway. 'Who do you think they were?' she asked. 'Those two men who tried to steal the backpack?'

Ryan shrugged. 'Thieves, I guess. I'm sure they work the ferries all the time.'

Cleo wasn't so sure. 'So you don't think they were especially targeting the writing tablets?'

'No one even knew we had the boxes from the museum apart from Dr Badawi,' Ryan pointed out.

'But it's strange that they only went for *our* bag.'

'The way we were guarding that backpack,' Ryan said, 'I bet they thought we had gold bars in there! Or an expensive camera at the very least . . .'

Ryan was probably right, Cleo thought. But as they entered a grove of glossy-leaved orange trees, she couldn't shake the feeling that the theft *hadn't* been random. Someone had followed them into Smenkhkare's tomb. Now someone had tried to steal the backpack containing Rahotep's writings. Surely there was a connection. 'I kept getting the feeling I was being followed at the museum,' she said.

Ryan bugged his eyes at her. 'You were. By me! I was stalking you the whole time. In a totally professional capacity, of course!'

Cleo couldn't help laughing. 'I don't mean *you*!' Then she remembered there was something else too. 'And there's the smell,' she added. 'It was in the tomb and at the Theban Museum this morning.'

Ryan frowned. 'Are you *sure* it was the same?'

Cleo pointed at her temple. 'The brain system that processes odours is closely linked to the memory and emotion systems. Olfactory memories are very powerful . . .'

'Olfactory?' Ryan stopped her. 'I take it that's the technical term for smelly?' He reached up, picked an orange from an overhanging branch and handed it to Cleo. 'Here's something for your olfactory system!'

Cleo breathed in the delicious sun-warmed scent.

'You overthink things, you know,' Ryan said.

'Well, you *under*think things!' Cleo wasn't even sure that was a real word but it was the best she could come up with.

She peeled the orange and was about to take a bite when she hesitated and glanced across at Ryan. His dark blond hair was flaked with dried mud and a bruise was coming up on his cheek where he must have bumped the side of the boat. He was being so nice and yet, she couldn't forget that if they *were* being followed it was almost certainly by someone working for Danny Farr and the Ancient Order of the Eternal Sun. Whatever Ryan said, there was no getting away from the fact that his mother was a member, and she was on first-name terms with Danny Farr.

Am I really meant to believe that Julie Flint isn't planning to steal the Benben Stone in time for the Return of the Phoenix? And that Ryan isn't just helping me so he can pass the information on to her?

Or am I just overthinking *again?* Cleo recalled the definition of *paranoia* from a course she'd taken in cognitive psychology: *an unfounded or extreme distrust of others, which can reach delusional proportions.*

Suddenly overwhelmed by confusion, the bittersweet smell of the orange caught in her throat.

She gave the fruit to Ali.

Cleo drew the blinds.

Although it was only early evening, it was dark outside.

She pushed books and papers off her desk and switched on the old reading lamp. Scorched dust rose from the metal shade. She'd brought the backpack home with her so that she could continue deciphering Rahotep's writings while Ryan went to the clinic to have the cuts on his legs cleaned and dressed. She took out all the writing tablets and the photographs of the papyri, laid them out under the pool of light and picked up where she'd left off.

Reading the mirror-writing hieroglyphs had been slow and tedious to start, but she had the hang of it now and soon had several pages of translation written up in her notebook.

She learned about Rahotep's daily life in the temple of Amun at Karnak. At dawn, noon and dusk, he and the other priests would cleanse themselves in the sacred stone pool before entering the shrine to carry out the rituals to honour the god Amun, whose *ka* – or spirit – resided in a golden statue encrusted with jewels. The priests would chant the dawn hymn, *Awake in peace, oh great Amun*, then wash the statue with fragrant oils and dress it in fresh linen garments before burning incense and setting out a sumptuous breakfast of roast meats, baskets of bread and fruit and jars of beer and wine.

She also found out a lot about the other priests: old Rekhmire always cheated when he moved his pieces in a game of *senet*, Ahmose was sneaking out to meet one of the girls from the spice market, Hori often made off with the jugs of wine and roast ducks from the offering table and hid them in a secret cache beneath a loose flagstone.

It seemed there wasn't much going on around the temple

that Rahotep missed! No wonder he'd taken to using mirror writing to keep his diary. The other priests would have been extremely interested – and upset – to know what he had to say about them!

Cleo was so absorbed in Rahotep's journal that she jumped when her phone buzzed in her pocket. She pulled it out to see a text from Ryan.

Clinic packed, still waiting to see nurse.

She kept looking at Ryan's words long after she'd finished reading them. She imagined him befriending everyone in the waiting room, playing with the children, charming the old ladies . . .

It was so confusing.

Cleo knew she was no expert on friendship. She'd never had friends of her own age – unless you counted the online classmates she discussed essay topics with over a video link now and then. Was Ryan her friend or not? He'd started out by laughing at her name. Then he'd saved her life by pulling her out of the deadfall. He'd made her laugh and told her they were a great team. He'd ruined everything by lying to her about his mum being in the Ancient Order of the Eternal Sun. Then he'd risked his life by jumping in the Nile to rescue the writing tablets.

This morning she'd hated him so much the sound of his breathing as he followed her round the museum had made her want to tear her ears off.

Now she was glancing at her watch, hoping there'd still be time for him to call round after seeing the nurse.

Was friendship *meant* to be this complicated? Or was she just doing it all wrong?

Cleo sighed and returned to her notebook. Compared

to friendship, translating encrypted hieroglyphic texts was simple. She stretched and rubbed her eyes. Rahotep's diary was a fascinating insight into his everyday life, but he still hadn't even hinted that he was on a top-secret mission to search for the Benben Stone. *Maybe my theory's wrong and he's just an ordinary apprentice.* But Cleo wasn't ready to give up yet. There were several more papyri to go. All she could was keep looking . . .

When Dad put his head round the door an hour later to say the team were all going out to dinner at the Moonlight, a garden restaurant on the next street, she barely glanced up long enough to say she'd rather stay at home.

She was on her way into the kitchen to make a sandwich when there was a knock at the door. It was Ryan, sporting dry jeans and T-shirt and a powerful pong of antiseptic cream. He held out the scarf she'd given him to dry off with when he'd waded out of the river. 'I've washed it as best I could,' he said.

Cleo took the neatly folded scarf. It was only a frayed old length of white cotton with some straggly fringing, but it was her favourite. It was still damp and had a whiff of Nile water about it, but she was happy to have it back. She hadn't really expected to see it again.

'Do you want a sandwich?' she asked, pulling bread and cheese and tomatoes from the fridge and sitting down at the kitchen table with a knife and chopping board.

'Sure,' Ryan said, joining her at the table. 'Swimming is hungry work.' He nodded towards her desk, which was visible through the open door of her room. 'Have you got any further with deciphering the papyri?'

Cleo stopped, her knife halfway through a tomato. She

was sure they were getting close to learning the truth about the Benben Stone. But she had to be sure she could trust Ryan before they went any further.

'Are you sure you didn't recognize the thief?' she asked.

'Are you *still* going on about that?' Ryan said, pinching a slice of cheese from the chopping board. 'Why would I recognize him? Do you think I've secretly spent my childhood working as a pickpocket with a gang of Nile ferry thieves? Like an Egyptian Oliver Twist or something?'

Cleo didn't laugh.

'Anyway,' Ryan pointed out. 'I only saw him from the back. Same as you.'

'What about the accomplice in the rowing boat?' Cleo pressed.

Ryan rolled his eyes. 'In case you didn't notice, I was busy swimming in the opposite direction.' Suddenly he jerked his head as if he'd taken an upper cut to the jaw. He nodded slowly. 'I've just realized what this is about. Why don't you come out with it? Did I recognize them as my mum's buddies from the Eternal Sun? Are they part of the evil plot she's masterminding to steal the Benben Stone?'

Cleo tried, but she couldn't look him in the eye. That was, of course, *exactly* what she'd been thinking. She laid four slices of tomato on a piece of bread and concentrated on lining them up so they were all an equal distance from the crust. 'Well?' she mumbled.

'Mum is not planning to steal the stone.' Ryan bit off each word in a quiet voice that throbbed with anger.

Cleo wanted to believe him. She *did* believe him. Almost. She knew she should leave it alone but it was like pushing her tongue against a mouth ulcer – it hurt but she couldn't stop. 'Did you tell her why we were going to the museum?'

Ryan let out a harsh yip of laughter. 'Yeah, I left a note saying I'd gone off to hunt for the Benben Stone and she should tell Danny Farr and the rest of the brotherhood to get their best phoenix-worshipping outfits ready!'

Cleo couldn't bear it. Ryan was making fun of her again! She slammed a piece of bread down on top of the tomatoes. Seeds sprayed out across the table. 'We're talking about one of the most sacred objects in human history and you think it's *funny*?'

Ryan shot to his feet, pushing back his chair which toppled over, clattering on the tiled floor. 'You think you're so smart, but you don't know anything about *anything*!'

Cleo stood up and glared at him across the table. 'This is all one big joke to you, isn't it?'

'If you must know, Mum's not working for the Eternal Sun,' Ryan flung back. 'She's the one trying to *stop* them!'

Cleo backed away, deflating as if someone had pulled out a stopper. 'W-what do you mean?' she stammered.

Ryan turned his back and made for the front door. 'Nothing! Forget it!'

But Cleo wasn't in the mood for forgetting. She grabbed his arm to pull him round. Then she ducked past him and stood in front of the door, her arms folded.

'Tell me what's going on!' she said.

20

HIDDEN

RYAN BACKED UP against the table.

Cleo looked more like an Egyptian goddess than ever, imperiously guarding the door as if it were the gate to the Underworld. Her nose only came up to the Superdry logo on his T-shirt, but Ryan knew he wasn't going to get past her. He opened his mouth and then closed it again as he tried to figure out what to say.

He had to protect his mother.

But he couldn't lie to Cleo again.

He'd only known her three days but somehow he was certain he could trust her. It was against all the rules but he was going to have to tell her truth.

'Mum is a reporter.'

Cleo made a growling sound. '*I know that!* She's doing this report on the dig for the Danny Farr Foundation. It's her cover story so she can snoop for the Eternal Sun . . .'

Ryan shook his head and stepped towards her. 'No, you don't understand.' He spoke so softly that Cleo had to lean in to catch the words. 'She's an *investigative* reporter. She's been looking into the activities of the Ancient Order of the Eternal Sun for months. That's the only reason she joined up. She's spent ages studying to be initiated – there are secret passwords and handshakes and that special symbol they have with the double ankh and the fiery sun. She's *undercover*.'

Cleo was silent for a long moment. Ryan listened to the rattle and thud of the building's dilapidated air-conditioning system. A door slammed somewhere upstairs.

'*Activities?*' Cleo echoed at last. They were standing so close now they could have been about to tango. Or wrestle.

'*Criminal* activities.' Ryan spoke in a whisper even though he knew the flat was empty. 'Mum's not interested in all their mad rituals and stuff. She suspects they have links to organized crime – smuggling antiquities and works of art, mainly.'

Cleo's eyes widened. 'She thinks they're planning to steal the Benben?'

Ryan shrugged. 'All she knows is that they may have someone operating here in Luxor, but she doesn't know who it is or what they're planning – yet. She thinks it could even be an insider on the dig team. I'm sorry I didn't tell you before . . .' He tensed, waiting for the fallout. Given how Cleo had reacted the first time she'd found out he was lying, he was fairly sure she was going to hit the roof now. In fact, she might even hit *him*. But she simply let her arms drop to her sides.

'You're not angry?' he asked.

Cleo leaned back against the door. 'No. It makes sense now. Being an undercover reporter is a perfectly logical reason for secrecy and duplicity.'

'Please don't tell anyone,' Ryan begged. 'If the Eternal Sun find out Mum's spying on them, who knows what they'll do.'

'First I can't tell anyone your mum *is* a member of the Eternal Sun,' Cleo said with a grin. 'Now I can't tell anyone she's *not* a member. Make your mind up!'

'So, you won't say anything?' Ryan asked again.

'My lips are sealed!' Cleo made a zipping gesture. 'We're a team, after all.'

'A great team!' Ryan laughed. 'The Dynamic Duo. No,' he said, correcting himself. 'That should be the Terrific Trio! You, me and Rahotep.'

Cleo moved away from the door. 'Does your mum know that we're trying to find the Benben by following Rahotep's trail?' she asked, as she wiped the tomato seeds from the table.

Ryan shook his head. 'I haven't told her. She'd only worry that we'll be in danger if we get involved. The Ancient Order of the Eternal Sun are a ruthless lot. She'd probably ground me if she found out.'

Cleo nodded. 'I think it's best if we keep my parents out of this for now as well. They'd panic too. Let's keep working on this by ourselves until we know what we're dealing with.' She handed him a plate of sandwiches and led the way back to her desk. 'I've made some progress but nothing says that Rahotep is planning to visit Smenkhkare's tomb yet.'

Ryan smiled. It felt good to be working alongside Cleo again. He was glad he'd come clean and told her the truth. 'So,' he said, grabbing a kitchen chair and bringing it through so he could sit at the desk next to her, 'have you come up with a theory yet?' He was reaching to push the writing tablets aside to make room for his sandwich plate when Cleo grabbed his wrist. 'Don't touch them with tomato juice all over your hands!'

Ryan's hand slipped and knocked one of the writing tablets off the desk.

He dived out of his chair to catch it, but it was too late. The tablet bounced off his outstretched fingers.

It skidded across the tiles, hit the wall and snapped in half.

The two friends stared in silence at the broken writing tablet.

The only sound was the soft thud of a moth headbutting the lamp bulb.

When, at last, Cleo spoke, her voice trembled. 'Look what you've done!'

'What *I've* done?' Ryan spluttered. 'You're the one who grabbed my hand!'

'*You* knocked it flying!' Cleo fired back.

Ryan knelt on the floor for a closer look. The wooden tablet had split like a cake into two horizontal layers. One piece was propped on its side in the corner. The other was caught up in the tassels of the rug.

Cleo slumped back in her chair. 'How are we going to tell Dr Badawi?'

Ryan didn't know. He picked up the two pieces, hardly daring to touch them in case they crumbled to dust in his hands. He blew away a ball of fluff. He was amazed to see that there were no splinters or cracks in the ancient wood. The newly exposed surfaces were smooth and white, with darker patches of what appeared to be dried-up glue dotting the edges. He looked up at Cleo. Her elbows were on the desk, her head in her hands.

'We haven't broken it,' he said. 'These two sections were stuck together like Lego bricks.'

Cleo glanced down at him through a veil of sleek black hair, but she didn't move.

'And there's more writing inside . . .'

Cleo's head snapped up.

Still on his knees, Ryan passed the pieces up to Cleo as if he were making an offering to a goddess.

Without a word, she picked up her magnifying glass and angled the pieces of the tablet towards the lamplight to pick out the rows of tiny symbols.

Ryan got up, sat back on his chair, reached for another of the writing tablets and turned it over. A hairline crack ran around the outside. He eased the tip of a sharp pencil into the join. With the slightest of twists the two halves of the tablet sprang apart. He tried another. It also popped in two. Just like the first tablet, the inner surfaces were covered in writing.

'Looks like we've found Rahotep's secret notes,' he said.

Cleo held out her hand without looking up from the magnifying glass. 'Quick, give me that pencil. I'll start translating. At least this part's not in mirror writing . . .' With that she began jotting in her notebook, eyes flicking back and forth between the page and the writing tablet, stopping only for the occasional high-speed riffle through her hieroglyphic dictionary.

Ryan peered over her shoulder. 'What does it say?'

Cleo waved him away with a don't-interrupt-me-now gesture, her pencil still flying over the page.

Ryan gave up. He began to copy a diagram from one of the other writing tablets into his sketchbook. It was a grid of five-pointed stars, just like the ones he'd seen on the ceilings in Smenkhkare's tomb. There were two rows of six larger stars down the middle, with a block of sixty-one on each side. *It was probably just Rahotep doodling during a particularly dull Advanced Priest Studies lesson,* he thought, *but, then again, it might be important.*

At last Cleo dropped her pencil. She blinked as if waking from a long dream.

'So, do you want to know what Rahotep says?' Without giving Ryan a chance to answer, she began to read from her notebook. '*After morning duties in the temple, High Priest Meryt, the Greatest of Seers, summoned me to his private chamber. Had I failed my studies so badly that I was to be sent home?*' Cleo looked up for a moment. 'This was while Rahotep was still in Heliopolis at the Great Sun Temple,' she explained. '*I trembled in fear. Not for my own ambitions – I would far rather leave the temple and train as an artist – but my mother has set her heart on me following my father into the priesthood—*'

'I know the feeling, Rahotep, mate,' Ryan cut in. 'My mum's always on at me about going to university instead of art college when I leave school.'

Cleo ignored the interruption. '*I entered the room and stared at the gold ornaments on Meryt's white sash, the leopard skin over his shoulder and the sceptre in his hand,*' she read, '*and waited for my punishment. But when at last he spoke, the Great Seer did not scold me. Instead he said, "Rahotep, I hear that you are a bright boy with a talent for noticing things and for solving puzzles. I have a puzzle for you now, one that you must breathe to no one. The Benben Stone has been stolen".'*

Cleo's green eyes glinted in the lamplight as she paused for breath. She picked up her pencil and made a small correction to a word in her notebook and then continued to read. *'At first I thought the Great Seer spoke in jest. Surely the Benben could not have been stolen from the Mansion of the Phoenix in the Great Sun Temple of Atum-Ra, for I had seen it only that morning, glowing in the first rays of dawn. But Meryt told me that the Benben Stone in the temple is a replica, fashioned in secret by skilled craftsmen. "The original disappeared almost fifty years ago," he explained. "We kept the truth hidden because we did not wish the people of the Two Lands to regard the loss as an omen of doom".'*

Ryan snorted. 'Or maybe the High Priests just didn't want to look like a bunch of idiots for letting someone nick their sacred object from right under their noses!'

'Are you *sure* you can't read hieroglyphs?' Cleo asked. 'Rahotep says exactly the same thing!'

Ryan grinned. 'Great minds think alike!'

'Well, whatever the real reason,' Cleo said, 'the High Priests clearly wanted to keep the theft of the Benben a secret – which explains why there's no mention of it in the Heliopolis Papyrus. *And* why they didn't just call in the Medjay – the police – to investigate.'

'So why is the High Priest telling Rahotep about it now?' Ryan asked.

'I'm just getting to that,' Cleo said. 'Meryt tells Rahotep that he's received some very interesting information. Just that morning, he says, the Medjay officers had brought a prisoner to see him in his chambers. This man offered to reveal the true whereabouts of the Benben Stone in return for a pardon for his crimes. He'd been sentenced to death by impalement on a stake, followed by burning, for killing a neighbour in a drunken brawl . . .'

Ryan grimaced at the gory details but Cleo didn't miss a beat. She got up and paced around the room as she read out High Priest Meryt's words. *The wretched prisoner fell to his knees and claimed to have heard a rumour from a distant cousin – a tomb guard in the Valley of the Kings – that it was no other than Pharaoh Smenkhkare who had stolen the Benben from the Mansion of the Phoenix, and that he had concealed it in his tomb as an offering to Osiris. It is almost certainly a lie, of course – a condemned man's feeble bid to avoid his fate – but it is worth looking into nevertheless . . .'*

Ryan jumped up. He could hardly believe it – Cleo's theory was right! 'Meryt's going to send Rahotep on a Search And Retrieve Mission, isn't he?'

Cleo stopped pacing, smiled triumphantly at him over her notebook and nodded. 'Meryt tells Rahotep that he will spend the season of Peret at the Temple of Amun-Ra in the Most Sacred of Places – that's the great temple complex of Karnak – under the supervision of a priest called Hori.'

'Just as we thought, the perfect cover story . . .' Ryan murmured, sinking back into his chair.

'Exactly. And here are Meryt's parting instructions,' Cleo went on. *'Rahotep, you will continue to be a Servant of God, but you will also carry out secret investigations. You must enter Smenkhkare's tomb under cover of darkness and if, by chance, the prisoner was telling the truth and the Benben Stone is indeed concealed within, you will bring it back to its rightful home in*

143

Heliopolis. Tell no one of your mission. A young apprentice priest travelling alone will attract little attention.'

'Wow!' Ryan breathed. 'So we've really found Rahotep's secret mission notes! Who could have guessed they were hidden away inside these tablets.'

Cleo nodded. 'I'm sure he was going to write all up in an official report when he returned to Heliopolis. Meantime, he had to keep it all well away from prying eyes. It sounds like the other priests were pretty nosy.'

Cleo sat back down next to Ryan in the pool of light from the desk lamp and looked back at her notes. 'Meryt promised Rahotep a magnificent Golden Collar of Honour if he found the Benben. He also gave him several precious amulets to protect him on his quest.' She looked intently at Ryan before reading out Rahotep's next lines. *'But the only talisman I need is my old green scarab, the one my father brought back from the coronation of Pharaoh Rameses II when I was ten years old. Since Father died, his* ka *protects me through the scarab.'*

Ryan felt in his jeans pocket for the scarab amulet – he'd remembered to transfer it from his muddy shorts – and stroked the smooth domed wing cases. *How often*, he wondered, *had Rahotep done the same thing, thinking of his father as he did so.* Ryan knew exactly how he must have felt. He reached for the St Christopher his own father had given him five years ago – only a few weeks before he'd disappeared. It was smooth and flat like a small silver coin, engraved with the image of the patron saint of travellers carrying a child across a river. He thought of Dad whenever he saw it.

Despite the three thousand years between their lives, at that moment Ryan felt as close to Rahotep as he had ever done to anyone. He knew they would have been instant friends, sitting at the back of the class, drawing pictures and sharing jokes. It was as if a thread connected them through time. He could almost feel Rahotep tugging on the other end of it.

Surfacing from his reverie, Ryan decided not to mention his time-thread moment to Cleo. No doubt she'd consider it unscientific or irrational or something. 'What does our man on the scene say next?' he asked instead.

'Rahotep followed the High Priest's instructions and went to Smenkhkare's tomb at night.' Cleo looked up and smiled. 'He was very clever. He *borrowed* the official seal of the Necropolis from one of the tomb guards. He took new wax with him and re-sealed the door of the tomb afterwards. That's why we thought the seal had never been broken.'

Smart move, Rahotep, Ryan thought. He felt another tug on the thread through time, knowing that he and Cleo had followed exactly in the young priest's footsteps: up the winding road into the dark hills, past the snoring night watchman – it must have been easy for Rahotep to pinch the key and the seal while the guard slept – up the steep path to the cleft in the ridge and into the black heart of the tomb. The Valley of the Kings had hardly changed in thousands of years. The only difference was that Rahotep probably hadn't gone by bike.

'Pressing my scarab amulet to my heart, and praying to Anubis and Osiris for protection, I opened the sarcophagus,' Cleo continued to read. *'I found Smenkhkare's Confession, just as the informant had predicted. It said that Smenkhkare had placed the Benben in the fourth house towards the realm of Osiris. Dawn was fast approaching when I found the secret*

entrance through the false wall, and I almost plunged into a deep pit—'

'Been there, done that!' Ryan muttered.

'*But at last I found the chamber,*' Cleo went on.

Ryan could hardly bear the tension. 'Was the Benben Stone there?'

SCORPION

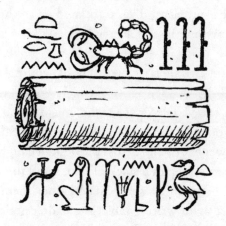

CLEO'S NOTEBOOK DROPPED to the desk with a slap that echoed in the silence.

'No,' she said. 'Rahotep found the fourth chamber empty, just like we did.'

Ryan groaned. 'So, that's it! End of story?'

Cleo shook her head. 'Not according to Rahotep.' She pointed to a line of hieroglyphs. 'He says *I now believe that Smenkhkare's Confession is no more real than a mirage in the desert, the lush green oasis that turns to sand as you draw closer.*'

'A mirage?' Ryan repeated. 'That's like an illusion.'

Cleo nodded.

'You mean Rahotep thinks the Smenkhkare Confession was a *fake*?'

Cleo nodded again.

'But if Old Smenkers didn't steal the stone, then who did?' Ryan asked. Suddenly he looked suspicious. 'And why does Rahotep believe the Confession is a fake? He must have found some sort of evidence.'

'That's the problem. I've translated everything and I can't find anything else,' Cleo sighed. She'd sorted all the writings into two piles on her desk: the scrolls of papyri which contained Rahotep's everyday-life journal in mirror writing, and the wooden writing tablets with extracts from the wisdom texts copied out on the outsides and his secret case notes hidden on the insides. 'We've read all this,' she said but, as she swept her hand across the desk, it caught the edge of a dictionary on top of a stack of books and the whole pile tumbled to the floor. As she bent to gather them up, Ryan reached for a small writing tablet she hadn't noticed before. It must have slid to the back of the desk behind the books.

They looked at each other. Cleo knew they were both thinking the same thing. *This could hold the final clue in the search for the missing Benben Stone!*

'Go on, open it!' Cleo urged.

Ryan prised the two halves apart.

Cleo leaned closer to get a first glimpse of the writing on the inner surfaces. But to her astonishment, there *were* no inner surfaces. The tablet had been carefully hollowed out to form a little box. Ryan tipped it up and a tiny scroll, as brown and brittle as an autumn leaf, rolled out onto the desk.

Cleo found a pair of tweezers and, with shaking hands, she unfurled the tissue-thin papyrus.

'What does it say?' Ryan asked.

'Give me a chance!' Cleo peered through her magnifying glass and read the first line. *Witness statement from Kaha, Scorpion Charmer of Set Maat village.* She looked up. '*Set Maat* is the old name for Deir el-Medina, the ancient tomb-workers' village near the Valley of the Kings.'

'Witness statement?' Ryan laughed. 'Sounds like old Rahotep fancied himself as the New Kingdom's answer to Sherlock Holmes. So, come, on, what does this scorpion charmer say? Does he know who really stole the Benben Stone?'

Cleo threw the magnifying glass down on the desk. 'It's not mirror writing, but I can't read the rest of it! I think Rahotep's started using some other kind of code.'

'Maybe old Hori, or one of the other priests, was getting even nosier and he had to upgrade his security measures,' Ryan suggested. 'I bet this little scroll contains the most sensitive information of all if Rahotep had to hide it like this *and* come up with a whole new code!'

Cleo felt so exhausted she could hardly hold her head up. 'I don't think I can face any more codes tonight.'

'I'm not surprised,' Ryan said. 'You've been translating for hours. Your brain must be fried.'

Cleo sighed. 'But we have to return everything to the museum first thing in the morning.'

'Don't worry. I'll take photos of the papyrus on my phone. Then we can carry on working on it tomorrow.' Ryan grinned as he positioned the papyrus under the lamplight. 'Just one question – I've heard of snake charmers, but why would anyone want to charm *scorpions*?'

'Scorpion charmers were magicians who were called

in to cast spells to rid places of poisonous creatures,' Cleo explained.

'Like Ancient Egyptian Rentokil?'

'Sort of. And, if that didn't work, they had other spells that were meant to heal the bites and stings.'

They both jumped as Cleo's phone buzzed. 'A text from my parents,' she murmured, glancing at the screen. 'They'll be back in fifteen minutes.'

Ryan looked at his watch. 'It's past eleven o'clock. I'd better go.' He started to get up. 'I'll meet you in the morning to take this lot back.'

Cleo's hand flew to her mouth. She stared at the writing tablets on the desk – each one split into two halves – as if seeing them for the first time. *What have we done? What were we thinking?* 'We can't take them back like this! Dr Badawi will lose her job. My parents will kill me!'

Ryan picked up two halves. 'I'm sure we can stick them . . .'

Cleo gaped at him as if he'd just suggested using the ancient writing tablets as firewood. 'You can't just superglue the past back together!'

'You got a better suggestion?' Ryan scratched at the flakes of dried glue on the tablet. 'If it was good enough for Rahotep . . .' He reached across to the computer keyboard and typed in ANCIENT EGYPT GLUE. 'Look! We can make something authentic. They used all kinds of natural adhesives.'

'Collagen extracted from cows' hooves?' Cleo read out from the screen. 'Gum prepared from the bark of the acacia tree?' She clutched at her hair with both hands. 'We haven't got time to start brewing up elaborate potions.'

But Ryan was undeterred. 'Egg white!' he said, pointing at the list. 'You must have some eggs in the—'

Before he could finish the sentence, Cleo had darted into the kitchen and flung open the fridge door. Three small white eggs lay on the shelf next to a wilted lettuce. She grabbed them, cracked them on the side of a bowl and separated the whites.

When her parents entered the flat ten minutes later, Cleo had just finished dabbing egg white onto the last of the writing tablets. Ryan pushed the two halves snugly together and weighted the tablet under the hieroglyphic dictionary to set.

'Cleopatra Calliope McNeil!' The shout came from the kitchen. 'What on earth have you been doing? There are egg yolks *everywhere*!'

Ryan and Cleo looked at each other and tried not to laugh.

'Calliope?' Ryan echoed.

'It means beautiful voice, if you must know!' Cleo shook her head. 'Shame I'm tone deaf. Sorry, Mum!' she called back. 'We needed the whites to . . . erm . . .'

'Make meringues,' Ryan shouted.

'Meringues?' Cleo mouthed. 'Is that the best we can come up with?'

Ryan shrugged and grinned. 'Yeah, I know! It's late. I've had a tough day!'

22

STARS

THEY STARTED OUT early the next morning.

A fresh river breeze whipped Cleo's hair across her face as she gazed out from under the canopy of the motorboat. The egg-white glue seemed to have held and the writing tablets were now safely encased in their boxes once more. Ryan was clutching the backpack on his lap so tightly, Cleo noticed, it would have taken the combined armies of the nine enemies of Ancient Egypt to wrest it from his grip, even though they were the only passengers; they'd decided to pay extra to cross the Nile in a private boat taxi to avoid any more run-ins with ferry thieves.

Cleo was thinking. Her thoughts were, of course, all about

the Scorpion Papyrus – which was the name she'd given to the tiny scroll they'd found inside the writing tablet. She was sure that the witness statement from the old scorpion charmer, Kaha, would hold the key to the location of the Benben Stone.

But first they had to crack the code and decipher its contents.

She glanced to the back of the boat to make sure the skipper wasn't listening, then asked Ryan for his phone, opened the photo of the Scorpion Papyrus on the screen and hunched over to shade it from the sun. She still couldn't make any sense of the writing. The hieroglyphs were perfectly formed, but they didn't make up words she understood – even if she reversed their direction, as she had done for the mirror writing in Rahotep's journals.

Ryan reached across and pointed out the border of ankh symbols – small crosses with looped tops – that ran around the edge of the writing. 'Maybe Rahotep's trying to give us a clue with these symbols,' he suggested.

Cleo was doubtful. 'The ankh was the symbol for life,' she said. 'Rahotep probably just added them for good luck. It's one of the most widely-used symbols in Ancient Egyptian iconography.'

Ryan nodded. 'You mean they crop up all over the place?'

Cleo frowned. 'Isn't that what I just said?'

The boat began to slow as they approached the east bank. The skipper steered a path through the throng of craft all making for the same stretch of the dock, and soon they were bumping up against the concrete landing stage. Cleo imagined Rahotep crossing the Nile to return to his temple duties at Karnak after visiting Smenkhkare's tomb. He might have come ashore at this very spot. Suddenly she had an idea.

'Let's go to Karnak after we've dropped off the tablets with Dr Badawi,' she said, as they balanced their way along the makeshift gangplank. 'It's only a few minutes' walk from the Theban Museum. I know it's a long shot – the temple complex is a big place – but perhaps we'll see *something* that will help us figure out the key to cracking the code.'

When Cleo said that Karnak was a big place, Ryan thought, *it might just have been the understatement of the century.*

It was like saying Everest was a big hill.

From the ticket kiosk they walked across a vast square fringed by tall swaying date palms, along a processional way flanked by ram-headed sphinxes and through a gateway between a pair of limestone pylons so stupendously enormous it was like walking into a fantasy film, set on a far-flung planet populated by giants. Ryan was still reeling, head thrown back, dizzy with the hugeness of it all, when Cleo marched past him.

'Right, we can ignore all this lot for a start,' she announced, wheeling round in the middle of the forecourt, sweeping her arms in an arc that took in, not only the monumental pylons, but also an assortment of massive statues, shrines, side temples and pillars.

A tour group of English tourists swivelled round to see who had uttered such barbaric words, all skewering Cleo with disapproving glares.

'Kids these days!' tutted a red-faced lady in a skimpy purple vest and shorts. 'No sense of history!'

Ryan grinned. *No sense of history?* Knowing Cleo, she'd probably been translating the hieroglyphic inscriptions on the wall reliefs of Karnak when most children were still struggling with *The Very Hungry Caterpillar*.

'Ignore all this?' Ryan asked, catching up with Cleo as she beetled towards the gateway in the opposite wall. Those stone pylons alone were over forty metres high. They weren't exactly *easy* to ignore. 'Why?'

'Too recent, of course,' Cleo said. 'We're only interested in structures that were in place when Rahotep was here. Anything that was added later than the first ten years of Rameses II's reign is too late.'

'Oh, yeah.' Ryan had been planning to say something more intelligent on the subject, but as they stepped through the gate his words simply evaporated on his tongue. They had entered a vast hall populated by columns so colossal it was like a forest of mighty redwood trees.

Cut from solid stone.

By human beings.

Without the use of cranes, diggers or computer-aided design systems.

And then carved to look like massive papyrus flowers at the top and decorated all over with perfectly chiselled scenes and ruler-straight lines of hieroglyphic writing.

Cleo smiled at Ryan's dumbstruck expression. 'I forgot you hadn't seen the Great Hypostyle Hall before. Impressive, isn't it?'

There she goes with the understatement again, Ryan thought. Manchester Town Hall was *impressive*. This was in a whole other league! His fingertips itched to pull out his sketchbook and capture it all on paper, but where would he even start?

Cleo plunged into the forest of stone. 'This part of the temple is in our timeframe,' she said over her shoulder. 'It was built by Seti I and Rameses II.'

Ryan hurried after her, one moment illuminated, the next in shadow, as he crossed the column-stripes of shade cast by the bright sunlight beaming down through the open roof. *How will we ever find a clue to Rahotep's code in here?* he wondered. *It's like looking for a single, specific blade of grass at Wembley stadium.* He was about to share this gloomy thought with Cleo – the words *needle* and *haystack* were all lined up ready – when he spotted the English tourists again.

'Two rows of six original columns line the central avenue,' their guide was telling them. He imitated an air steward demonstrating the emergency exits on a plane. 'With sixty-one slightly smaller pillars on either side. Anyone here good at maths?' he chuckled. Nobody volunteered. 'That's one hundred and thirty-four in total,' he said. 'Although,' he added, 'seven have gone missing. We'll be checking your pockets on the way out!'

Cleo rolled her eyes, but Ryan had barely noticed the cheesy patter.

One hundred and thirty-four columns?

Two rows of six down the middle?

He recognized those numbers. He shucked off his backpack, pulled out his sketchbook and found the copy he'd made last night of the star diagram hidden inside Rahotep's writing tablet. He did a quick count just to be sure. Yes, he was right: one hundred and thirty-four stars, with twelve bigger ones down the middle. 'It must be something to do with this,' he murmured. 'The star pattern corresponds exactly to the layout of these columns.'

It seemed like a breakthrough and yet, after searching the columns for over an hour, they still hadn't figured out what – if anything – the star pattern was telling them to look for.

Hot and tired, they finally left the hall and moved on to the sanctuary, the most ancient part of the temple of Amun, where they trailed through a maze of small rooms. Ryan was about to suggest giving up and finding the café when they entered yet another dimly lit chamber. He looked up to see that the ceiling was painted with gold five-pointed stars on a deep blue background. He'd seen stars like these in lots of places – it must have been the height of fashion for Ancient Egyptian ceiling decoration – but then he did a double take.

The pattern looked familiar.

He began to count the stars on the ceiling, faster and faster as he neared the magic number. 'One hundred and thirty-four!' he yelled at Cleo.

Cleo blinked at him in the gloom. 'The same as the original number of columns in the Hypostyle Hall,' she said, 'but what does it mean?'

'I don't know,' Ryan admitted, 'but Rahotep obviously thought it meant *something*. This is definitely the pattern he copied down on his writing tablet.' He waved his sketchbook up at the ceiling. 'It's got the twelve bigger stars in the centre and everything.'

Cleo nodded. 'We're right next door to the shrine here. Rahotep probably spent a lot of time in this room while the lector priest was reciting all the rituals to the statue of Amun. They must have gone on for ages. If he was bored, he might have counted those stars over and over, but why would he draw them in his secret journal?'

That's what I've been trying to figure out, Ryan thought. But, as Cleo spoke, he suddenly saw the answer. She was standing in front of a wall relief of a group of gods gathered around Amun. The long curved beak of the ibis-headed god, Thoth, looked as if it were sticking out from her left ear, but that wasn't what had caught his eye. It was the ankh Thoth held in his raised hand that interested Ryan. It was pointing up to the ceiling. 'Right at that star there!' Ryan said aloud, as he stretched over Cleo's shoulder and traced a straight line from the end of the ankh to the third star in the third row. 'This could be the clue that Rahotep left us. That's why he added the row of ankh symbols to the Scorpion Papyrus.'

'Of course!' Cleo cried, so excited she could hardly get her words out fast enough. 'Thoth is the god of writing and knowledge! It makes sense that *he's* the one pointing to the answer.' She peered up at the ceiling. 'But I can't see anything special about that star . . . Why that one?'

Suddenly Ryan slapped his forehead. 'The stars on the ceiling are a map of the columns in the Great Hypostyle Hall.' He began pulling Cleo towards the door. 'And Rahotep is telling us' – he panted as they ran out of the chamber, almost barrelling into a group of Japanese ladies and a member of the tourist police checking something on a clipboard – 'that we'll find the answer on the column that corresponds to the star Thoth is pointing at . . . the third one in the third row . . .'

23

ANKH

RYAN RACED INTO the Hypostyle Hall, checked a large map on the wall to get his bearings, and wove in and out of the giant columns, dodging holidaymakers walking backwards with their cameras held high, temple sweepers with old-fashioned brooms made of bundled twigs and a family of stray dogs begging for scraps. If the stars on the ceiling were lined up to match the columns, the one he wanted should be in the north-east corner. *Three along and three down,* he repeated under his breath as he counted his way along.

He was so intent on finding the right column he didn't notice the thick red rope until it was too late. Until, in fact, it had caught round his chest and was flapping like the finishing tape of a hundred-metres sprint.

It wouldn't have been so bad if the rope hadn't been tethered to a line of plastic posts, which scraped and clattered along behind him.

'What on earth are you *doing*?' Cleo hissed, catching up with Ryan as he tried to disentangle himself from the rope. She pointed at a large sign on a wooden trestle. DO NOT ENTER – RESTORATION WORK IN PROGRESS had been chalked on it in bossy capitals. Ryan looked round and took in the scaffolding and stepladders and the buckets containing the stone-coloured cement that was being applied to damaged columns. 'There's no one working here at the moment,' he said. 'I'm sure they wouldn't mind if we had a quick recce.'

Cleo glanced around nervously and started standing the posts back up. 'I don't think we should . . . restoration work can be very delicate . . .' But at that moment her foot knocked against the signboard. It keeled over and smacked the ground with a bang that rang round the columns like a volley of fireworks.

A temple sweeper appeared from nowhere, a tiny, wizened man in a dusty blue *galabaya,* wielding his broom like a battleaxe. Ryan didn't need to speak Arabic to guess that his yells of *Yallah!* translated roughly as *Get out!*

Possibly with an *Or else!* thrown in for good measure.

And now three tourist police officers, black-uniformed and armed with a lot more than broomsticks, were hotfooting onto the scene. With a crouching military-style run, their eyes flicking side to side, they were clearly primed for a major security incident.

Rubbernecking tourists looked up from their guidebooks, bristling with curiosity and outrage. 'Kids running riot!' they muttered. 'I blame the parents!'

'We'd better get out before we're thrown out,' Ryan whispered.

As stealth operations go, he thought, *we've totally fluffed this one!*

'We'll come back tonight during the sound and light show,' Cleo panted as they beat a hasty retreat past the ram-headed sphinxes. 'I've been before. There aren't so many guards around and it's dark away from the illuminations for the show. We should be able to slip under the rope undetected.'

Ryan sneaked a glance at his friend. What had happened to *I don't think we should?* he wondered. Was this really the Cleopatra McNeil who'd given him a lecture about procedures and protocols only three days ago?

The afternoon seemed to go on forever.

Cleo spent it helping her mum in the storeroom cleaning and cataloguing their meagre finds from the Smenkhkare tomb. The team had not made any progress in finding more chambers beyond the fake wall. All they'd found were some small stone vases and statues that had stood in niches along the tunnel.

Although it was hot and dusty it was usually a job Cleo enjoyed, working side by side with her mum, sorting through the trays, checking that every fragment was correctly stored and labelling it neatly with site code, date and location, just as archaeologists had done ever since the early days of Flinders Petrie and Howard Carter. But today she was impatient for evening to come around.

'Ryan wants to go to the sound and light show. He's not seen it before,' she said casually, sticking to the truth, if not the *whole* truth. 'I thought we might go tonight?'

Mum smiled. 'As long you stay together, that's fine.'

Rachel looked up from her work at the next bench. 'You two are getting *very* friendly,' she teased. 'How romantic!'

Cleo stared at the motes of dust suspended in a shaft of sunlight from the small high window and pretended she hadn't heard. She'd only just started to get to grips with friendship. She'd read *Romeo and Juliet* and *Othello* and enough Russian novels to know that romance was even more complicated!

Rachel went back to chatting with Max Henderson, who was taking close-up photos of all the finds. 'I've just called in to see J.J. in his hotel room,' she said. 'He's got a nasty case of food poisoning. Can't keep anything down. Must have been something he ate at the Moonlight restaurant last night, poor lamb.'

Max adjusted his light meter. 'He should have stuck to egg and chips like me,' he said, 'not dabbled with that foreign grub.'

They worked in silence for a while. Cleo could tell Mum was on edge. She kept dropping things. 'What's wrong?' Cleo asked as yet another pile of paperwork cascaded to the floor.

Mum pushed her hair out of her eyes and propped her elbows on the bench. 'There were some reporters hanging around at the dig this morning. They said they'd heard rumours we're looking for the Benben Stone. Dad got rid of them, but it seems that word has leaked out somehow. I just don't know how . . .'

Cleo felt as if all her internal organs were turning inside out.

This is all my fault.

She'd checked the *Mystical Times* website every day and had been relieved to see that so far Nathan Quirke's DAUGHTER REVEALS MCNEIL TEAM IN TOP-SECRET SEARCH FOR MAGIC STONE story hadn't appeared. She'd almost started to hope that he'd had a change of heart and decided not to write the article after all. But perhaps the *Mystical Times* had turned it down for some reason and he'd published it somewhere else. *I'm going to have to come clean,* she thought, *and confess that* I'm *the leak.*

But before she could say anything, Mum started up again. 'And to make matters worse,' she groaned, 'Sir Charles has been on the phone from London again this morning. He wants to organize a press conference to announce the plans for the new visitor centre soon. He's even trying to get Danny Farr to fly in to the Valley of the Kings in person – with a TV crew in tow, no doubt – to open the centre and unveil the Benben Stone!' She snorted rather hysterically. 'That'll be tricky if we can't find it!'

Cleo swallowed. *That's not even the worst of our problems,* she thought. *If Ryan and I are right, Danny Farr's more interested in* stealing *the Benben than unveiling it . . .*

Unless we stop him first!

She was on the verge of telling the whole story. At least it might make Mum feel better to know that she and Ryan were on the trail of the Benben Stone. But what if they were wrong? All they had to go on was a witness statement in Rahotep's three-thousand-year-old case notes.

Which they couldn't even read yet!

And, Cleo thought guiltily, it would involve revealing a few details she'd rather keep to herself for now – like the fact that she'd borrowed Dad's key and crept into the tomb at night, and the way she and Ryan had broken open those writing tablets. She couldn't risk being banned from going back to Karnak tonight.

As soon as we've deciphered the Scorpion Papyrus and found out whether Kaha knows the true location of the Benben Stone, she thought, *I'll tell everything . . .*

It was dark when Cleo and Ryan joined the coachloads of tourists heading across the square for the sound and light show, but the air was still warm and thick with exhaust fumes and smoky cooking aromas from the stalls of the street vendors. Somewhere, a horn blared above the muted roar of traffic. A blast of Egyptian pop music swelled and then died away.

Cleo noticed a row of souvenir sellers near the ticket office and made a detour. 'I bought you this,' she said, catching up with Ryan and shaking a paper bag under his nose.

Ryan took the bag and tipped a scarab amulet onto his palm. It was similar in size and colour to the one from the tomb, although the turquoise glaze was rougher. He turned it over. The plaster base had been stamped with a slightly wonky ankh sign.

'It's only a cheap machine-carved version, I'm afraid,' Cleo explained. 'I noticed how attached you've got to Rahotep's amulet but you'll have to hand it in to my mum sooner or later. Maybe this will do as a stand-in?'

Ryan clasped the amulet to his heart with both hands. 'I'll treasure it forever.'

Cleo stepped back in dismay. She felt her skin flush as she remembered Rachel Meadows' words: *how romantic*! Had she accidentally made Ryan think she was in love with him or something?

'Yes, whenever I look at this dung beetle's bottom,' Ryan murmured, a vacant, dreamy look on his face, 'it will remind me of you.'

Cleo laughed with relief. *He's joking!* Then she jumped as a dramatic voice suddenly boomed out from concealed loudspeakers.

'Welcome to Karnak!' As the narrator began to tell the story of the temple complex, coloured lights played over the towering first pylon. The immense carved figures of gods and kings seemed to come to life.

Every few minutes the soundtrack paused and the guards ushered the crowd along to the next gathering point. Eventually they came to the Hypostyle Hall, where the illuminated columns seemed taller even than in daylight, thrusting upwards into the deep brown-black sky.

Ryan and Cleo dawdled at the back of the group and waited for their chance. The narrator described the papyrus flower shape of the tops of the columns. Every head tipped back to gaze upwards. Even the guards looked up, as if expecting the gods to descend from the heavens.

'Now!' Ryan whispered. They slipped behind the nearest column and crouched, motionless, until they heard the audience shuffling away to the next vantage point. When all was quiet, they began to thread through the columns.

Although the main avenue was floodlit, the rest of the hall was deep in shadow. Now and then the flickering projections in the other parts of the temple would flare up and throw a carved scene into sudden relief. It was disorientating, as if the columns were moving around like gargantuan pieces in a chess game played by titans. Cleo realized she had no idea of the way to the north-east corner, but Ryan seemed to know where he was going. She stayed close.

They came to the rope barrier. Ryan ducked underneath and held it up for Cleo. She glanced over her shoulder and followed. She thought for a moment she'd glimpsed movement behind her, but when she looked again there was no one there. They crept further and further into the cordoned-off area, searching for the third column on the third row.

Ryan stopped at last. 'It's this one!' he whispered.

Ryan switched on his torch and shone it at the column. The light was a risk but there was no way they'd find *anything* in the dark.

Especially as they didn't really know what they were looking for.

Something – which may or may not involve an ankh symbol – that might help us crack Rahotep's code and read the Scorpion Papyrus, Ryan thought.

It wasn't exactly much to go on!

Cleo had switched on a tiny penlight and was circling the

pillar examining the inscriptions. 'Cartouches of Seti I,' she muttered. 'The standard scenes, offerings to Amun . . .'

Ryan was about to ask if she'd spotted anything useful – like a sign saying BENBEN STONE CLUES THIS WAY, for example – when he thought he heard something. He shrank back against the stone.

Yes, he'd *definitely* heard something.

'Footsteps!' he gulped. Grabbing Cleo by the arm, he pulled her round to the other side of the column. They both clicked off their torches and hunkered down.

Ryan squinted into the grainy dark. He *thought* he could make out a figure. Suddenly the scene was lit up by a series of flashes from the light show. Only a few metres away, a temple sweeper was padding between two columns, but it wasn't the ferocious little old man who'd accosted them on their first visit. This guy was much taller. He flickered silently from one flash to the next like a flip-book cartoon. At last he melted away into the shadows.

After a long, nail-biting wait, Ryan finally allowed himself to breathe again. 'I think he's gone,' he whispered.

Cleo stood up. 'Keep looking.'

Ryan *kept* looking – but looking was one thing, finding was another. There were dozens of ankhs on the column. Just about every god was holding one. And not one of them contained mysterious inscriptions or meaningful-looking symbols. Ryan was starting to think this was a waste of time.

'What about that ankh right up there above Seti's head?' Cleo whispered. 'I can't reach it.'

Ryan stretched up and ran his fingers over the stone. This ankh was so deeply carved that the centre of the loop stood out like a doorknob. Without really thinking, he gripped it and gave it a twist. To his amazement, the circle of stone clicked round in a clockwise quarter-turn.

Cleo sprang backwards. 'Something moved!' she gasped, pointing at her feet. 'There's a hole down here!'

Ryan knelt to look. A corner of one of the flagstones had sunk down, and the opposite edge had flipped up – just like the loose paving slab you always stepped on when you were in a hurry, the type that squirted muddy water right up your trouser leg. It was more a trip hazard than a hole, but he could understand Cleo's over-reaction; she *did* have a history with holes.

Cleo crouched next to him and wobbled the slab. 'When you turned the centre of that ankh it must have activated some kind of release mechanism that runs down inside the column . . .'

But Ryan wasn't listening. This was no time for discussing the details of Ancient Egyptian engineering design. He grasped the upended corner and tried to tug it free. 'Come on, give me a hand.'

Together they heaved. The stone shifted and slid to one side. Ryan cringed at the scraping noise, his heart in his throat – surely the tall tomb sweeper would come scurrying back any moment – but all was quiet. It seemed they'd got away with it.

Cleo shone her torch into the cavity that had opened under the floor. It was only about twenty centimetres deep and thirty across. *Not the sort of hole you could fall down,* Ryan thought, *even if you were Cleo, but* exactly *the sort of hole you could hide something in.*

Cleo felt inside and pulled out a wad of ancient mud-coloured leather. A string had been threaded through a row of holes at one end. 'It's a pouch,' she whispered, starting to pull apart the stiff folds. The dry leather creaked and a cloud of dust puffed up into her face. She clapped her hand over her mouth to hold back a cough.

Ryan took the pouch from Cleo and fumbled to loosen a knot in the fraying string. 'This had better not just be one of old Hori's food stashes . . .' he muttered.

But before they could find out, he heard footsteps slapping across the stones.

There was more than one set this time.

They were moving fast and they were closing in from all directions.

Ryan grabbed Cleo's arm and pulled her to her feet. 'Run!'

24

FLIGHT

CLEO DARTED IN and out of the columns.

She had lost all sense of direction and ran blind, searching for a way out of the hall. At last she came to a small doorway she'd never noticed before. She turned to beckon to Ryan to follow.

But Ryan wasn't there! The ragged breathing and hammering footsteps behind her belonged, instead, to an officer from the tourist police – she glimpsed thickset shoulders, a full beard, her own reflection in mirror-effect sunglasses . . . *Sunglasses at night? That's odd* . . . but she didn't have time to finish the thought. The man lunged at her. She dodged his grasp, bolted out of the door, and ran through the dark ruins.

Stumbling over potholes, cobbles and fallen masonry, the bones and ligaments in her right ankle – still not fully healed after her fall onto Smenkhkare's sarcophagus – pulsed with pain. Her heartbeat pounded in her ears, so loudly she couldn't tell whether the guard was still in pursuit.

But she didn't dare stop to look back.

Fight or flight. The basic physiological reaction to perceived threat . . .

She'd read all about it. Now she knew what it felt like.

Had Ryan got away?

Cleo reached the Sacred Lake, where the final part of the sound and light show was being projected onto the buildings across the water. She ran behind the rows of seating. Orange and violet lights played across her body as she passed the projector.

'The timeless secrets of the ancient world unfold . . .' the narrator intoned. At that moment the shadow of a giant girl sprinted across the film of the sunset over the pyramids.

Uncertain laughter rippled through the audience.

Cleo glanced back and saw the even more giant shadow of a man with a torch not far behind her.

Her lungs were burning but the new jolt of fear spurred her on. *Adrenaline triggers increased heart and lung function,* she remembered . . . She was almost at the outer wall of the temple complex. She spotted an opening. It wasn't the main entrance, but a narrow gateway with a barrier. *Probably just for people who work here . . .*

She propelled herself towards it, rolled under the barrier and kept on running: past a guards' hut, across a small square, across a busy junction, weaving around cars and minibuses and motorbikes, and into a crowded shopping centre. At last she staggered into an alley between two dress shops and collapsed against the wall behind the dustbins, hands on her knees, gulping for air.

Something clanged behind her. *The guard!* She whipped round, ready to flee again, but it was only a plump young man with a shiny face trying to navigate past her with a barrow full of olive oil cans. 'You need help, lady?' he asked.

Cleo pulled her scarf over her head and shrank back against the wall.

The man smiled and shrugged and continued on his way.

She tried to talk some sense into herself. *The guard won't find me here.*

But her fear was out of control, twisting every sound, every movement, into a potential attack. It fed on her thoughts too.

It's nothing to worry about, she told herself, *just the guards doing their job, shooing people out of the closed-off area.*

No way! Cleo's fear fired back. *It was much more than that. Ordinary guards wouldn't have given chase all the way out of the temple. And then there's the smell! Don't pretend you didn't notice it – that soapy, chemical smell!* Cleo couldn't deny it: it was only the faintest trace, but when the guard had been so close she could see her reflection in his sunglasses, she'd definitely caught the scent from the tomb and the museum again . . .

Cleo glanced up and down the alley. She could almost feel the gaze of watchful eyes peering out from every shady doorway and shuttered window.

And where was Ryan?

She crept to the end of the alley and looked out onto the street. A group of ladies swathed from head to toe in *niqabs* and long black *abayas* had stopped to admire the display in

172

the dress shop window. Talking and laughing, they went inside. *Hidden,* Cleo thought. *Hidden and safe.* She slipped into the shop after them, walked straight past the frothy wedding dresses and sharp designer suits, and picked out the longest and blackest *niqab* and *abaya* she could find.

Meanwhile, Ryan was on the run too.

He zigzagged his way through the Hypostyle Hall, trying to throw off the guards. Suddenly he noticed that Cleo was no longer running beside him. In the time it took to glance back for her, the tall temple sweeper had ambushed him from behind a pillar. Putting long hours of school rugby practice to use at last, Ryan dummied the man, ducked under his arm and ran, head down, for all he was worth.

The temple sweeper was surprisingly fast. Ryan could feel him gaining ground. He was never going to be able to outrun him to the main exit. He looked around frantically for a Plan B. He glimpsed a tower constructed of rickety scaffolding. It was about three metres tall topped with a wooden platform. Craftsmen must have been standing up there to repair cracks high up in the wall.

Ryan doubled back.

He threw himself at the structure and began to scramble up. The spindly metal poles wobbled alarmingly, but it was easy to climb – at least it would have been, if he hadn't still been clutching the leather pouch in one hand. With no time to stow it in his backpack, he clamped it in his teeth instead.

As he hauled himself up onto the platform, Ryan felt the scaffolding judder beneath him. He looked back over his shoulder. The man had grasped one of the poles and started to climb up after him!

His heart hammering like a drum solo, Ryan crouched, frantically trying to work out his next move. It was too high to jump down; he'd almost certainly break a leg. He looked at the wall behind him. A section at the top had crumbled away so it was lower than the rest. If he could just jump across and push the scaffolding away with his feet, he could make his getaway. He inched to the edge and sized up the gap. The wall was carved with a relief of Rameses II holding out the severed heads of his enemies to Amun-Ra. It was much higher and much further away than he'd first thought. *You'd have to be totally insane to even attempt it . . .*

But the temple sweeper's long fingers were already gripping the edge of the platform.

There was no going back.

25

SERPENT

RYAN LEAPED.

He wedged his right foot onto the top of the largest decapitated head, stretched up and found a shaky handhold in a deeply carved cartouche. But as he was swinging his left leg across towards the ostrich plumes on Amun's headdress, he felt something tug him back. The temple sweeper had swung from the side of the scaffolding and grasped him by the left foot.

Ryan kicked hard. His trainer flew off in the man's hand. Carried by momentum, Ryan hit the wall. Somehow he scrabbled up, gritting his teeth as the rough stone scraped against the weed-scratches on his legs, and hoisted himself onto the top of the wall.

He heard a cry of *Whooooaaaaah!* a clang of metal poles on stone, and then a single, very loud swear word. The scaffolding had toppled over. The man's weight as he swung must have pulled it down on top of him.

Ryan didn't hang around to hear more. He crawled along the wall until he was within jumping distance of the flat roof of a smaller building but, as he sprang, he was engulfed in a twittering frenzy of beating wings; a flock of wagtails, startled from their roosts in the crevices in the stonework, fluttered up into flight. Hundreds of little yellow and grey bodies batted into him, soft feathers brushing against his face. Ryan gasped with fright, and then with horror, as the leather bag dropped out of his mouth. Reaching out instinctively, he caught it before it plummeted to the ground far below. Off balance now, he almost fell, saving himself only at the last moment by grabbing at a decaying parapet.

Ryan clung on to the ancient stone, catching his breath and letting his heartbeat slow. But he knew he couldn't wait any longer. He ran, leaping from roof to roof, with only starlight and luck to guide his steps. He'd always thought parkour looked like fun when he'd seen it on YouTube, but now he wasn't so sure. As he jumped onto a petrifyingly narrow ledge, he could hear Cleo's words from the first day in Smenkhkare's burial chamber: *It's not all just running around and grabbing treasure . . .*

He'd have to take her up on that point – if he ever got out of this alive!

He came, at last, to the outer wall of the temple complex and found himself looking down into an alleyway. Below him stood a skinny white donkey hitched between the shafts of a cart laden with oranges.

Ryan jumped.

He landed spread-eagled on the oranges. The donkey barely looked up from chewing on a bundle of clover. Ryan pushed up onto all fours and brushed off an orange that had split and shmushed all over his T-shirt.

That's when he noticed he wasn't alone.

He was looking into the pale copper eyes of a snake.

The snake's hypnotic gaze didn't waver as it began to unwind its coils from among the fruit, head swaying from side to side, tongue flicking in and out, its scales rustling softly as it moved.

Ryan gulped. The taste of the ancient leather pouch turned rancid in his mouth. He wished he'd paid more attention to the section on *Venomous Creatures of North Africa* in Mum's guidebook on the plane journey. Or *less* attention. All he could remember was that there were thirty-six varieties of snake in Egypt, of which nine were poisonous – If you didn't count the other nine whose venom fangs were at the back of the jaws so they had to get a good mouthful of their prey first. Was this one of the deadly nine? It didn't have the flared hood of a cobra or the little slug horns of a horned viper, but that still left at least seven *game over* options.

Ryan looked at the snake. The snake looked at Ryan.

Words from the guidebook – nightmarish words like *neurotoxin, haemorrhage* and *necrosis* – ricocheted around his head, along with the curse from Smenkhkare's tomb. *He will be devoured by the serpent . . .*

Ryan couldn't keep still any longer. He had cramp in his calf and his arm was going to sleep. *I've got Rahotep's scarab amulet in one pocket, Cleo's in the other pocket, and Dad's St Christopher round my neck,* he thought. *Surely I've got enough luck on my side?* Very slowly he opened his fingers, closed them round a large orange and took aim.

This had better work, he thought.

He threw the orange at the snake.

It worked! The snake slithered away. But there was no time to celebrate. The orange bounced and struck the donkey on its bony hindquarters. The donkey brayed, flicked its oversized ears, bucked and bolted.

The cart careened along the alleyway, slewing wildly from side to side on its single pair of wheels. A taxi swerved, missing them by millimetres. The driver honked his horn in fury. The donkey veered off down an even narrower alley, the cart tipping so far over as it took the corner that Ryan clung onto the sides, fearing it would capsize at any moment.

They were hurtling through a bustling evening market now. Women scooped children out of the path of the runaway cart. A man carrying a tray of white eggs jumped backwards and landed in a basket of chilli powder. The eggs flew up and rained down like hail, to splatter all over the mounds of ground spices and bunches of herbs. 'Sorry!' Ryan shouted in all directions, ducking as the items for sale, hanging from lines festooned between the buildings on either side of the alley, zoomed towards him: dresses, towels, blankets, radios, kettles, furry toys, baskets of live chickens, sides of meat, bike tyres and flip-flops. It was like being in the most random 3D film ever.

As they rampaged on, through a mobile-phone stall, a juice stand and an underwear stall, Ryan scrambled over the avalanching oranges to the front of the cart. At last, with a heroic lunge, he grabbed hold of the reins. The donkey – now sporting a lacy black bra on one ear – pulled up just in time to avoid a head-on collision with a child on a tricycle.

The donkey seemed none the worse for its exploits and trotted at a genteel pace as Ryan steered out of the market and along a tree-lined avenue. But the crisis wasn't over yet. He had to get back to the temple and find Cleo. He had no idea what had happened to her. He twitched the reins and the donkey broke into a canter. They were racing towards a shopping mall when Ryan noticed a lone woman shrouded in a black veil and cloak. She kept stopping, turning round, taking a few steps, then stopping again.

Suddenly Ryan laughed. He drew up. 'Want a lift?' he called.

'Go away!' the mystery woman yelled. This was followed by a stream of Arabic so fierce that, for one stomach-lurching moment, Ryan thought he must have made a mistake.

But, no, he recognized that tattered white cotton scarf poking out from under the *abaya* . . . 'You're lost, aren't you?' he shouted.

'Ryan?' Cleo folded the veil back from her face. 'Of course I'm not lost!' she blustered. 'I was looking for *you*. What happened?'

'Long story!' Ryan said, hauling her up onto the seat next to him.

'Have you got the . . .'

Ryan held up the leather pouch. He clicked his tongue to gee the donkey forward and drove until they were under the light of a street lamp. Then he eased the strings open and tipped the contents out onto Cleo's black-cloaked lap: a wooden game board, some playing sticks, broken reed pens, ink pots – and a large gold ankh with two lines of hieroglyphs inscribed along the side.

'Result!' Ryan cried. 'Now we're getting somewhere!'

26

SUSPICION

'**COME ON, YOU** two! We're playing volleyball!'

The shouted invitation came from Alex Shawcross. It was the next morning, a Friday, the Islamic day of rest, and there was no work on the dig. Instead, Rachel Meadows had organized a team outing, a picnic lunch in a scenic banana grove near the riverbank.

'No, thanks,' Cleo called back to Alex. 'We're fine here.' She and Ryan had piled up their plates and found themselves a secluded spot curtained by the thick foliage of a clump of bushy banana palms.

'They want to be alone!' Rachel cooed.

Cleo heard her dad start whistling *It Must Be Love*. She

stuck her head out through the paddle-shaped leaves. 'No, it's *not*!' she protested, her face flushing as pink as a pomegranate.

But Ryan pulled her back. 'Let them think that! At least they'll leave us alone.'

Cleo saw his point. They had far more important things than love on their minds, but they *did* want to be alone. After their narrow escape from Karnak last night, they had a lot to talk about. And they couldn't risk being overheard. Cleo sat back down on the picnic blanket. She tore off a strip of pitta bread, scooped up some hummus and got straight to the point. 'Those were no ordinary guards last night.'

Ryan agreed. 'And I'm sure that temple-sweeper guy was creeping around following us for ages. I reckon he was waiting to see what we found.'

'Exactly,' Cleo said. 'Those two men weren't after *us*.' She patted Ryan's backpack. 'They were after *this*!'

Ryan grinned. 'If I'd known my old school bag, complete with genuine Manchester United keyring and biro stains, was going to be so in demand in Egypt, I'd have left it at home.'

'I didn't mean the backpack,' Cleo said. 'I meant the *contents*!' She reached in and took out the pouch they'd found in the secret hidey-hole. 'Someone else is after the Benben Stone and they think we'll lead them to it.' She bit into a falafel. 'It's obviously the Ancient Order of the Eternal Sun. Those two men must be working for them. Did you recognize them?'

Ryan shook his head. 'It was too dark to see much.'

'Did that temple sweeper say anything when he was chasing you?'

'We didn't exactly stop to exchange business cards!' Ryan

paused. 'Oh, wait a minute! He did say *one* word, when the scaffolding fell on top of him.'

'What word?'

Ryan spat out a salvo of olive stones. 'You sure you want to know?'

Cleo groaned with impatience. 'Tell me!'

Ryan mouthed the swear word. 'That,' he said. 'Only louder – and with a lot more feeling.'

Cleo sighed in disappointment. 'A basic Anglo-Saxon obscenity. That doesn't tell us much . . .'

'It tells us one thing,' Ryan pointed out. 'He's probably a native English speaker. If you've got a shed-load of metal poles crashing down on your head, you're not going to yell rude words in a foreign language, are you?'

Cleo smiled at Ryan in admiration. 'Excellent deduction! That would mean he's not really Egyptian in spite of wearing the traditional *galabaya* and *shaal*.'

Ryan took some more olives. 'What about the guard who chased you? Knowing you, you got a full identity profile, including his blood type and inside leg measurement.'

But Cleo had to admit that she had very little to go on either. 'All I know is he had a heavy build, light-brown skin, a dark beard . . . oh, and he was wearing sunglasses . . .'

'In the dark!' Ryan snorted. 'That's obviously a disguise.'

Cleo agreed. She took a sip from her glass of Ribena-pink *karkade*, a favourite Egyptian drink made from hibiscus flowers. The fruity fragrance triggered her olfactory memory and reminded her of the mystery smell. She'd detected it again when the guard had come close to catching her last night. She was sure he must be the same man who'd followed them before. Perhaps their stalker was a heavy karkade drinker, then? She sniffed the pink liquid again but, no, it was too cranberry-like. The mystery smell was different. For some reason, it had made her think of opening presents on Christmas morning . . .

'You're meant to drink that stuff, not inhale it,' Ryan laughed. 'I think I'll stick to this,' he added, reaching for a can of Coke and taking a swig.

Cleo decided not to mention the Christmas morning memory. She had a feeling Ryan would roll around laughing at her. 'How's your mum's investigation going?' she asked instead. 'Does she still think that there's an insider on the dig who's working for the Eternal Sun?'

Ryan nodded. 'She doesn't say much because she thinks the less I know, the safer I'll be, but she's tearing her hair out because she's not getting far. The Eternal Sun are very clever at keeping their members secret. They have false identities and everything, and she can't risk asking too many questions in case anyone gets suspicious and sees through her cover.'

'So it's up to *us* to find out who it is,' Cleo said.

Ryan nodded. For once he looked serious. 'Any ideas?'

Cleo had thought of nothing else all night, of course. She'd even got up at two in the morning and started compiling lists of suspects. She took a computer printout from her shorts pocket, unfolded it and smoothed it out on the blanket.

Ryan's eyebrows shot up. 'You've made a *spreadsheet*?'

Cleo couldn't understand why he was so surprised. Surely they studied basic data handling in normal schools?

'It's the most efficient way to tabulate and analyse a large set of variables,' she explained.

'Of course!' Ryan laughed. 'I never tabulate my variables any other way!'

Cleo still wasn't sure what was funny so she carried on regardless. 'I've entered all possible suspects down the side,' she explained. 'Then there are columns for times, places, alibis, possible motives and so on.'

'Is there a column for suspicious smells?' Ryan asked.

'Excellent idea,' Cleo said, making a note in the margin.

They lay on their stomachs, side by side, poring over the spreadsheet, but the longer they looked, the clearer it became that it raised more questions than it answered. *What was Max Henderson doing on the ferry when the backpack was stolen?* Cleo wondered. *Was he spying on us, or was it chance? Could Mum's student, J.J., be involved? He fits the description of the tall English-speaking temple sweeper in the blue* galabaya*, but Rachel said that when she called to see him yesterday he was too ill to leave his bathroom!*

And the members of the dig team weren't the only suspects. *Scores of people could have overheard us in the El-Masry Café planning the dawn mission to Smenkhkare's tomb,* Cleo thought. *Any one of them could have sneaked after us to see if we were right about the Benben Stone never having been in the fourth chamber because of the lack of light. They could have been hoping we'd lead them closer to finding out where the stone's really hidden.*

Which we have done, of course! Cleo reflected.

And anyone could have listened outside Ryan's apartment door and heard us talking about the inscription on the scarab amulet leading us to Rahotep's papers in the museum, and then to Karnak, and followed us to see whether we unearthed any more clues as to the location of the Benben. Cleo's mind ranged over the local diggers, the drivers, the site guards . . . Were any of them secret members of the Eternal Sun, gathering information and reporting back to their masters?

Her suspicions slithered out in all directions like the tentacles of a giant squid. Was Dr Leila Badawi in league with the ferry thief? What about the cloaked woman who'd come into the storeroom when they'd been working on the writing tablets at the museum? And how about the old lady with the shopping on the ferry, or the tourist policeman with the clipboard outside the star-ceilinged chamber at Karnak or Yusuf, the waiter at the El-Masry Café, whose computer Ryan had used to look up the time of sunrise . . .

Shuddering at the thought of a faceless network of *unknown variables* watching their every move, Cleo sank her forehead onto the picnic blanket and closed her eyes. Maybe she should stick to something simple like linear algebra.

'Well, whoever it is, we're way ahead of them,' Ryan said. '*We've* got the secret weapon.' He sat up, opened the leather pouch and took out the ankh. It was the size of a chunky old-fashioned door key, made of a gold metal that glinted in the sunlight dappling through the palm leaves. 'If only we knew how it worked!'

Cleo took the ankh from Ryan and examined it. At the point where the loop and the crossbar intersected, the Bennu Bird symbol had been engraved. It had been crudely scratched by hand, but there was no mistaking the stately grey heron with the crest of two tall feathers. Along the length of the ankh were two neat rows of hieroglyphs. Cleo had already translated them, of course. She recited the verse.

'*In radiant fire you fly up to every corner of the heavens and the Two Lands*

We worship you in the temple at dawn, Oh Mysterious One.'

It probably wasn't unusual for a young priest working at

Karnak to carry an ankh with a religious verse inscribed on it as a talisman, she thought. But there had to be something special about these two lines. Cleo was sure that somehow they held the key to cracking the code Rahotep had used in the Scorpion Papyrus. Why else would he have hidden the ankh so carefully? And why else would he have scratched the symbol of the Bennu Bird onto it? That had to be a clue that the verse was connected to his search for the Benben Stone.

Cleo looked at the baffling lines yet again. '*In radiant fire you fly up . . .*' she murmured. 'Those words must be something to do with the Bennu Bird, the Ancient Egyptian phoenix, rising up in flames from the Benben . . .' She looked up at Ryan. 'It's got to mean something. What are we missing? What's Rahotep trying to tell us?'

Ryan shrugged. 'I don't know. But we managed to solve the Mirror Code, didn't we? With your brains and my luck I'm sure we'll crack this Phoenix Code as well. Eventually!'

Deep in thought, Cleo set the ankh down on the blanket next to the spreadsheet.

That's when two strange things happened at once.

A plate of cakes appeared through the banana leaves, and Ryan dived on top of her.

27

HERON

'**QUICK!' RYAN HISSED** in Cleo's ear. 'Pretend we're kissing.'

Cleo's first instinct was, of course, to push him away. But, just in time, she realized that Ryan's bizarre manoeuvre had a higher purpose; he was hiding the spreadsheet and the ankh from the bearer of cakes, who was now poking their head in through the foliage.

Cleo did her best. She sort of nuzzled in and moved her head around. Beyond her ultra-close-up view of the cinnamon-coloured freckles on Ryan's slightly sunburned nose, she could see a flash of purple jungle-print kaftan.

Rachel Meadows held up a plate. 'Knock! Knock!' she chirped. 'I thought you lovebirds might like some baklava.'

'Yum, thanks,' Ryan said, trying to sound enthusiastic.

He twisted round and took the plate, all the while keeping his body in shield-position. It might not have been as heroic as a soldier throwing himself on a live grenade to protect his fellow men, but the way Cleo had looked at him when he'd leaped on her, it might almost have been as dangerous.

As soon as Rachel had gone he swiftly disengaged and sat up. He was rubbing his ribs where the ankh had jabbed into him, when he thought he saw something move under the blanket. He sprang back in horror, grabbed a stick and began to beat the ground.

'What are you doing?' Cleo asked.

'Checking for snakes.'

'I didn't know you were ophidiophobic!'

Nor did I, Ryan thought. In fact, he didn't even know what *ophidiophobic* was, but he made an educated guess. 'I *wasn't* until last night,' he said. He'd left out his close encounter with the snake in the donkey cart when he'd told Cleo about his escape from Karnak earlier. Now he recounted the full story.

'Ooh, was it sizzling?' Cleo asked.

'Sizzling!' Ryan spluttered. 'It was a snake not a stir fry!'

'It's the sound that some snakes make with their scales,' Cleo explained.

Ryan thought back. 'Yeah, there was a sort of rustling sound. It might count as sizzling.'

'Wow, a horned viper!' Cleo said enviously. 'The Ancient Egyptians used it as the hieroglyph for the "f" or "v" sound

189

because of that noise it makes. I've always wanted to see one . . .'

'No horns,' Ryan told her.

Cleo looked disappointed. Then she brightened. 'It must have been a saw-scaled viper. They sizzle too.'

'Totally harmless, I expect?' Ryan asked.

Cleo smiled. 'Deadly, actually.'

'You're kidding!' Ryan looked at Cleo waiting for her to laugh. She didn't. He should have known. Cleo didn't really *do* kidding. He glanced at the dense undergrowth all around them. 'You don't know any of those scorpion-charmer spells for getting rid of unwanted reptiles, do you?'

All of a sudden his voice tailed off and he spun round. But it wasn't a snake he'd heard. Footsteps were rustling on the dry grass, not far from their hideout. This time Ryan was quick enough to bundle the ankh and the spreadsheet into his backpack before peeping out through the leaves.

Max Henderson was crouching in the bushes, holding a pair of binoculars to his eyes.

'He's spying on us,' Cleo breathed from just behind Ryan's shoulder.

Ryan decided to go for the direct challenge. 'What are you looking at?'

Max Henderson almost dropped his binoculars 'Ooh, you gave me a fright there, lad.' He patted his chest in a heart-attack gesture. 'Superb heron.'

'A heron!' Cleo gasped. Ryan knew what she was thinking. *Max must have seen the Bennu Bird on the ankh.*

'What heron?' Ryan bluffed. 'I don't know what you're talking about.'

Max chuckled. 'You have to know where to look! Juvenile

male black-headed heron – just over there in the reeds, he was, bold as brass.'

Ryan almost laughed out loud. 'You're a *bird-watcher*?'

The pouches and creases of Max's face slowly rearranged themselves as he smiled. 'Guilty as charged,' he said. 'I had to drop out of a hummingbird safari to Colombia with the West Yorkshire Birders Society when this job came up, you know!' He turned to Cleo. 'Anyone else, I'd have told them where to get off, but your mum's an old friend. She twisted my arm. But it's not that bad for birds here. I spotted a lovely little bittern from the ferry the other day.' Max suddenly cocked his head on one side and snatched up the binoculars. 'Clamorous reed warbler! Notched!' He took a smartphone out of his jacket pocket and typed in some details. Then he stood up, reverting to his usual grumpy self as he stomped away. 'Don't suppose there'll be any food left worth eating.'

Ryan fell back on the blanket, trying to stifle howls of laughter. 'Clamorous reed warbler?' he gasped. 'Tell me that's not a real bird!'

'It is, actually,' Cleo giggled. '*Acrocephalus stentoreus!*'

'You are *definitely* making that up.'

Cleo shook her head. 'No, that's its Latin name. Phew, I really thought Max was our stalker for a moment there. He was on that dig I told you about in Peru when the Bloodthirsty Grail went missing. I figured he must have stolen that and now be after the Benben Stone too.'

'Well, we can delete him from your spreadsheet now,' Ryan said. 'He wasn't spying on *us* on the ferry the other day, he was spying on bitterns. In fact, the phoenix is probably the only bird in Egypt he's *not* interested in.'

Ryan leaned back against a tree trunk and thought about

the ankh. He was sure the engraving of the Bennu Bird was Rahotep's way of telling them they were on the right track. The young priest must have known his mission was dangerous and had left clues so that someone else could complete it if he didn't make it. He probably didn't think it would take three thousand years.

Ryan gazed around, wondering whether Rahotep had ever sat in this spot, and how much it had changed in all that time.

Probably not that much, he thought – the sun blazing in a deep blue sky, rushes with silvery plumes swishing along the banks of the Nile, clamorous reed warblers chirping their heads off, a girl with long black hair frowning over a spreadsheet . . . *Well, maybe Rahotep wouldn't have encountered the spreadsheet part . . .*

If they could just crack the Phoenix Code and decipher the Scorpion Papyrus!

'*In radiant fire you fly up to every corner of the heavens . . .*' Ryan repeated to himself. 'Thanks for the clues, Rahotep, mate,' he murmured, 'but couldn't you have made them a bit easier to figure out?' He felt in his pocket for Rahotep's scarab amulet. *If this were a movie,* Ryan thought, *the amulet would turn out to be a magic portal, and it would transport us back through time to find the answer.* But it was just a piece of stone. *And I should have given it in to Cleo's mum by now,* he remembered guiltily. For some reason he really didn't want to let it go . . . *This must be how Bilbo felt about the Ring in* The Hobbit. Ryan reached into his other pocket for the plaster amulet Cleo had given him. They were more or less the same size and shape. *I wonder*, he thought, *whether anyone would notice if I handed the new one in instead?*

He had a feeling the substitution wouldn't fool Professor McNeil for long!

Substitution, he mused. *That's an idea . . .*

He sat up so fast he sent the baklava plate flying into the undergrowth.

Maybe Rahotep's amulet *had* worked some magic after all – he might just have figured out the Phoenix Code!

28

NEFERTITI

RYAN'S BRAINWAVE TURNED out to be right. The Phoenix Code was a substitution code.

It had nothing to do with the *meaning* of the verse, after all. Rahotep had simply used the verse on the ankh as a cipher key because he had it to hand. He could just as well have picked any two lines of writing. Looking for the deep, hidden meanings of the words had been leading them astray all along!

The genius of the Phoenix Code lay in its simplicity. When Rahotep had written down Kaha's statement in the Scorpion Papyrus, every time he needed to use a symbol in the top line of the verse on the ankh, he substituted it with the one that occurred directly beneath it. Likewise, if he wanted to write a symbol from the bottom line, he used the one above it instead.

Although there were only about thirty symbols on the ankh altogether, they were all commonly used ones; switching them around was enough to make the Scorpion Papyrus unreadable.

Unless you went through and reversed all the swaps, of course.

Which is what Ryan and Cleo had been doing all afternoon.

They'd slipped away from the picnic and established their code-breaking headquarters in Cleo's room. They'd downloaded the photo of the Scorpion Papyrus from Ryan's phone onto Cleo's computer, enlarged it and printed it out. Then Ryan had set about the task of copying it out again, this time with all the substituted glyphs swapped back to the correct ones, so that Cleo could start translating.

As soon as they'd decoded the first few lines they knew they were onto something big.

After eavesdropping among the craftsmen and tomb servants of Set Maat village for many days, Rahotep wrote, *I learned of an old scorpion charmer named Kaha, who lives in a hovel outside the village wall, a man who has seen more than eighty harvests. From a group of Medjay guards, their tongues loosened by beer, I heard a rumour that old Kaha knows the real story behind Pharaoh Smenkhkare's burial. I resolved to find this scorpion charmer, for I was sure he could lead me to the Benben Stone . . .*

It was now four hours later. Ryan finished work on his last section of the papyrus and slid it along the desk to Cleo. Cleo didn't look up from her notes.

He took his sketchbook from his backpack, and wandered out to the balcony, where a small metal table and two chairs

195

had been squeezed in under the shade of a scrambling apricot-coloured bougainvillea. He brushed the confetti of fallen petals from one of the chairs and sat down, wincing as his legs brushed against the metal; the slashes of the sharp Nile weeds were itching as they healed. His shins were striped pink and puce and scarlet, like a technicolour zebra.

He looked back through the open balcony door and watched Cleo working at the desk. She was like a translating machine! She was sitting cross-legged on her chair, wearing a faded orange T-shirt – another of her dad's by the look of it – and her zip-off shorts. Her teeth and lips were stained with blue ink where she'd been chewing the end of her pen.

Somehow she still managed to look like an off-duty supermodel.

Ryan's thoughts drifted to the kiss-that-wasn't in the banana grove. Should he have tried to kiss her for real? he wondered. But no, he was glad he hadn't. She'd probably never have spoken to him again. He'd almost lost Cleo's friendship once and he didn't want to risk it a second time.

He opened his sketchbook. He'd drawn a gecko basking on the wall and a yellow butterfly resting on the bougainvillea by the time Cleo joined him on the balcony.

'I think we've got enough to work with now,' she said. 'I've had to fill in with a bit of guesswork where the papyrus was damaged but . . . could you please stop drawing me? It's very distracting.'

'How d'you know I'm drawing *you*?' Ryan asked, quickly slipping his sketchbook under the table.

'Why else would you be staring at my right eyebrow?'

Ryan put his pencil down.

'Listen to this,' Cleo said. 'You won't believe it!' She

began to read out her translation of Rahotep's interview with Kaha.

"'I may be a poor scorpion charmer now, but when I was young I had a very different life. My mother was a cook in the Grand Palace of Pharaoh Akhenaten and I was a kitchen boy." The old man turned his cloudy eyes up to me, waiting for my reaction. It is customary these days to spit on the ground upon hearing the name of Akhenaten, and to say the words "The Accursed One, may he be forgotten by time".'*

Cleo looked at Ryan over her notebook. 'Akhenaten was the pharaoh who ruled for about seventeen years before we think Smenkhkare came to power,' she explained. 'He was quite a character. He rejected all the traditional Egyptian gods like Osiris and Amun, and replaced them with a new religion with a single god, the sun disc or Great Aten. Akhenaten means *Servant of Aten.* He established a new city . . .'

'Like Milton Keynes?' Ryan suggested.

Cleo frowned at him. 'A fabulous new city in the desert. Its modern name is Amarna. Akhenaten ruled from there with his queen, Nefertiti. But not long after he died, everyone went back to the old religion. Amarna fell into ruin and Akhenaten's memory was reviled. His name was even hacked off statues and plaques . . .'

Ryan looked up from his sketchbook, which was balanced on his knees where he'd surreptitiously started work on his portrait of Cleo again. He'd never heard of Pharaoh Akhenaten, but he *had* heard of Queen Nefertiti. 'Wasn't she meant to be the most beautiful woman in the world?'

Cleo nodded. 'Nefertiti means *the beautiful one has come,*' she said. 'According to Kaha, she was more beautiful than the stars of the skies.' She put down her notebook. 'Wait, I'll show you.'

Cleo disappeared inside and returned with a reference book of Ancient Egyptian art. She set it on the table and opened it to a glossy photograph that Ryan recognized as a famous head-and-shoulders sculpture of Nefertiti, with high cheekbones, elegant nose and perfect skin beneath a tall blue headdress. Although, Ryan noticed, the artist *had* left one eye unfinished.

Cleo turned the page to a painting of a man making an offering to the sun disc. 'And that's Pharaoh Akhenaten,' she said.

Ryan stared. It was unlike any of the other Ancient Egyptian art he'd seen. Akhenaten's face was long and narrow, with sloping heavy-lidded eyes and full lips. It was one of those strange faces that was somehow ugly and fascinating at the same time. He also had man boobs, a pot belly and long spindly arms.

Cleo pointed out the round object at the top of the picture. Sun rays descended from it, each ending with an odd little hand holding an ankh. 'That's the sacred sun disc, the Great Aten.'

Ryan examined the image. The combination of the sun and the ankh symbols reminded him suddenly of the logo of the Ancient Order of the Eternal Sun he'd seen in his mum's research notes. There the ankhs were enclosed within the circle of the sun rather than held at the end of long, straight rays, but the meaning of the symbols – power and eternal life – had changed little over thousands of years.

Cleo picked up her notebook and continued to read from Kaha's statement. *'Akhenaten loved Nefertiti more than life itself. But by the twelfth year of his reign, whispers began to ripple through the palace like the breeze through the rushes. Nefertiti, the Perfect One, had fallen in love with Akhenaten's younger brother, Smenkhkare.'*

Cleo stopped reading and looked up, her eyes shining. 'Do you realize how *significant* this is? Historians have always thought that Smenkhkare was related to Akhenaten in some way, but we didn't know how. This document *proves* that they were brothers. It's a breakthrough. And that's not all.'

Cleo continued to read Kaha's words.

'Smenkhkare was Akhenaten's great favourite. When Smenkhkare was only sixteen years old, Akhenaten appointed him as co-regent to rule at his side. Akhenaten was preparing his younger brother to take over as sole ruler of the Two Lands when Akhenaten himself made his journey to the Western Horizon, which he felt would not be long in coming, for he was an ailing man.'

'You mean Akhenaten was dying?' Ryan asked.

Cleo nodded. 'This is the best bit!' she said. 'The reason Akhenaten was so ill is that Nefertiti was slowly poisoning him or, in Kaha's words, *She was lacing the remedies he took for discomforts of the belly with antimony and arsenic.'*

'I get it,' Ryan said. 'Nefertiti and Smenkhkare were plotting to bump Akhenaten off so they could be together.'

'And rule Egypt together!' Cleo added. 'According to Kaha, Nerfertiti and Smenkhkare weren't just having a love affair, they were also plotting with a group of powerful priests from Heliopolis and Karnak to overturn Akhenaten's beloved new religion and bring back the old gods.'

Ryan shook his head in awe. 'Wow! They were quite the double act!'

Suddenly Cleo leaned across the table and threw her pen at him. 'You're drawing me again! I can tell!'

Ryan held up his hands in surrender and laughed. 'Sorry, I just had to finish it off. You looked too freaky with half an eyebrow.' He closed his sketchbook and looked over the rail of the balcony. The pen had missed him and sailed over to land in the bushes below. He heard a rustle of leaves. It must have surprised a sleeping cat or a stray dog. 'So, did the perfect Nefertiti and Old Smenkers get away with their evil scheme?' he asked.

Cleo shook her head. 'According to Kaha, the plot to poison Akhenaten was rumbled. Akhenaten was furious, of course, but before he could do anything, Nefertiti and Smenkhkare escaped south to Nubia together. Years later, Akhenaten received word that Nefertiti had killed herself and had left a note saying that she was truly sorry for betraying him. Akhenaten still loved her in spite of everything, so he sent one of his top Medjay officers to bring her body back to Amarna, and had her buried in a magnificent secret chamber hidden beneath his own tomb.'

Cleo stood at the rail of the balcony gazing out over the rooftops. Her voice quivered with emotion as she turned back to face Ryan. 'This is even more important than finding out about Smenkhkare! Nefertiti's fate has always been one of the greatest mysteries of Egyptology. No one has ever known what happened to her. It's as if she vanished into thin air. But the Scorpion Papyrus explains *everything*!'

'And what about Smenkhkare?' Ryan asked. 'What happened to him after Nefertiti killed herself?'

Cleo grimaced and made a chopping action at her throat. 'Alex and Dad were right about his head being cut off *before* mummification. Kaha says here that Akhenaten's men executed Smenkhkare and then hijacked that half-finished tomb of Nakhtmin's and buried him in there.' Cleo looked up, her face glowing the way it always did when she was in full-throttle Theory Mode. 'That explains why it was such a strange burial, with none of the usual grave goods. So it seems Smenkhkare never did get to rule on his own as pharaoh, after all. He only had the royal cartouches because he'd been co-regent with Akhenaten many years earlier, before all the trouble with Nefertiti started. This is so exciting! It could be the solution to a question that's puzzled historians for decades . . .'

But Ryan had stopped listening. Cleo might be excited about boring details like which pharaoh was co-regent with which, but he'd thought of a much more interesting historical puzzle of his own – and he might just have solved it! 'Rahotep said that Smenkhkare's Confession was a fake,' he said slowly. 'What if *Akhenaten* was the one who really wrote it?'

Cleo gazed at Ryan across the table. 'Yes, of course! That would fit. It would all be part of his revenge against Smenkhkare.'

Ryan nodded. 'Akhenaten helpfully popped a confession in the coffin to be sure everyone got the message about what a treacherous slimeball his little brother had been.'

'So now we know what the *double abomination* meant,' Cleo added.

'Abomination Number One,' Ryan counted on his fingers, 'getting cosy with Akhenaten's lovely wife, Nefertiti, the Not-Quite-So-Perfect.'

'Abomination Number Two,' Cleo chipped in. 'Plotting

with the priests to overthrow the new Aten religion.'

Ryan grinned. 'So, you were right, mate!' he said, addressing the invisible presence of Rahotep and raising his hand for a high five, as if the young priest were sitting at the table next to him. 'Smenkhkare's Confession *was* a fake. You figured it out from Kaha's evidence.' He turned back to Cleo, so excited that he grabbed her hand. 'You know what this means, don't you?'

Cleo stared at Ryan's hand on her own but didn't pull away. 'The Confession also says that Smenkhkare stole the Benben Stone,' she breathed. 'If Akhenaten forged the Confession . . .'

Ryan finished the sentence for her. 'Maybe *he's* the one who stole the stone too.'

Cleo nodded.

Ryan leaned back in his chair. 'Wow! No wonder Rahotep wrote Kaha's statement down in top-secret code. It's pretty explosive stuff. You couldn't make it up!'

Then he paused and let go of Cleo's hand as a thought suddenly hit him. *What if old Kaha was making it up?*

29

RIDDLES

CLEO TURNED BACK from the railing. 'What's wrong?'

'I hate to burst our bubble,' Ryan said, 'but how could old Kaha know all this stuff was going on in the Grand Palace if he was just a kitchen boy at the time?'

A sphinx-like smile flickered across Cleo's ink-stained lips. In the dying light of dusk, Ryan thought, she looked so like the sculpture of Nefertiti in the art book that it was almost frightening. When she spoke he wouldn't have been surprised if her words had come out in Ancient Egyptian.

They didn't.

'It's so weird,' she said. 'You and Rahotep *always* think the same thing. Rahotep asked Kaha that exact question – *How can I be sure that this is the truth and that you are not spinning me a tall tale in return for my gifts of beer and bread?'*

Ryan mimed a knuckle touch with invisible Rahotep. 'Couldn't have put it better myself, mate!'

Cleo pointed to her notebook. 'Wait until you hear Kaha's reply! It's amazing . . .' But before she said any more, she went inside and came back with matches to light the coil of citronella incense that hung from a branch of the bougainvillea to keep the gathering insects at bay. A tendril of pungent smoke curled up into the evening air.

'So is *that* your mystery smell?' Ryan asked.

'How on earth did you know I was thinking that?' Cleo started.

Ryan laughed. 'Just my incredible telepathic abilities,' he said. 'Or maybe it was because your nose is twitching like a rabbit with hay fever!'

Cleo shook her head. 'No, I thought it was for a moment. But the mystery smell wasn't as smoky as this. It was more sort of Christmassy.'

'*Christmassy?*' Ryan repeated. 'I'm seriously starting to wonder whether you need to see somebody about this.' He pushed Cleo's notebook into her hands. 'Come on, tell me Kaha's amazing story, then. I'm dying of suspense here.'

Cleo smiled. 'OK. Kaha says that Akhenaten selected one hundred trusted advisors, craftsmen and servants to help construct and furnish a magnificent hidden tomb for Nefertiti. They were all sworn to utmost secrecy. If word had got out that Akhenaten had forgiven Nefertiti it would have made him look weak – which would be unthinkable for the pharaoh. Kaha was lucky – or unlucky – enough to be one of the hundred. He says he'd become something of a favourite at the palace because he used to take Akhenaten's young daughters special sweets and pastries that his mother had baked.' Cleo paused, her voice dropping to a dramatic whisper. 'When the tomb was sealed, the one hundred people who knew about it were shut inside so that the secret would be buried with them . . .'

Ryan stared at Cleo. Someone in a nearby flat had switched on their TV and the frenetic soundtrack of an Egyptian football match drifted out from an open window. 'Are you serious? They were just walled up inside the tomb to die?'

Cleo checked her notes. 'They drank a potion of wolfsbane and hemlock first, so they were probably already dead . . .'

'Oh, that's all right then!' Ryan snorted sarcastically. He tried to shut out thoughts of what it must have felt like to know you'd been buried alive in an underground tomb with ninety-nine other people. *Kaha can't have been much older than us when this happened* . . . 'How did he escape?'

'He only *pretended* to drink the poison!' Cleo said. 'Once everyone else was dead, he tunnelled out. He went into hiding for a while then came to Luxor and worked as a tomb guard in the Necropolis here before becoming a scorpion charmer.'

Ryan shook his head. 'It's an incredible story, but what's it got to do with the Benben Stone?'

But before Cleo could reply, the pieces fell into place. Ryan slapped his palms down on the table with a bang that sent all the geckos on the wall scuttling for cover. 'Of course! It's got *everything* to do with it! It's the whole reason why Akhenaten stole the Benben Stone in the first place. He wanted to put it in Nefertiti's tomb. That was the biggest secret of all. But Kaha knew because he was there! He saw it . . .'

Cleo snatched her notes up off the table and flicked through the pages. 'Yes! That must be it!' She ran inside to her desk and returned to the balcony with the Scorpion Papyrus and her magnifying glass. 'You're right,' she said, after several minutes of poring over the tiny scroll. 'Kaha says: *To complete the adornment of Nefertiti's tomb, Akhenaten took some great treasure from* . . . Then there's a little rip in the papyrus so the name of the place is missing.' She frowned and scribbled out something in her notebook. 'I assumed Kaha was talking about Akhenaten just taking some special objects from one of his palaces or something, but when you look closely you can see the edges of the missing hieroglyphs.' Cleo held out the papyrus and magnifying glass. 'There. See?'

Ryan nodded wisely, although in the dim light all he could make out was a close-up of her pointing finger.

'When you complete those partial glyphs and decode them,' Cleo went on, 'they make up the name Iunu. That's Heliopolis. And now I look at it again, Kaha doesn't actually say Akhenaten took *some* great treasure – it says he took *the* Great Treasure.'

'Akhenaten took the Great Treasure of Heliopolis,' Ryan repeated slowly.

Cleo nodded. 'That has to mean the Benben Stone. Akhenaten must have feared that Nefertiti's heart would be so heavy with sin that she would be denied entry to the afterlife . . .'

'. . . so he placed the Benben in her tomb as a bribe to Osiris to let her enter the Underworld,' Ryan finished.

'Or as an offering to the Great Aten,' Cleo corrected. 'Remember, Akhenaten didn't believe in traditional gods like Osiris.'

Ryan fell silent for a moment, trying to take it all in. Pigeons cooed from the sycamore trees and, on the neighbours' television, a crowd roared at a goal. It seemed Akhenaten had thought of *everything*! He'd stolen the Benben Stone himself and placed it in his beloved Nefertiti's tomb. Then he'd written the fake confession and framed Smenkhkare for the theft instead – just in case beheading him wasn't revenge enough for the fact that he'd run off with Nefertiti! On top of all that, stealing the mega-sacred Benben Stone must have seemed like the perfect way of getting back at those disloyal Heliopolis priests for plotting against him with Smenkers and Nefertiti. 'So,' Ryan asked, 'what happened? Did Secret Agent Rahotep go to Nefertiti's tomb and find the Benben Stone?'

Cleo sighed. 'I don't know. The Scorpion Papyrus ends suddenly. There are just some riddles . . .'

'Riddles?' Ryan asked. 'What kind of riddles?'

Cleo picked up her notebook. Then she let it fall back to the table and rubbed her eyes.

Ryan reached over for the notebook and peered at Cleo's translation. No wonder her eyes were tired; her writing was almost as tiny as the hieroglyphs on the Scorpion Papyrus itself and the glow of the smouldering end of the citronella coil was the only light. He cleared his throat and began to read Rahotep's words aloud. '*Kaha complained that he was too tired for more talk and asked me to return the next day. But when I came back to the hut at dawn, I found the old man huddled on the dirt floor, his skin burning with fever. He gripped my arm and pulled me to his side, addressing me as sweet Meritaten . . .*' Ryan paused. 'Who's Meritaten?'

'One of Pharaoh Akhenaten's young daughters,' Cleo said. 'It sounds like Kaha was delirious.'

'I sent a child to fetch a healer from the village,' Ryan went on. 'While we waited, Kaha gazed past me, unseeing, but suddenly his eyes cleared like the moon appearing from behind a cloud. "The Perfect One lies hidden deep beneath the chamber where the Servant of the Aten now rests, only a short walk from here . . ." he croaked. I squeezed drops of water from a cloth to his dry lips. "How shall I find the hidden place?" I asked.

'The old man rambled of honeyed cakes and almond pastries. His words wandered like the rivulets of the Nile through the reed beds, but I was able to make out, "take the wrong path and you will roam the labyrinth for eternity". As the healer arrived, chanting incantations, Kaha closed his eyes and departed for the Far West.' Ryan looked up. 'I take it the Far West doesn't mean Cornwall.'

Cleo frowned at him. 'Of course not. It means . . .'

'Dead,' Ryan said. 'I know. I was joking. Oh, I see, here come the riddles. Rahotep says these were Kaha's dying words.

'In the tomb of the Great Warrior,

Look through the new eyes of Ra to the creature himself and you will see the hidden way.

In the tomb of our Royal Grandfather,

Follow the path of the World Encircler through the hours of the night,

To the cry of the Bennu Bird in flight . . .'

Ryan turned to the next page but it was blank. 'Where's the rest?'

'That's it,' Cleo said. 'It just stops mid-sentence. Kaha must have died.' She regarded Ryan across the table, her eyes made dark and enormous by the evening shadows. 'But I think he was trying to tell Rahotep where he'd hidden the directions to find the way into Nefertiti's tomb. He must have left clues in other tombs: the tomb of the Great Warrior, the tomb of the Royal Grandfather . . .'

Ryan nodded. It made sense. Kaha had worked as a tomb guard before he became a scorpion charmer, so he would have been in and out of the tombs all the time. He probably couldn't read or write so he must have made up the riddles to help him remember where to find the directions. Ryan leaned back in his chair and swatted a mosquito from his leg. *But why are there no more writings after the Scorpion Papryus?* he wondered. What happened to Rahotep? Had he found the secret tomb of Nefertiti and reclaimed the Benben Stone for his bosses in Heliopolis?

Or had he tried and failed and come to a sticky end?

Well, Ryan thought, *there's only one way to find out . . .*

'We'll just have to solve all these riddles, find the clues and discover the tomb of Nefertiti ourselves,' he said. 'How hard can it be?'

Cleo didn't reply.

Ryan looked up. Her head was down on her arms. Her shoulders gently rose and fell. She was fast asleep.

'We'll start in the morning!' he said quietly.

30

EYES

THEY MET FOR breakfast at the El-Masry Café.

At least, *Ryan* thought it was for breakfast.

Cleo had other ideas.

'Quick,' she said, before he could sit down or stroke Snowball, who had trotted out to greet him. 'There's a bus coming now.'

'Where are we going?' he asked as they ran to the stop.

'I've told my parents we're going to spend the morning looking round the tombs in the Valley of the Nobles because you're really keen to see the artwork.'

'And are we?' Ryan asked.

Cleo glanced over her shoulder. 'No, we're going to the

Valley of the Kings.'

Ryan stared at her. 'You *lied*? Surely that goes against approved protocols?' he teased.

'This way, if anyone who happens to be a member of *you know what* asks Mum or Dad where we are, they won't be able to give away our true location,' Cleo explained as the bus pulled up. She refused to say another word in case any of the other passengers were eavesdropping.

'Hang on,' Ryan said. 'This bus is going the wrong way. We're going *down* the hill.'

Cleo silenced him with a look. It was all part of her plan. 'We'll change at the next stop,' she hissed. 'If anyone's following us, it'll throw them off the trail.'

She gazed out of the window as the bus overtook a donkey plodding down the road laden with bundles of sugar cane. She could hardly contain her excitement. It wasn't just about finding the Benben Stone now: Nefertiti's secret tomb would be the biggest find in the history of Egyptology! It could be filled with untold treasures that would make Tutankhamun's tomb look like a jumble sale! It *But if it's hidden somewhere beneath the tomb of Akhenaten,* she thought, *the entrance must be* extremely *well concealed.* That tomb had been thoroughly explored and no one had reported finding any secret passages to another tomb underneath it . . .

But no one had ever had Kaha's secret directions before, either!

Cleo had been puzzling over those riddles all night and she was sure she'd figured out exactly where Kaha had hidden the clues.

'First stop,' she whispered to Ryan, when they finally

arrived at the Valley of the Kings after three changes of bus, 'the tomb of Thutmosis III.'

'How do you know that's where to look?' Ryan asked. Then he grinned. 'You've got your Theory Face on again!'

Cleo shook her head. 'Not so much a theory as a logical deduction.'

'Of course!' Ryan laughed. 'That's *totally* different. Go on then, deduce away.'

'Thutmosis III conducted seventeen military campaigns in twenty years. He was at war with *everyone*. That's why he was known as—'

Ryan finished the sentence for her. 'The Great Warrior!'

The tomb of Thutmosis III was one of the oldest in the Necropolis.

Ryan and Cleo merged with the crowds of tourists and climbed up to the entrance high in the cliff at the end of the valley, down steep flights of steps, along corridors and through a vestibule. At last they came out into a large oval burial chamber.

Ryan stood next to the sarcophagus of gleaming red quartz, slowly circling it in wonder. It was like being inside a vast graphic novel. The curved white walls were divided into panels, just like comic strips. The drawings were simple, little more than stick figures, in muted tones of rust and rose, picked out with black, but the complexity and scale of the scenes was breathtaking.

'It's the *Book of the Amduat*,' Cleo explained. 'The same as in the passage beyond the fake wall in Smenkhkare's tomb.

It's the sun god Ra's journey through the twelve hours of the night.'

Ryan began to pace along the painted walls, muttering the words of the riddle under his breath. *'Look through the new eyes of Ra to the creature himself and you will see the hidden way.'* He peered into every image of an eye. There were hundreds of them. 'How do we know which eyes are the right ones?'

'I don't know,' Cleo admitted. 'Kaha didn't say . . .' Suddenly she stopped. 'No, wait! He said *the* new *eyes of Ra.*' She hurried to the east wall. 'It's those up there!' she whispered. 'Those *wedjat* eyes with the falcon markings. This panel shows the eleventh hour of Ra's journey, shortly before sunrise. It's when the eyes of Ra are *renewed.*'

Ryan looked up past a figure grappling with a winged serpent to see a large pair of staring eyes. There was just one minor problem – those eyes were so high on the wall that he couldn't reach to see them properly. Even when he jumped up. How was he meant to look *through* them?

'Don't make it so obvious,' Cleo hissed. 'Any of these people,' she waved her hand at the groups of tourists admiring the frieze, 'could be members of *you know what* . . .' Without finishing her sentence Cleo suddenly bent over as if tying her shoelaces. 'Don't look now,' she whispered, 'but that tomb caretaker over there keeps looking at us.'

Ryan slid his eyes towards the corner. A young man in a blue *galabaya* and white *shaal* was reminding a Chinese couple that no photography was allowed in the tombs. He caught Ryan's eye and started towards him.

'Oh, no,' Cleo muttered, grasping Ryan's arm. 'He's one of the men who's been following us. The ferry thief . . .'

But Ryan laughed. Cleo was definitely getting paranoid! The man wasn't the thief. It was Yusuf, from the El-Masry Café. Ever since Ryan had helped him with his computer on their first visit to the café, they'd chatted many times. They shook hands.

'Hey, Yusuf,' Ryan said. 'I didn't know you worked here as well as at the café.'

Yusuf grinned. 'The café belongs to my brother,' he said in halting English. 'I help there sometimes. This is my real job.' He gestured at the wall. 'You want to see high things?' He held up a finger. 'Wait one minute!'

Cleo still looked doubtful, but moments later Yusuf returned carrying a small wooden stool with a woven rush seat. 'You stand on.'

Ryan climbed up. At last his eyes were level with the eyes on the wall.

He wasn't quite sure what he'd been expecting – maybe some kind of little window at the centre of each pupil, behind which would be revealed the creature that would magically show them the way to the hidden tomb.

But there was nothing! Just solid black paint on solid white plaster.

All Ryan could see were his own eyes reflected in the protective glass that had been installed in front of the ancient artwork. *Oh, no!* he thought. *If this turns out to be one of those trick riddles where the answer is that the creature you see through the eyes of Ra is yourself, and it's meant to be all deep and meaningful because you have to look into your own heart to find the way or something, I'm going to scream!*

'What can you see?' Cleo demanded.

Ryan was about to tell her about his look-into-your-heart

reflection when he realized that it obviously *couldn't* be the answer. 'They hadn't invented glass in Kaha's day, had they?' he asked, just to be sure.

'Well, glass-making *was* known to the Ancient Egyptians,' Cleo corrected him.

Ryan groaned. Maybe it was the look-into-your-heart thing, after all.

'But they could only make beads and vases and things,' Cleo went on. 'Nothing like this.' She tapped on the sheet of glass.

'That's a relief!' Ryan laughed. *But what else is there to see through those eyes?* He stared at them. They stared back at him. Suddenly it clicked. *What if Kaha meant look* out *through the eyes, not* in *through them?*

He turned on the stool and surveyed the burial chamber from the viewpoint of the eyes on the wall behind his head. He found himself looking over the sarcophagus directly at a large white rectangular pillar embellished with a procession of figures. There was only one creature on it; it looked like some sort of mutant cat-rabbit-leopard hybrid . . .

Cleo spun round to see what he was looking at. 'Of course!' she breathed. 'The clue is *look through the eyes of Ra to see the creature himself.* That animal *is* Ra himself, in the form of the Great Cat, Mau.'

The Great Cat, Mau? Sometimes Ryan wondered whether Cleo was making this stuff up. And there was more . . .

'In some versions of the legend,' Cleo was saying, 'the Great Cat was the protector of the Tree of Life in the Mansion of the Phoenix, the home of the Bennu Bird. This has to be leading us closer to the Benben Stone.'

'I'll take your word for it,' Ryan said.

Then he jumped down from the stool, took his sketchbook from his backpack and began to make a copy of Mau.

Cleo waved hello to Mr Mansour and ran up the stairs to the apartment.

She was feeling very pleased with the morning's progress.

She didn't know *how* the Great Cat would show them the door to the hidden tomb, but she was sure they'd work it out.

Ryan had gone home for lunch with his mum and they'd agreed to meet later to follow up Kaha's second clue: *in the tomb of our Royal Grandfather, the path of the World Encircler will lead you through the hours of the night.* Cleo was sure that the *Royal Grandfather* was Rameses I, the grandfather of Rameses II, who had been pharaoh at the time that Kaha told the riddle to Rahotep.

Mum and Dad were clearing the lunch table. Mum smiled. 'You must be hungry after being out all morning. There's plenty left.'

'I'll be there in a moment,' Cleo called, hurrying into her bedroom to jot down the latest update on the Great Cat clue in her notebook. She lifted the corner of the mattress where she'd taken to hiding her notes for safekeeping.

She pushed her hand into the gap, feeling for the corner of the plastic folder and the cover of her notebook. She pulled away the sheets and heaved the mattress up higher and stuck her head right in underneath it.

Her notes had disappeared.

31

APEP

CLEO RAN BACK into the kitchen. 'Have you taken anything from my room?'

'Only your laundry,' Mum laughed. 'Come and sit down.'

'Sorry, no time!' Cleo flung the words over her shoulder as she hurtled out of the flat, leaving her mum holding out a plate of sandwiches.

She raced back to the bus stop calling Ryan's number on her mobile as she ran. Her thoughts raced even faster. She and Ryan had been so sure they were miles ahead of whoever was following them; they'd found the ankh key and deciphered the Phoenix Code Rahotep had used to write the Scorpion Papyrus. But now someone had her notes – all her translations and research – she might as well have handed them the Benben Stone on a golden offering tray.

Ryan wasn't answering his phone.

Cleo groaned. There was no time to lose. They had to find Kaha's second clue straight away. She punched in a text.

Urgent. Meet me at Rameses I.

After ten minutes there was no bus. Further along the road Cleo noticed a coach loading up with a party of tourists. She ran up to a woman sporting a sharp silver bob and elegant black-and-white linen trouser suit at the back of the group. 'Is this the Valley of the Kings tour?' she asked.

The woman nodded. '*Si! Naturalmente.*'

'Oh, good, I thought I might be late,' Cleo replied with her best confident smile and climbed on the bus after her new friend.

She was first off the coach, barely waiting for it to roll to a halt in the car park. As she ran across the dusty tarmac towards the entrance she was beset by doubts and suspicions. *What if the people who stole my notes have worked out the riddles and are here already, searching for Kaha's clues?* She glanced around at the crowds, seeing malice and threat in every face. The shadowy operatives from the Ancient Order of the Eternal Sun could be disguised as tourists, or guards or drivers . . . *and if they see me here, they'll do anything to stop me finding the clues before them . . .*

Two can play at that game! she thought. *I need a disguise.*

Cleo darted into the crowded souvenir bazaar near the entrance kiosk and wove through the stalls of canopic jars, beaded jewellery, shisha pipes and tea towels. She grabbed the first shawl she saw, dumbfounding the salesman by paying full price without even attempting to haggle, and threw it over her head and shoulders.

The searing afternoon sun beat down, bouncing off the limestone cliffs, stoking the heat in the valley like a furnace. By the time Cleo reached the tomb of Rameses I, the Royal Grandfather, sweat poured down her face. When she saw the sign that said *Closed for Private Tour* she almost sank to her knees in tears of frustration.

'Are you all right?' a voice asked in Italian. Cleo turned to see the smart lady from the coach. She and her group were gathering around the sign.

'Just a little hot,' Cleo replied, drawing on the Italian she'd picked up when her parents had been working in Rome last summer. She peeped out from under her new shawl, which she noticed for the first time was bright purple, sequinned and dotted with shiny gold Tutankhamun masks.

'Would everyone who's with the Ferrari Corporate Tour please come this way,' a guide blared in Italian into a microphone.

The lady took Cleo's arm and steered her through the entrance. 'Your parents work for Ferrari, I assume?'

Cleo recoiled, eying the woman warily. Was she another spy from the Ancient Order of the Eternal Sun? Or was she just making polite conversation? *At least it's getting me free passage into the tomb!* 'My father is with the, er, British office . . .' she mumbled, still speaking Italian, but sure that the lady would have noticed her English accent by now.

As she descended into the subterranean gloom, Cleo glanced over her shoulder. Two men were standing at the top of the stairs. They looked familiar somehow. It took Cleo a moment to recognize them: the Italian archaeologists from the dig near Smenkhkare's tomb. Her heart began to thump. *Of course! It's them! They were in the El-Masry Café with Rachel the first day I met Ryan there. They must have overheard us talking about the Benben Stone.* They're *the ones who've been following us all along!*

Cleo sniffed. She couldn't detect the mysterious smell that had haunted her, but the men were probably too far away. No doubt it was some kind of fancy Italian cologne!

She pulled the Tutankhamun shawl further over her head and hurried into the burial chamber. The tour guide had begun to describe the beautifully painted wall scenes from the *Book of Gates*. Keeping an eye out for the two Italians, Cleo sidled around the fringes of the group, reciting Kaha's riddle under her breath: *follow the path of the World Encircler through the hours of the night.*

Cleo knew who the World Encircler was, of course – Apep, the evil serpent of the Underworld and great enemy of Ra. That was the easy part. The hard part was that he was *everywhere.* He wasn't called the *World Encircler* for nothing. Which of the hundreds of Apeps was the one that would lead them to Nefertiti's tomb? *Through the hours of the night*, she mused. There were twelve hours. For want of a better idea she began to count the loops and coils of each snake. *Seven, five, twenty, six . . . twelve.* Only one image of Apep had exactly twelve coils. They were laid out in two stacks of six, scrolling like the flourishes on an ornate signature.

Could this be the one?

The only drawing materials she had were a leaky pen and the back of her bus ticket, but she set about making a copy. It wasn't easy, especially trying to keep pen and paper out of sight under the shawl. She was contemplating trying a sneaky photo on her phone when she felt a tap on her shoulder. She sprang backwards and almost screamed out loud. Was she about to be thrown out and sued by Ferrari for gate-crashing their corporate event? Or kidnapped by the Italian branch of the Ancient Order of the Eternal Sun?

'You really need to chill out!' Ryan said. 'And you've got that all wrong,' he added, taking the pen and paper from her hands. 'You've drawn these coils going over the top of these ones, when they should go under. If we're going to have any chance of following the path that Apep is taking here, we need to get it right.'

'How did you get in?' Cleo asked. 'This is a private tour!'

Ryan grinned. 'I had a word with Yusuf. He got me in. I came as soon as I saw your text. Why the sudden panic anyway?'

Cleo told him about the theft of her notes. The smile faded from Ryan's face.

'*And* those two Italian archaeologists are snooping around,' Cleo whispered. 'I'm sure they're the ones who stole my notes. They're looking for the clue too.'

Ryan twitched his eyebrows.

Cleo could tell he didn't believe her. 'Why else would they just turn up in Rameses' tomb?' she demanded.

A man at the back of the group glared and put his fingers to his lips. 'Shh!' he hissed.

At that moment the Italian guide raised his voice. 'Please welcome your guest lecturers . . .' Two men stepped forward and were greeted by applause.

Ryan barely glanced up from his drawing. 'You mean those two? They're giving a talk by the look of it.'

'Obviously a cover story!' Cleo shot back.

'If you go over and start sniffing to see if their aftershave matches your mystery smell, I'll disown you,' Ryan said.

Cleo didn't admit she'd tried that already. 'But they keep *looking* at us,' she insisted.

Ryan shrugged. 'It's not surprising. We're jabbering all through their talk. Or,' he added with a grin, 'it could be that you're wearing the most hideous shawl in the history of the universe!' He tugged the spangled trim. 'Come on, let's get out of here before we're chucked out.'

Cleo gave up and followed.

'Purple sequins are so not you!' Ryan said as they stepped out into the glittering sunlight. 'If the Eternal Sun don't get us, the Fashion Police certainly will.'

'I vote we go to the Italians' camp this evening and see what they're up to,' Cleo whispered, as they walked from the bus stop through the village. 'I want my notes back.'

Ryan wasn't convinced that the Italian archaeologists were the note thieves, but he agreed. After all, he didn't have any better ideas. And although he'd been trying to hide it from Cleo by making jokes, the disappearance of her notes had really rattled him. Whoever was after the Benben Stone obviously meant business and would stop at nothing to get it. They might just be the kind of crazed fanatics who wanted to use the Benben to start World War Three or trigger the apocalypse.

As they rounded the corner into Cleo's street, a small red-tracksuited figure bundled towards them with a shout of, 'Hey! Manchester United!'

Ryan laughed. 'Ali! My man!' He held his hand out to the little boy for a knuckle touch. 'We'll play football later, OK?'

But Ali pointed proudly to his chest. 'Spying!' he said. 'Like James Bond.'

Ryan turned to Cleo. 'The other day I asked Ali if he'd keep an eye out for any suspicious characters hanging around the apartment building.'

'I see two men,' Ali said, with an ear-to-ear smile. 'This morning.'

'Where?' Cleo asked.

'I show you.' He tugged Ryan by the T-shirt and led them to the bushes at the side of the building near the apricot bougainvillea.

'This is just below my room!' Cleo gasped. 'Ali must have seen the thieves who stole my notes! Did they climb up there?' she asked, pointing to the balcony on the second floor.

But Ali shook his head. 'No, they just like this.' He did a pantomime impression of a dodgy lurking action. 'I see them here before. Two, three times.'

Ryan groaned. 'Of course! I heard someone here last night. When you threw the pencil at me. I thought it was an animal in the bushes.' He looked under the bougainvillea. Sure enough, there was a patch of flattened leaves and grass. 'They must have heard the entire translation of the Scorpion Papyrus.'

'Ali, were these men you saw *Italian?*' Cleo asked in Arabic.

Ali shrugged. 'Egyptian like me, I think.' He pointed to himself. 'In *galabayas.* He thought for a moment. 'One maybe from south.' He pointed to his face. 'Very dark skin.'

Suddenly Ryan had an idea. He took out his sketchbook

and showed Ali the portraits he'd drawn of the local diggers and workmen on the first day at Smenkhkare's tomb. 'The men you saw. Were they any of these?'

Ali shook his head.

'Did either of them *smell*?' Cleo asked.

'Smell?' Ali looked at her as if she'd taken leave of her senses. Then he did a double take at the sketchbook. It had fallen open at a page covered with doodled sketches of various members of the McNeils' team. 'Maybe this one.'

Ali was pointing to a picture of Professor Lydia McNeil's graduate student.

The tall black American student Ryan had played basketball and eaten pizza with only a few days before – J.J. Jennings.

32

TRAP

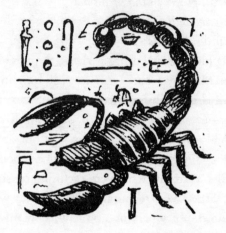

DID ALI REALLY *see J.J. lurking beneath Cleo's balcony?* Ryan wondered.

He reached the end of the pool, flipped over, and began another length of front crawl. Cleo's parents had announced an outing to the Golden Nile Hotel for swimming and afternoon tea on the terrace in honour of their wedding anniversary. Ryan had been invited to join them. The plan for a surveillance expedition to the Italian camp had been postponed.

But if Ali was right, the Italians weren't the ones they had to worry about anyway.

Ryan chased the questions round and round in his head as he sliced through the water.

Could J.J. be the Eternal Sun insider?

Could J.J. have been following us?

The man who chased me in the temple was tall and dark-skinned like J.J. and he did swing from the scaffolding like a basketball player from a hoop.

And the thief on the ferry did throw my backpack over the side like a basketball player lining up a shot.

J.J. plays basketball.

But J.J.'s been ill for days!

He could have been faking it, Ryan supposed, but Cleo said Rachel Meadows had been to visit him in his room. Apparently he'd been hugging the toilet!

Ryan got out and sat on the side dangling his feet in the pool. The chlorine was stinging his legs but at least there were no crocodiles or Nile perch to worry about here. He waved to Cleo's parents who were reclining on sunloungers. He could tell they were trying to relax, but they were talking intently – no doubt worrying about what would happen if they didn't find the Benben Stone.

'Whoever stole my notes must be someone we know.'

Ryan looked down. The voice came from the water near his feet where Cleo was gliding to the wall.

At least there was no chance of being overheard here. The only other swimmers were a family playing a noisy game of pool Frisbee. Bubbling water filters, swishing lawn sprinklers and piped Europop music from the poolside bar drowned out any remaining sound. 'Ali was spying on the apartment building all day yesterday,' Cleo added, pushing up onto the side. 'He saw J.J. and another man hanging around, but he didn't see anyone climb into my room through the balcony. That means someone must have gone in

226

through the front door. Someone Ali wouldn't be suspicious of.'

Ryan watched a hoopoe with zebra-striped wings and flashy orange crest hopping about on the grass drinking from the puddles made by the sprinklers. 'Which would include J.J.,' he said. 'He's definitely looking like our prime suspect.'

Cleo shook water from her hair. The drops made tiny rainbows in the sunlight. 'And he was at our flat today. Mum and Dad had the whole team round for lunch again while we were at the Valley of the Kings. Mum said he was still feeling delicate after his food poisoning so he only drank mint tea.'

'But even if J.J. *was* in your flat for lunch,' Ryan pointed out, 'how could he have sneaked into your room without anyone noticing? And, anyway, we can't be *sure* that Ali was right about it being J.J. He only recognized him from my sketch. It wasn't exactly a police photofit . . .'

Cleo tucked her knees up under her chin. 'You're right. And even if it *is* J.J., he's not working alone. There's at least one other man – the guard with the mysterious smell who chased me at Karnak – who may or may not be the same as the man in the rowing boat. There might even be more of them . . .' She gazed down at the sunlight breaking up in the ripples of the pool. 'And they've got my notes now. They know everything that we know. There's only one more clue left to solve – *the cry of the Bennu Bird in flight*. They might not even bother following us to see if we solve it any more. If they're smart enough they could solve it themselves and figure out how to get into Nefertiti's tomb and find the Benben Stone before we do.'

Ryan sighed. 'Yeah, especially as we don't have the foggiest idea what the Bennu Bird clue means.' He thought for a moment. 'Hey! Perhaps *we* should try spying on *them*. See if they can solve it for us!'

'Some hope, if we don't even know who *they* are.' Cleo grabbed her towel and stood up. 'There's only one thing for it. We're going to have set a trap and flush them out.'

Ryan pretended to shake water out of his ears. 'Sorry, for a moment I thought you said *set a trap.*'

Cleo didn't smile. 'You heard right,' she said. 'I've been thinking about it. It's the logical solution. Whether it's J.J., or someone else, let's turn their snooping to our advantage. We'll act as if we think we know where Kaha's next clue is. We'll talk about it really loudly in public . . .'

Ryan got the picture. 'Then we lie in wait?'

Cleo nodded. 'And see who turns up to see if we find the answer to the clue . . .'

Ryan reached out and caught a wayward Frisbee as it soared past. He couldn't resist teasing her. 'That sounds as if it might involve breaking one or two teensy little protocols.'

'Oh, we're *way* past protocols now,' Cleo said seriously, as she stood up and snapped her towel round her shoulders. 'We just have to decide when and where to set the trap!'

Cleo and Ryan spent the rest of the evening dropping pyramid-sized hints about their plan to search for the third clue – *the cry of the Bennu Bird in flight* – that very night.

The place, they'd decided, would be Smekhkare's tomb; they knew their way around and had access to a key. As for the time, they'd settled on midnight, for no other reason than that it sounded suitably significant. They blabbed this information loudly at the El-Masry Café, on the balcony of Cleo's room, and as they walked along the street. They even called each other to discuss the operation in greater detail – just in case someone was tapping their phones.

Just as on their previous secret visit to the tomb, Ryan waited until his mum was asleep before slipping out into the dark night and hurrying to meet Cleo outside the McNeils' apartment building. He'd almost given up on her when she appeared at last.

'My parents decided to stay up late and watch a film,' she panted, pulling a jumper on back to front over her T-shirt. 'I thought they'd never go to bed!'

They borrowed the Mansours' bikes again to make the journey up the winding road to the Valley of the Kings. It took some heroic pedalling, but somehow they made it into position in Smenkhkare's tomb with a few minutes to spare.

They hunkered down behind the sarcophagus which, to Ryan's relief, was now firmly sealed up. They turned off their torches, switched their phones to mute and waited.

That's when Ryan heard a scuttling noise on the ground near his leg.

He clicked his torch on and directed it towards the sound.

The scorpion glowed in the light, the pale translucent yellow of old Sellotape. Ryan watched, his eyes fixed on the barbed stinger as it arched its tail over its back only millimetres from his bare kneecap. He wished he'd worn long trousers. 'Scorpion,' he breathed.

'How big are its claws?' Cleo whispered.

'Not too bad. Quite weedy-looking, in fact.'

'No, that *is* bad,' Cleo said. 'The smaller the claws, the

229

more likely they are to sting rather than pinch. What colour is it?'

Ryan gulped. 'Yellowish.'

'Sounds like a deathstalker,' Cleo murmured.

'Deathstalker,' Ryan echoed weakly. 'You're kidding.' He had a horrible feeling she wasn't.

'Whatever you do, don't move.'

Move? Ryan thought. He was incapable of breathing, let alone *moving,* right now. Had that curse from the fourth chamber finally caught up with him? *He will be devoured by the scorpion.* Paralysed by terror, he watched as Cleo opened the bum bag on her tool belt and took out her archaeologist's trowel.

Very slowly, she leaned over his legs.

Very slowly, she lowered the trowel to the ground.

The deathstalker wheeled round and quivered, braced to strike. With a flick of the wrist, Cleo caught the scorpion on the end of the trowel and sent it spinning into orbit.

There was a soft click and a scuffle as it landed in the furthest corner of the chamber and scurried away into the stonework.

'Th-thanks,' Ryan stammered.

Cleo smiled. 'Don't mention it. You saved me from the deadfall. Now we're quits.'

All of a sudden, a tiny sound made them both fall silent and flatten themselves against the base of the sarcophagus. Ryan turned off his torch.

They strained their ears towards the entrance.

Yes! The door was creaking open . . .

Someone was walking right into their trap!

33

ROMANCE

CLEO PEEPED ROUND the side of the sarcophagus.

A figure was framed in the doorway of the tomb, black against the grey rectangle of moonlit sky.

Cleo held her breath.

Was it J.J.?

Or maybe his accomplice?

Cleo sniffed silently, searching for a stray molecule of the mystery smell on the cool air.

Her pulse thudded in her ears. She was sure she could hear Ryan's heart beating in time at her side. She realized that they hadn't actually thought of what they would do *after* they saw who entered the tomb, but it was too late now.

The figure took a step forward. Cleo could tell now that it wasn't J.J. Whoever it was wasn't tall enough, but they were broad and solid and wearing some sort of cape or robe. The figure turned and a shaft of moonlight picked out a springy mass of chestnut-brown hair with a silvery gleam.

'Rachel!' Cleo exclaimed. 'What are *you* doing here?'

Rachel stumbled on a loose rock, but she quickly found her footing. She strode into the tomb and switched on a high-powered torch. Cleo's hands shot up to shield her dark-adapted eyes as the chamber flooded with bright white light.

'What do you *think* I'm doing?' Rachel's huge shadow loomed on the wall among the painted gods. 'Looking for you, of course!'

Cleo scrambled to her feet. 'But why?'

Rachel stood facing Cleo across the sarcophagus. She swept her tartan shawl across her shoulder. 'I overheard you and Ryan planning a secret meeting at midnight . . .'

Ambushed by a wave of anger, Cleo slammed her fists down on the lid of the sarcophagus. 'You mean you *snooped* on our private conversation?' She knew she was being irrational – making sure they were overheard had been the whole point of the exercise – but that just fuelled her fury. She couldn't believe she and Ryan had been so stupid as to overlook the obvious flaw in their brilliant plan: that their deliberate attempts to lure the spies into their trap might have the unintended consequence of alerting Rachel or their parents to their midnight outing!

Rachel looked hurt. She shook her head. 'Of course I wasn't *snooping*. I was just behind you in the market. I couldn't help hearing. You weren't exactly being discreet.' She looked around, the blazing torchlight throwing her pale face into deep contrast like an old black-and-white photograph. 'I assume he's here, too? Your partner in crime?'

Ryan popped his head up from behind the sarcophagus. 'Er, yeah, that'd be me. Hello, Dr Meadows.'

'I don't know what you two think you're doing running around in the middle of the night . . .' Rachel paused for breath and at that moment Cleo thought she heard a sound outside the entrance – the soft clatter of small stones trickling down the cliff as if dislodged by a footstep. She ran from behind the sarcophagus, past Rachel and peered out through the door into the night.

There was nothing there.

Maybe it had just been a night-hunting animal, a jerboa or a fox, passing by. *But what if it was the spy, or spies?* Cleo thought despairingly. *If they heard us plotting to meet and followed us up here, they'll have been scared off by seeing Rachel parked in the tomb entrance, shouting at us and lighting the place up like a landing strip with her searchlight. They'll be long gone by now . . .*

Cleo ground her teeth. Rachel had totally ruined their brilliant trap!

'I'm surprised at you, Cleopatra,' Rachel went on. 'You of all people must know how dangerous it is to creep around up here at night. This tomb isn't a playground, it's a working dig. What if you fell and hurt yourself? How would your parents feel if anything happened to you? Don't you think your mum has enough on her plate at the moment?' She shook her head sadly. 'I didn't want to worry them, so I followed you up here myself.'

Cleo's anger drained away as quickly as it had started. She

hung her head. Rachel was right, of course. It *was* dangerous to come up here at night.

Rachel's stern expression softened to her usual motherly smile. 'Now, what's going on? You can tell me, dear. I *was* young once, you know. I do remember what it's like to be in love, but why all this secrecy? I hope you're not thinking of running away together . . .'

Cleo couldn't help a snort of laughter. 'You don't seriously think I'd stay up half the night and climb up a cliff in the dark for a romantic meeting with Ryan, do you?'

'Cheers,' Ryan muttered. 'The feeling's mutual.'

Rachel sighed. 'You've been acting very strangely lately, Cleo. Ryan seems to have been a bad influence . . .' She turned to Ryan. 'Have you got anything to say for yourself, young man?'

'No, no!' Cleo stammered, before Ryan could speak. 'It's not Ryan's fault.' *It might have started out that way,* she thought, but, since then, any influencing had mostly been in the other direction. Suddenly Cleo felt as if the earth were giving way beneath her feet, just as it had when she first fell into Smenkhkare's tomb all those months ago. Rachel was right.

Mum would be beside herself if she knew I was here. I've been completely irresponsible, playing at being some kind of action hero. I should have known better . . .

'This was all my idea,' she mumbled, gulping back tears of guilt and shame.

Rachel skirted the end of the sarcophagus and put her arm round her, which made Cleo feel even worse. 'So, if it's not romance, what *is* this all about?' she asked gently.

Cleo glanced at Ryan. This was their secret quest. Well,

theirs and Rahotep's. It didn't feel right to tell anyone else about it when they were so close to finding the Benben Stone themselves. Not even Rachel.

Rachel's shoulders sagged with disappointment. 'Well, if you can't come up with a sensible explanation, I'll have to tell your parents about this. I wouldn't be surprised if they ground you and stop you seeing Ryan. They can't have this sort of distraction when there's an important excavation to run . . .'

'No!' Cleo gasped. She stared at Rachel in horror. If she was grounded, the Eternal Sun spies would *definitely* find their way into Nefertiti's tomb first and steal the Benben Stone.

She felt Ryan nudge her elbow. 'We've got to tell,' he said quietly. 'It's not like we're about to crack the Bennu Bird clue anyway . . .'

Cleo agreed. They had no choice. Now that their trap had failed, they'd probably never get another chance to catch the Eternal Sun spies. 'We're looking for the Benben Stone,' she sighed. 'We came across some documents that contain clues about where it's really hidden. We need to find it before the Eter—' She broke off at a shake of the head from Ryan. *Yes,* she thought, *best not to mention that part. I'll just sound even more hare-brained if I start going on about being stalked by unidentified members of a secret society.* 'Well, we just want to find it,' she said flatly.

Rachel gave her a squeeze. 'You silly billies! Why didn't you discuss this with the rest of the team, instead of all this cloak-and-dagger nonsense?'

'I'm sorry. I didn't think. I just felt so bad about the Benben Stone not being here when I was the one who found the tomb in the first place.' *Not to mention that I spilled the information to a journalist,* Cleo thought, although she decided to skim over that part too. 'It feels like everything is my fault. I thought it would make up for it if we could find the stone by ourselves.'

'Yeah, we were just trying to help,' Ryan chipped in.

Rachel smiled. 'Well, no harm done, eh? How about we go back and tell your parents all about it over a cup of tea?' She wrapped her shawl tighter and turned towards the door. 'I'll see if I can rustle up some biscuits too.'

Cleo suddenly felt sick. 'Mum's going to be furious when she finds out how many excavation rules I've flouted. And that I took the key to the tomb. They'll probably ground me anyway!'

'Don't worry,' Rachel said. 'I'm sure I can smooth things over.'

Cleo mustered a weak smile of thanks. There wasn't much Rachel couldn't sort out with a cup of tea and a plate of biscuits!

Half an hour later they were all sitting around the kitchen table.

True to her word, Rachel glossed over the more dangerous tomb-raiding elements of Cleo and Ryan's rendezvous and simply said she'd caught them having a late-night meeting. Ryan phoned his mum to let her know where he was and she hurried to join them at the McNeils' flat.

Then, while Rachel bustled around filling the teapot and searching the cupboards for biscuits, Cleo and Ryan told their story: how they'd found Rahotep's scarab amulet in the fourth chamber which had led them to the writing tablets in the Theban Museum; how they'd discovered the Scorpion Papyrus inside one of the tablets and deciphered it to read old Kaha's witness statement, which told of the tragic love triangle between Pharaoh Akhenaten, his beautiful Queen Nefertiti and his younger brother, Smenkhkare.

They left out some of the dicier parts – like jumping in the Nile to save the writing tablets, being chased out of Karnak by the guards and their suspicions that J.J. had stolen Cleo's notes.

They had also agreed – in a whispered conversation on the way down the cliff – not to mention the other major element of the story: that Danny Farr, the man everyone thought of as a loveable old rock star who'd set up a charity to do good works, was, in fact, a secret member of the sinister Ancient Order of the Eternal Sun and was trying to get his hands on the Benben Stone in time for the Return of the Phoenix.

'If Mum finds out this has anything to do with the Eternal Sun,' Ryan had pointed out, 'she'll freak out at me for getting involved and *I'll* be the one getting grounded and forbidden from seeing *you*.' He'd paused for a moment. 'And given how madly in love we are, I couldn't stand that.'

Cleo had started spluttering that she was not even the slightest bit in love, before she'd noticed the big grin on Ryan's face.

It took a while for Cleo's parents to make sense of what they were hearing. A few moments before, they'd been fast asleep – and had assumed that Cleo was too. Mum was trying to tie back her unruly black hair in an elastic band, while doing up her dressing-gown belt and finding her slippers. Dad rubbed his face and kept blowing on his tea even though

237

the steam was fogging up his glasses. Only Julie Flint, who, Cleo figured, was probably used to late-night briefings as a journalist, looked wide awake, her blonde hair as spiky as ever. She asked Rachel for coffee instead of tea, flipped open a lined pad and filled page after page with notes.

But Mum soon forgot all about her hair and her dressing gown and her slippers. 'You *really* think you know where the Benben Stone is?' she asked.

Cleo nodded. 'Well, sort of.'

'So, let me get this straight,' Dad said, stirring his tea with the earpiece of his glasses. 'You're saying that Pharaoh Akhenaten stole the Benben Stone and installed it in a top-secret hidden tomb for Nefertiti. Then he executed Smenkhkare, faked that confession and placed it in Smenkhkare's coffin as an act of revenge.'

Cleo grimaced. 'I know it sounds a bit far-fetched when you put it like that . . .'

'Oh, no, I can believe it,' Dad said. 'People have done far worse things in the name of love. And we were pretty sure from the tests on the mummy that Smenkhkare had been decapitated. Wait till I tell Alex it *was* an execution. She'll be over the moon.'

Mum had been pacing up and down the kitchen. Now she sank into a chair. 'But if the Benben Stone is hidden in a secret chamber beneath Akhenaten's tomb, that means it's up in the Royal Tomb at Amarna, not here in the Valley of the Kings.'

Cleo smiled. 'That's what I thought, at first. But remember, Kaha was telling Rahotep all this about fifty years *after* Akhenaten died. The new city of Amarna had fallen into ruin by then. I've checked my translation over and over, and

Kaha definitely says Nefertiti lies *deep beneath the chamber where Akhenaten now rests*.

Rachel gave a triumphant cry as she found a forgotten pack of custard creams at the back of a drawer. 'Well,' she said, tipping the biscuits on to a plate, 'we know that when Amarna was abandoned, Tutankhamun ordered the mummies of the royal family to be removed from the tombs there and brought here to be reburied in the Valley of the Kings. Most of them probably in KV55.'

'Exactly!' Cleo said. 'KV55 is the abbreviation for the fifty-fifth tomb discovered in the Valley of the Kings,' she explained to Ryan. 'And,' she went on, 'Kaha specifically told Rahotep, *it's only a short walk from here*. That proves he *can't* have been talking about the Royal Tomb in Amarna, because the interview took place just up the road from here in *Set Maat* village and Amarna is hundreds of miles away!' Cleo paused and poured herself some more tea from the pot. She'd given this a lot of thought and could see only one explanation. 'Somehow, word of Nefertiti's secret tomb must have slipped out so that, when Akhenaten was moved to KV55, some of the people who were still loyal to him moved Nefertiti as well, and reburied her mummy and all her treasures in just the same way as before – in a chamber beneath the new Royal Tomb – so that the pharaoh and his queen could remain close together in death.'

Julie looked up from her notebook. 'But KV55 is only a small tomb. Why has nobody reported a passageway leading down to Nefertiti's chamber before?'

'It's *hidden*,' Cleo and Ryan said in unison.

'And there's a labyrinth of some sort. Kaha left clues to find the way in, in the form of riddles,' Ryan explained.

'We've found the first two – the Great Cat and the World Encircler . . .'

Dad hooked his glasses back on over his ears and smiled. 'It seems that you two have it all figured out . . .' He bit into a stale custard cream, then frowned at it and grimaced. 'I wouldn't be surprised if this pack of biscuits had been buried with Nefertiti too!'

Mum swiped him with a tea towel. 'Just imagine – if we found Nefertiti's long-lost tomb *and* the Benben Stone, it would be one of the truly historic discoveries of our time. We need to get a permit to excavate in KV55 as soon as possible . . .'

Cleo was about to agree when there was a knock at the door. Rachel looked at her watch. 'Goodness, it's four o'clock in the morning. Who could that be?'

Cleo glanced at Ryan. Was it J.J.? If he'd been frightened off from the trap at the tomb, maybe he'd been unable to resist coming to see what was going on at the flat.

But it was only Alex Shawcross, in white tracksuit and trainers, her ivory skin flushed a delicate shade of pink. 'I couldn't sleep, so decided I might as well do my morning run extra early,' she puffed. 'It's best to go before it gets too hot.' She looked around the kitchen, taking in the crowd. 'I saw your light on. Nothing wrong, is there? Ooh, am I missing a breakfast party?'

'Looks like we might find the Benben, after all,' Dad told her.

Cleo and Ryan told the whole story again.

'The secret hidden tomb of Queen Nefertiti?' Alex marvelled, reaching for a custard cream. 'With ninety-nine poisoning victims, you say? Now that *would* be worth seeing!'

34

BLOOD

THE SUN WAS barely above the horizon.

Ryan shivered in the chill morning air, warming his hands on the plastic mug of sweet milky tea Rachel had poured him from her flask. It was two days later and the McNeil team had gathered outside Tomb KV55, in the slate-grey shadows of the valley's limestone crags. Ryan had been expecting the entrance – not far from the world-famous tomb of Tutankhamun – to be something spectacular. After all, several royal mummies from the Amarna period had been reburied here. But it turned out to be an unpromising-looking hole in the ground.

Ryan exchanged a glance of anticipation with Cleo.

Swathed in a thick brown jumper that looked as if had been handwoven with chopsticks from the hair of a particularly shaggy and poorly groomed mountain goat, she was bouncing up and down on the toes of her walking boots. He couldn't tell whether it was an attempt to keep warm or impatience to get started.

Ryan could hardly believe how quickly things had moved since the night of the prehistoric custard creams.

Phone calls had been made and emails sent.

Cleo's mum had spoken to Sir Charles Peacocke back in London, and he'd persuaded his contacts in Egypt to arrange for a survey permit to be granted at short notice.

And now, only two days later, they were about to enter. There were some final heated discussions with the tomb guards, but at last they were filing into the tomb down a steep flight of steps and along a sloping passageway. Lydia and Pete McNeil led the way, closely followed by Ryan and Cleo, Rachel Meadows, Alex Shawcross, J.J., several of the guards and local workmen and Max Henderson with his photography equipment, grouching about the substandard lighting conditions as always. Ryan saw his mum at the back of the group, her voice recorder, notebook and pen poised to record the momentous events.

Ryan watched J.J. carefully as he loped along the passageway, discussing the layout of the tomb with Cleo's mum. He seemed to have recovered from his stomach upset and was acting normally – as friendly and laid-back as ever – but Ryan and Cleo had resolved that they would be keeping a *very* close eye on him. After all, members of the Ancient Order of the Eternal Sun were renowned for their secrecy. J.J. was hardly going to give himself away by starting to recite magic spells or waving a flag emblazoned with the mysterious double-ankh-and-sun symbol in public.

The main burial chamber was just as unimpressive as the entrance: small, empty and unadorned. But the buzz of excitement was like the super-charged hum around an electricity pylon. Lydia McNeil and J.J. began to sweep the roughly plastered walls with handheld laser scanners that could detect changes in the structure of the stonework. The others divided the area into sections and scoured every millimetre for any sign that might point them towards a hidden entrance to a secret chamber: a giant cat or a coiled serpent or a Bennu Bird . . .

Nobody said it out loud but Ryan knew everyone was thinking the same thing. It was as clear as if they had thought bubbles over their heads: *We could be about to find the long-lost sacred Benben Stone, solve the mystery of Nefertiti's disappearance* and *maybe discover treasures even richer than those of Tutankhamun's tomb into the bargain!*

All apart from Alex Shawcross and Pete McNeil, that was. They were more interested in finding the ninety-nine dead bodies.

'A toxicologist's dream!' Alex enthused, as they discussed the symptoms of poisoning by wolfsbane and hemlock: paralysis, palpitations, burning of the limbs . . . When they started on the sensation of ants crawling under the skin, Ryan stopped listening.

'Are you *sure* this is the right tomb?' he whispered to Cleo. 'There's nothing here.'

Cleo didn't answer but Ryan could tell she was having doubts. She pulled her ponytail tighter and jutted her chin further as she continued to search.

243

Ryan moved through to a small, unfinished antechamber. Ancient red draughtsman's marks on the walls showed where further stonecutting had been planned but never carried out. He clambered up on a heap of fallen stones for a closer look. It seemed that the draughtsman had got bored and started doodling. He'd sketched a pile of duck carcasses on a table, ready for roasting. A four-legged animal was under the table, stealing one of the ducks, its teeth clamped round a long neck. *It looks like a dog or maybe a fox,* Ryan thought. *Or it could be a cat.*

'What do you think of this?' he called to Cleo. But as he reached up to brush away flakes of stone he lost his footing on the rubble. He stumbled forward, grabbing at a nub of stone protruding from the wall. It came away in his hand. Suddenly, he was being showered by a mini-avalanche.

The entire section of wall had given way.

The archaeologists instantly flocked around him.

'Don't worry,' Ryan said, shaking out fragments of stone and plaster from his T-shirt. 'I'm fine.'

No one answered. Ryan realized that they weren't interested in *him*. They were all shining their torches into the hole that had opened up in the wall. Max Henderson's camera began to flash.

'This must be it!' Professor McNeil cried. 'Hard hats, everyone. Let's clear this loose stone . . .'

One by one, they all climbed through and walked along a low tunnel, the palms of their outstretched hands flat to the walls, the lamps on their helmets bobbing up and down.

But Ryan couldn't shake the feeling that something wasn't right. Yes, the cat – if it even *was* a cat – had led them to the tunnel, but only because he'd tripped and knocked the wall down. He'd been expecting the Great Cat clue to be something more *sophisticated* somehow. 'And what's this tunnel got to do with following *the path of the World Encircler*?' he whispered to Cleo. 'It's not exactly a labyrinth.'

'Maybe the old man was making it sound more complicated than it really was to put Rahotep off,' Cleo suggested.

Ryan wasn't convinced but, before he could argue the point, a call came from up ahead. 'There's a cave-in here!'

Ryan and Cleo hurried to catch up with the others. Large boulders had tumbled from the roof, blocking the passageway.

'We should be able to get through this gap on the left side,' Professor McNeil said after a short inspection. 'We just need to move these stones and insert a wooden prop . . .'

While the work was underway, Ryan lay on his stomach and directed his head torch through a small hole near the ground on the right side of the rock pile. He thought he could see a smaller tunnel branching away from the main passage. The light picked out an odd shape some way along. The rest of the team were all crowded around the workmen, who were shoring up the roof on the left. Ryan tugged at a stone. It came away easily. He pulled another one out. And another. Soon the hole was the size of a dog flap.

'What are you doing?' Cleo hissed. 'We've got to wait for a safety check . . .'

But Ryan *couldn't* wait. Something was driving him on. He'd been troubled by a sense of foreboding ever since entering this tomb, and somehow he was sure that the cause of it lay in the tunnel ahead.

He wriggled through the hole and walked towards what he could now see was some kind of large cage-like contraption of wood and metal. It was like watching a gory medical programme on TV: the less he *wanted* to look, the more he knew he *had* to.

He was close enough now to see that the cage was a battery of long metal-tipped spikes that projected diagonally upwards from the walls on each side, interlocking to form a latticework.

And there was something caught up in them . . .

Ryan reeled round at the sound of footsteps, his heart flailing in his chest, but it was only Cleo. She must have decided she couldn't wait either.

'It's a booby trap,' she said. 'And it's been sprung. The stakes have all shot out and impaled that poor guy . . .'

They stood in silence, staring at the skeleton skewered on the spikes like a fly ensnared in a spider's web. The body had been lifted from the ground and was held upright by a spar through the rib cage. A second spike had pierced the vertebrae at the neck. Tatters of cloth hung from the pelvis. A woven sandal dangled from one fleshless foot. The stone beneath was stained sooty brown where blood had pooled.

Ryan reached up to touch a shoulder blade. 'It's Rahotep, isn't it?'

Cleo nodded. Her voice was almost inaudible. 'I think so.'

Ryan jumped back in horror as the skull fell from the neck, hit the ground with a thud and rolled over. As he stooped to pick it up he noticed a small scroll lying next to it. He handed it to Cleo while he balanced the skull back in place. Cleo unfurled the scroll. 'The Great Cat of Ra, the twelve-coiled serpent, the Bennu Bird,' she read. 'Rahotep must have solved the riddles too. He was carrying this note with him when he . . .' She shook her head, unable to say the words.

Ryan reached out and squeezed her hand. Rahotep's mission had ended here on these cruel spikes. *He must have cried for help, but nobody knew he was here.* He imagined Rahotep's mother back home in Heliopolis, waiting for news that never came. He felt for his St Christopher and closed his fingers around it. The ache of Dad's disappearance clawed at his heart. He dug in his pocket and pulled out Rahotep's scarab amulet. Now Ryan knew why he hadn't been able to hand it over to Professor McNeil. This was where it belonged. He ran his thumb over the beetle's smooth blue-green wing cases for the last time. Then he unclasped the silver chain from his neck, slid the St Christopher pendant into his palm and put it into his pocket. He threaded the chain through the small hole in the scarab and gently hung it around Rahotep's neck. The amulet dangled between the time-blackened ribs, where the young priest's heart would once have beaten.

'I know it's been a long time,' Ryan mumbled, 'but your father's *ka* is here to protect you again.'

Cleo looked away. Ryan could tell that she'd seen, but she was pretending not to have done.

Suddenly she grabbed hold of Rahotep's skeletal hand and stretched his arm out to the wall, until the finger bones brushed the stone.

'What are you doing?' Ryan asked.

Cleo didn't reply. Instead she bent to examine the wall by the light of her head torch. Ryan leaned closer. He could see faint brown marks. He couldn't be sure, but he thought they looked like . . .

'Hieroglyphs?' he asked.

Cleo nodded. 'Rahotep's left us a message. He must have written it in his blood.'

'What does it say?'

'Akhenaten, I think.'

'But we *know* this is Akhenaten's tomb,' Ryan said. 'Why does he need to tell us that?'

'No, wait! It's not Akhe*naten, Servant* of the Aten, it's Akhe*taten, Horizon* of the Aten. That's the original name of the new city he built in the desert before it changed to Amarna.' Cleo looked up at Ryan. 'And there's another symbol but it's not clear . . . it looks like a bee . . . that could mean *king* or *Lower Egypt* or *bee* or even *honey*.'

Ryan shrugged. 'Honey? That's a bit random.'

At that moment a shout came from the other side of the rockfall. 'This must be it! We've found the hidden tomb!'

35

HONEY

AS SHE SQUEEZED back through the rocks and ran down the left-hand fork of the corridor, Cleo could hardly see for the tears filling her eyes. She scrubbed them away with the end of her scarf. *It's logically impossible to be grieving for Rahotep,* she told herself. *He died over three thousand years before you even knew he existed!*

But he was still our friend!

And she'd thought being friends with *Ryan* was complicated enough.

At least we can complete the quest for him, she thought. Any minute now, they would finally set their eyes on the Benben Stone . . .

But as soon as she saw the team clustered around a low doorway roughly hewn into the stone at the end of the tunnel she knew something was wrong. Mum's face was as stiff as a death mask. Rachel was leaning against the wall, holding her mini electric fan to her face. J.J. had slumped next to her, his head between his knees as if he'd been taken sick again. Cleo stepped over his long legs and entered a large chamber lit by a swaying lamp that one of the diggers had hooked onto the ceiling. The room was filled with wooden boxes and coffers. Scrolls of leather and papyrus were piled up in the corners and writing tablets and stone ostracons were stacked against the walls.

'What is all this?' Cleo asked.

Mum followed her inside. 'Official records from Amarna. It looks like they cached them here for safekeeping after the city was abandoned.'

'Never mind! Could be worse!' Dad boomed in the cheerful voice he saved for catastrophes like missed planes and stolen wallets. 'It may not be Nefertiti's tomb, but this'll be a treasure trove for historians.' He began to whistle *Walking on Sunshine*.

But Mum thumped the wall. 'No, Pete, it *couldn't* be worse. I promised the Danny Farr Foundation an *actual* treasure trove with *actual* treasure. Oh, yeah, and the Benben Stone! They wanted *media impact*. I know this archive is important but old records won't impress them.'

The only one who'd truly got over the disappointment was Alex Shawcross. She was happily rummaging through a box of papyri, her blonde hair knotted in a blue-and-white dotted scarf. 'This is amazing. Some of these are medical records,' she enthused. 'This could tell us why they abandoned Amarna so quickly. I've always suspected a devastating plague epidemic.' She held up a scroll. 'And here's a surgeon's notebook. Wow, it's a list of amputations!'

Cleo was backing out of the chamber when Ryan shouted in her ear. *'Honey cakes!'*

Cleo jumped. She hadn't even realized Ryan was standing behind her. She turned and stared at him. So did everyone else.

'Er, sorry about that,' Ryan mumbled. He tugged Cleo out into the tunnel.

'That bee wasn't random!' he said, as soon as they were out of hearing.

Cleo had no idea what he was talking about.

'I *knew* that cat was a dog.'

'Arggh!' Cleo groaned, sliding down the wall to sit on the stone floor. 'Non-random bees? Cats that are dogs? Stop speaking in riddles!' she snapped. 'You're worse than Kaha!'

Ryan sat down next to her. 'You're not the only one who can have a theory! I've just figured out what Rahotep was trying to tell us with that message he wrote on the wall. You said that Pharaoh Akhenaten's original tomb was in this new city of his, right?'

'That's right – Amarna.'

'And after the city collapsed, the royal mummies were brought here and reburied?' Ryan went on.

'Yes, they were hidden away for safety, just like these records. There was a lot of anger towards Akhenaten's memory by that time, so there was a risk that anything connected with him would be vandalized.'

'But nobody knew about Nefertiti's tomb hidden away under Akhenaten's tomb, did they?' Ryan asked. 'Everyone

251

who helped with it had been locked inside and killed . . .'

'Well, yes, everyone except Kaha,' Cleo said impatiently. They'd been through all this before. 'But word must have got out somehow. It would've been hard to keep something that important a secret.'

'What if it didn't? What if Akhenaten's people *didn't* relocate Nefertiti's tomb here and it was left behind in Amarna, completely forgotten about?'

Cleo rested her chin on her knees. It was a good theory, but the Scorpion Papyrus had been clear. 'Kaha definitely told Rahotep that Nefertiti was buried beneath the chamber *where Akhenaten now rests, only a short walk from here* . . . Like I told Mum, he can't have meant the tomb in Amarna. It's hundreds of miles north.'

Ryan held up a finger. 'Yeah! That's the part that fooled Rahotep, too. He only realized his mistake when he was dying.'

Cleo jerked her head up. 'Mistake? What do you mean?'

'Kaha was *delirious* when he told Rahotep about where to find Nefertiti's tomb, remember? He called him *Meritaten*. He was going on about pastries and honey cakes . . . poor old Kaha thought he was back in his youth, talking to Princess Meritaten and sneaking her cakes from the kitchens. My gran was the same when she got really old. She kept calling me Eddie. She thought I was Dad when he was a boy.'

At last Cleo understood. She couldn't believe she hadn't worked it out before. 'Of course!' she said, jumping to her feet. 'In Kaha's fevered mind, *here* meant the Great Palace in Amarna, and *now* meant fifty years ago when he was a child.'

'Exactly!' Ryan stood up. 'That's what Rahotep was trying

to tell us by writing the name of the new city and *honey* on the wall. He was trying to write *honey cakes* but I guess he ran out of time when . . . well, you know.' Ryan puffed out his cheeks and shook his head. 'I *knew* this wasn't the right tomb. No wonder the clues didn't fit properly. I always thought it seemed unlikely that anyone would have recreated the whole secret tomb here, and now I'm sure that they didn't.' He turned to face Cleo. 'When Tutankhamun brought the royal mummies back to Luxor, he had no idea he'd left Nefertiti behind in her secret tomb.'

Cleo gazed back along the dark tunnel.

No one did, she thought.

Not until now.

'I'm sorry Cleo, but there's no way on this earth we're trooping up to Amarna on another wild-goose chase!' Lydia McNeil yanked the fridge door open and glowered at a bowl of salad. 'It's a four-hour drive!'

Cleo gripped the cheese grater so hard her knuckles turned white. 'But Mum,' she pleaded. 'That's where we'll find Nefertiti's tomb. I'm sure of it.'

Mum banged the salad down on the table. 'You were *sure* it would be under Tomb KV55!'

'I know,' Cleo sighed, 'but we got it wrong. We've figured out why. The scorpion charmer was muddled. He was talking about when he was young . . .'

'I'm starting to wonder whether you and Ryan invented this whole story.' Mum snatched handfuls of cutlery from the drawer. 'Where's your evidence?'

Cleo grabbed another big chunk of Parmesan and began to grate furiously. 'All my notes and my translations got stolen.'

'Stolen?' Mum repeated. 'By whom?'

Suddenly Cleo realized she'd said too much. If she started going into her suspicions about the Eternal Sun following them, and Mum's favourite graduate student, J.J., quite possibly being one of their spies, Mum might just have a nervous breakdown. And anyway, she'd promised Ryan she'd keep that part quiet for now . . . 'I don't know who stole them,' she mumbled, 'but they disappeared from my room.'

Mum didn't say anything, but the way she was thumping knives and forks onto the table told Cleo she didn't believe a word.

'You can ask Dr Badawi at the Theban Museum. She'll show you the writing tablets. We had to break them open . . .' Cleo's hand slipped and she grated her thumb instead of the Parmesan. *Why did I go and say that?*

'You *damaged* Eighteenth Dynasty artefacts?' Mum shouted. She slammed the fridge door so hard the bottles rattled inside.

'Dad?' Cleo tried. He could usually talk Mum round. But he looked up from his laptop and sighed. 'Cleo, love, we don't have time for this.'

Cleo stared at him in disbelief. If *Dad* couldn't see the upside, things *had* to be bad. 'What do you mean?"

Mum turned back from the fridge. 'We have exactly forty-eight hours to pack up and leave!'

Surely Mum's just being dramatic, Cleo thought. But Dad was nodding.

'I'm booking the tickets now,' he said. 'Your mother's been called in to see Charles Peacocke as soon as we get back to

London. This episode has caused a major embarrassment for the Department of Museums and Culture. They pulled a lot of strings to get that permit fast-tracked for us . . .'

'Episode?' Mum snapped. '*Fiasco*, more like! The Danny Farr Foundation wants us to repay all their money.'

'Why?' Cleo gasped.

'They say we've broken the terms of our contract. Apparently someone gave an interview to the press. We weren't meant to talk to anyone apart from Julie Flint . . .'

Dad got up, stood behind Mum and squeezed her shoulders. 'They must have made a mistake. I'm sure nobody would have been that foolish. We'll appeal.'

And just when Cleo thought things couldn't get any worse, they did.

A knock at the door was followed by the appearance of Rachel Meadows. She slapped a newspaper down on the table next to the salad bowl. 'Have you seen this?' she demanded.

'The *Mystical Times*?' Mum glanced up at her friend in bemusement.

'A colleague sent it to me.' Rachel shook her head. 'I'm surprised at you, Cleo.'

Horror seeped through Cleo's veins like ice water through a sponge.

There, between a story about an alien abduction and a woman who thought her cat was the reincarnation of Queen Victoria, was her own photograph above the headline *CLEOPATRA CONFIRMS SEARCH FOR STONE*.

She forced herself to read on.

In an in-depth interview with our reporter, Nathan Quirke, Miss Cleopatra McNeil (14) confirmed that the top-secret

goal of her parents' excavation of the tomb of Pharaoh
Smenkhkare is to search for the long-lost Benben Stone.
Miss McNeil would neither confirm nor deny rumours that
the project's sponsor, Danny Farr, is linked to the Ancient
Order of the Eternal Sun . . .

Mum stood up and then sat back down again. 'How could
you have done this, Cleopatra?'

'And what's all this about the Eternal Sun?' Dad asked.

Cleo looked down to see that she had clumped the entire
plate of grated cheese into a sweaty ball in the palm of her
hand. 'I'm sorry. Quirke tricked me. And then I wanted to
stop him bothering you . . .' She pushed back her chair. It
clattered to the floor. She fled to her room and threw herself
on her bed.

At first she tried to block out the conversation still going
on in the kitchen, but suddenly she sat up and pressed her
ear to the wall. 'Tell you what,' Rachel was saying. 'If you
like, I could pop up to Amarna, just to see if there's anything
in this story of Cleo's. I could make some calls. I'm sure
the site guards would let me have a quick look around the
Royal Tomb. I'll get one of the drivers to take me. If we leave
tonight and get there for the first ferry crossing over the Nile
in the morning, we could be back in twenty-four hours.'

'I don't know,' Mum said. 'Is there any point now we have
to leave anyway?'

'If I see anything that looks promising I'll take photos,'
Rachel went on.

'Well, I think it's a brilliant idea,' Dad said. 'Rachel can
do that while we're getting the dig packed up here. And if
she sees any evidence of a concealed tunnel we can use her

photos to make a case to come back and excavate properly next season.'

Cleo catapulted from her bed and threw open the door.

Mum, Dad and Rachel all swung round to face her.

'Before you ask,' Dad said. 'No, you *can't* go with Rachel.'

Ryan was about to knock on the front door of Cleo's apartment building when she flung it open from the other side and barrelled out so fast that she almost knocked him down the steps.

There was a shell-shocked expression on her face, as if she'd been caught up in some kind of natural disaster.

Ryan turned and followed her.

They walked in silence for a long time. They left the village streets and entered a track through a grove of mango trees, where the branches met overhead to form a tunnel of deep green shade.

Finally, Cleo began to pour out her troubles. 'Mum will lose her job,' she said in a voice that was only a gulp away from a sob. 'They'll go bankrupt paying back the money to the Danny Farr Foundation. We have to leave Egypt. And it's all my fault.'

'But what about finding Nefertiti's tomb in Amarna?' Ryan asked gently.

'Not happening.' Cleo stopped walking and picked a spire of pinky-red blossom. 'Rachel's offered to go up tonight to check it out but I'm not allowed to go with her.'

Ryan stared at her. He couldn't believe that after all they'd been through they wouldn't be able to complete Rahotep's mission. 'But there's no way Rachel will find it without us to figure out the clues.'

Cleo shredded the delicate flowers from their stem. 'I know. She'll probably just end up leading the Eternal Sun people there so they can break in and steal the Benben Stone the minute we've all left the country!' Suddenly her face brightened. 'What about your mum? Would she take us?'

Ryan sighed. 'No. She's getting worried that her cover story is starting to crack. I was on my way to tell you – Mum's contacts at the Danny Farr Foundation have suddenly broken off communications. She thinks we need to get out of Egypt as soon as possible. We'll probably be on the same plane home as you.'

They stood in gloomy silence for a long moment, watching the crushed flowers fall from Cleo's fingertips. Red petal juice stained her hands like blood.

'We've got to go to Amarna,' Ryan said. 'We owe it to Rahotep.'

Cleo shook her head. 'Rachel would never agree.'

'That's why we don't ask her!' Ryan's voice grew urgent now as a plan started to take shape in his mind. 'She'll be in a pick-up truck, right? So we can stow away in the back.'

'We can't . . .'

'Why not?' Ryan demanded. 'Because it's not *protocol*? What happened to the girl who broke into Smenkhkare's tomb and set a trap and . . .'

'Let's think!' Cleo's voice was bitter. 'Oh, yes, she made a total and utter mess of *everything*!'

'Well, *I'm* going!' Ryan began to march back along the track. 'You don't have to come with me.'

Cleo ran after him. 'What do you think's going to happen when you get to Amarna?'

Ryan stopped and turned on his heel. 'Rachel will blow her top, of course! But I'll be there by then, won't I? I'll persuade her to let me help look for Nefertiti's tomb.'

Cleo folded her arms across her chest. 'You wouldn't have a hope of finding it without me.'

'Ha!' Ryan's honk of laughter startled a pair of doves from the branches overhead. 'You're joking! You have the worst sense of direction I've ever known. You could get lost in a cardboard box!'

'I could *not*!' Cleo spluttered. 'Anyway, you can't read hieroglyphs!'

Ryan turned and kept walking. 'I'll manage.'

'No, you won't!' Cleo shouted after him.

'And what are you going to do about it?' Ryan threw back.

'I'm coming with you.'

36

AMARNA

EVERYTHING WENT TO PLAN.

Ryan was waiting beneath Cleo's balcony shortly before midnight when she climbed over the railing and scrambled down through the bougainvillea. He reached up to catch her as she jumped the last metre. She was wearing the old black jumper she'd worn on their first dawn mission and she'd zipped the legs onto her shorts. Her trusty tool belt was strapped round her waist and her old white scarf dangled from her neck.

Keeping to the shadows, they crept round to the front of the apartment block.

The driver who was taking Rachel Meadows to Amarna

had parked his dust-grey Land Cruiser pick-up truck at the kerb and was leaning on the bonnet, smoking a cigarette. Ryan recognized him as Rashid – the man he'd helped change a flat tyre on that very first day in the valley below Smenkhkare's tomb. He'd seemed friendly enough, Ryan thought, although he was the only one of the men who hadn't wanted his portrait drawn. It was hard to believe that had been little more than a week ago.

It felt much, much longer. Over three thousand years longer, in fact.

And the journey wasn't over yet.

Rachel's silhouette appeared against the security light. She hurried down the steps lugging an oversized shoulder bag. Rashid ground out his cigarette with his toe and opened the cab door for her – a phone-in on an Arabic radio station wafted out – then walked back round to the driver's side. Ryan and Cleo picked their moment, scooted to the back of the pick-up and crawled under the tarpaulin that had been stretched over the equipment in the back.

The engine sputtered into life and they were off.

It rapidly turned into the most uncomfortable four hours of Ryan's life. The truck bed was made of some kind of unnaturally hard metal with ridges that dug into him no matter how often he changed position. They were sharing the ride with crates, reels of rope, shovels and toolboxes that buffeted them with every swerve and jolt. Maybe Rashid was in training as a stunt driver, Ryan thought, as they took another sharp bend at breakneck speed.

They soon left the village and drove north on the main road, following the west bank of the Nile. Ryan had finished his water and all the food in his backpack – apples, oranges and two Snickers bars — in the first hour. He gazed up through a hole in the tarpaulin at a navy-blue sky studded with fat gold stars. It was just like the painted ceilings of the tombs and temples. The celestial vaults, Cleo had said the Ancient Egyptians called them. By the time they rolled onto the car ferry and pitched gut-lurchingly across the Nile, daylight was beginning to glow through the weave of the canvas cover. A few more miles and the truck juddered to a halt. The road trip was finally over.

The doors of the cab opened and slammed shut. There were voices and the crunch of footsteps on gravel.

'Here we go!' Ryan whispered to Cleo.

The tarpaulin was thrown back. Light flooded in.

Ryan blinked. A lone vulture circled high in the pearl-pink sky. He shuddered, hoping it wasn't an omen of their impending doom.

He pulled his focus in closer. Rachel's large round face loomed into view, framed by her brown curls, and then shot out of it again as she jumped back. 'You gave me such a fright!' she exhaled, patting her mountainous bosom under its multicoloured tropical-flowered tunic. She'd been in the middle of dousing herself with mosquito spray, and coughed and spluttered as she accidentally sprayed far too much and it shot up her nose. 'I think you two have some explaining to do!' she said sharply.

Ryan sat up. He winced as every muscle jabbed with pain. He coughed too as the industrial-strength insect spray hit his nostrils. He looked around. They'd parked on a pebbly dirt patch outside a cluster of concrete huts on the edge of a rock-strewn desert plain, ringed by high flat cliffs.

Apart from the huts it could have been a moonscape.

'We've come to help you find the Benben Stone,' Ryan said.

'Sorry about this, Rachel,' Cleo added, 'but we had no choice.'

Cleo was still struggling to believe that she'd actually gone through with it!

Had she really left a note on her bed for her parents, sneaked out at midnight *again* and travelled hundreds of miles as a stowaway? Had she lost her mind? If this trip backfired, her parents would have every right to disown her.

But, to her surprise, things had gone just as Ryan had predicted. After a long lecture about irresponsible behaviour, Rachel had agreed that now they were here they might as well help with the search for Nefertiti's tomb. She would phone their parents to let them know the friends were safe and that she'd bring them back tonight. 'Then,' she warned, fixing them both with a severe look, 'you'll have to face the music on your own.'

They sat on the steps of the hut while Rachel disappeared inside to discuss the plan for the day with the site guards. Cleo was ignoring the triumphant told-you-so looks from Ryan when she heard the distant drone of an engine. A moment later a plume of dust signalled a vehicle approaching along the ribbon of tarmac road. A white jeep swung onto the gravel. The glare of sunlight on the windscreen blocked their view of the driver.

The door opened and a tall man began to unfold himself from behind the wheel.

High-top trainers, long legs in faded jeans, white T-shirt – it was J.J.

He looked as astonished to see Cleo and Ryan as they were to see him, but he quickly masked his shock with a friendly smile. 'Hey, cool, I didn't know you guys would be here,' he said as he loped towards them. 'I thought I'd come and give Rachel a hand. I'm not really needed back at base.'

Ryan hooked a thumb in the direction of the site hut. 'She's in there.'

As soon as J.J. was inside, Cleo grabbed Ryan's arm. 'I *knew* it! Ali was right when he said he recognized J.J. as one of the men hanging around outside my room.'

Ryan agreed. 'He's come to see if Rachel finds Nefertiti's tomb so he can steal the Benben Stone for the Ancient Order of the Eternal Sun!'

Cleo jumped to her feet. 'We have to warn Rachel.'

But there was no chance. When Rachel emerged from the hut moments later, she was side by side with J.J., laughing at something he'd said. She stopped and squinted out across the sun-bleached plain and pointed to the cliff wall to the east, where a valley cut a notch out of the rock. 'It's a few more miles up to the Royal Tomb,' she said. 'Luckily there's a road all the way up. One of the site guards will come with us to show us the way and unlock the tomb.'

'You two can ride in the jeep with me,' J.J. said with a grin. 'More comfortable than hiding in the back of the pick-up, eh?'

Cleo didn't see how they could refuse without letting J.J. know they were on to him.

They drove in convoy around the curve of a headland. Ryan kept up a conversation with J.J. about basketball, while Cleo stared out of the window across the arid plain, imagining the magnificent city of Amarna as it must once have been – opulent palaces, spectacular temples, lush gardens, wide avenues and courtyards, bustling workers' quarters – sparkling under the rays of the all-powerful sun disc, the Great Aten. Now all that remained of Akhenaten's dream city was a tracery of mud brick walls slowly being reclaimed by the drifting sands.

Soon they were turning off and climbing into the Royal Valley and then into a smaller *wadi*, where they parked near the entrance to the Royal Tomb. The heat hit them like a wall of fire as they stepped out of the air-conditioned vehicles and walked to the simple rectangular opening near the base of the cliff. Rachel stopped to take photographs as the others hurried down the steep flight of steps and waited for the guard to unlock the padlock on a portcullis-like metal gate.

Cleo hung back with Rachel, gazing down over the plain. In the distance a team of archaeologists were digging a trench. They were dwarfed to ant-size by the vast expanse. 'We think that J.J. is up to something,' she said out of the side of her mouth.

Rachel Meadows lined up a shot of the tomb entrance, but her brow furrowed above the viewfinder.

'I know this sounds weird.' Cleo dropped her voice to a whisper. 'But we're pretty sure that he's involved with the Ancient Order of the Eternal Sun . . .' She paused as the metal gate swung open with a screech that rebounded from the cliff faces all along the valley. 'And that he's planning to steal the Benben Stone,' she added.

Rachel couldn't have looked more stunned if Cleo had informed her that Queen Nefertiti was planning to meet them in person inside the tomb. 'Where on earth did you get that idea?' she laughed. 'J.J. is your mum's student!'

'I know.' Cleo had to admit that now she said it out loud it did sound a little unlikely.

'I'm sure you're mistaken,' Rachel said, smiling as she slotted the lens cap back on, 'but I'll keep an eye on him.' With that, she was off down the steps, the camera bouncing on her chest.

Cleo followed her into the tomb. There was nothing more she could do.

The entrance flared out into a wide sloping corridor, which led to a large burial chamber. The Royal Tomb must have been spectacular once, Cleo thought, but it had been badly damaged over the years. The stone was corroded by floodwater, and everything of value had either been destroyed by those who wished to remove all memory of the heretic Pharaoh Akhenaten, or plundered by tomb robbers. Even the decorated plaster covering the walls had been sliced away in sections to be sold to collectors. Here and there, fragments of wall scenes remained; the rays of the Aten could be seen everywhere.

The search for the concealed entrance to Nefertiti's secret tomb began. Rachel, J.J., Cleo and Ryan explored systematically, looking for any sign of the clues Kaha had given with his dying breath – Ra himself as the Great Cat, The World Encircler as the twelve-coiled serpent, the cry of the Bennu Bird in flight. Even Rashid, the driver, and Mohammed, the site guard, came in to help with the search.

But as the morning wore on, it seemed they were doomed to failure.

They found nothing.

While the others focused on a long curved passageway off to one side of the main corridor, Cleo and Ryan wandered back in to a suite of smaller burial chambers that had belonged to one of the young princesses. The plasterwork was in better condition here and it was possible to make out the scenes of the royal family mourning the dead girl. 'She was called Meketaten,' Cleo told Ryan. 'It's thought she died in childbirth.'

'Wasn't she Kaha's favourite when he was a boy?' Ryan asked. 'The honey-cake girl he told Rahotep about?'

Cleo shook her head. 'No, that was Meritaten.'

'They could have picked names that weren't all basically the same,' Ryan grumbled.

'I think these are some of the other sisters,' Cleo said, pointing to a section low down in the corner. A group of girls could be made out among the cracks and craters in the plaster. 'Meritaten might be one of those.'

Ryan lay on his stomach and shone his torch over the group. Suddenly he twisted round and pulled Cleo down next to him. 'Look! This one's carrying a cat.'

Cleo knelt.

Ryan was right. A spotted cat with a long tail was bundled up in the arms of a small girl. It was much too big to be an ordinary pet.

Cleo reached out and ran her hand over the cat. The carving looked as though it went right through the dilapidated plaster into the limestone beneath. The centre of the eye was hollowed out into a little round hole. Had it been carved that way or was it just pockmarked by time? she wondered. She tried to push her finger in, but the hole was too small. 'Have you got a pencil?' she asked Ryan.

Ryan *always* had a pencil!

'HB or 3H?' he asked.

Cleo rolled her eyes. 'Anything!'

Ryan fished in his backpack and passed her a long yellow pencil with a freshly sharpened lead. She inserted the tip into the hole. It went in a surprisingly long way before meeting an obstacle.

The obstacle moved.

Next thing she knew, Cleo was tumbling head over heels into nothingness.

37

LABYRINTH

RYAN NOSEDIVED INTO the dark.

The ground beneath him had opened up and then tilted downwards to form a long, steep chute like a waterslide without water. Bodysurfing on a stream of rubble, images of Rahotep's impaled skeleton flashed before his eyes.

Don't they always have spikes at the bottom of these booby traps?

He crumpled to a halt. He barely had time to check he hadn't been punctured when Cleo landed on top of him.

'It was a trapdoor,' she said.

'You don't say!' Ryan muttered. 'You'd think a pharaoh would have designed a more stylish entrance.'

'I don't suppose you're meant to be standing *on* the trapdoor when it opens!' Cleo said. 'If you used a long thin rod to release the catch in the cat's eye you could stay further back and not fall in.'

'Well, you're the world expert on falling down holes!' Ryan said with a grin. 'You should know.'

'Oh, no!' Cleo groaned. 'The bulb in my torch has broken.' Ryan was relieved to find that *his* torch was still working after the high-speed descent. He directed the beam up the steep incline. A dim rectangle of light far above showed where they'd dropped through. Steps had been cut into the stone down one side of the chute. Cleo was right. That was the way sensible people would enter, but at least they had completed the first of Kaha's clues: *look through the new eyes of Ra to the creature himself and you will see the hidden way.* Check!

Ryan looked around to size up the situation. They were at the bottom of a pit. On the opposite wall from the ramp, he could see a dark smudge – the entrance to a small tunnel. He got to his feet and held his hand out to pull Cleo up.

Her eyes sparkled in the torchlight. 'This is it!' she breathed. 'We're actually going to find the lost tomb of Nefertiti!'

Ryan grinned. He felt just as excited, but they still had work to do. He pointed to the tunnel. 'Looks like we have to go through there.'

Cleo nodded. 'The second clue. *Follow the path of the World Encircler . . .*'

'As if we were snakes burrowing through the sand behind the serpent, Apep,' Ryan chipped in. He pulled his sketchbook out of his backpack and turned to the page with his copy of the twelve-coiled snake from Rameses' tomb. 'This shows us the path to take. It's like a road map. Come on!'

They made their way along the tunnel, keeping a careful watch for deadfalls and booby traps. It sloped steeply downwards before widening out and forking in two. Cleo hesitated, but Ryan checked his diagram. 'Apep turns left first.'

Cleo hurried off into the right-hand tunnel. Ryan watched her for a moment, shaking his head, then called her back. '*This* left!' he laughed, pointing to the other fork. 'You'd better just follow me.'

The tunnel made a hairpin bend and then, at the next choice point, there was one opening above the other. 'We take the lower one,' Ryan explained, consulting his map. 'This is where Apep crawls under his previous coil.' They continued until the next fork. 'And now we turn right . . .' Ryan's words faded away. He stood raking the torch beam up and down and side to side.

They'd come face to face with a wall of solid rock.

'A dead end,' Ryan groaned. 'It can't be!'

They retraced their steps. Ryan double-checked his snake map. They tried again. Again they found themselves standing in front of the wall.

'Let's try another way,' Cleo said, heading towards a side tunnel.

Ryan dragged her back. 'We can't just wander round at random! Remember what Kaha told Rahotep: *take the wrong path and you will roam the labyrinth for eternity*. And we have to stick together. We've only got one torch.'

Cleo stumbled. Suddenly Ryan noticed her face was pale

271

and slick with sweat. 'What's the matter?' he asked. 'Are you feeling claustrophobic down here?'

Cleo closed her eyes and shook her head. 'It's not that. It's my bad ankle. I must have knocked it when we fell through the trapdoor.'

Now Ryan thought about it, she *had* been limping a bit. 'Why didn't you say something?' he asked. 'We could have gone back up and got some ice on it.'

'Because I knew that's what you'd say. And there was no way I was going to wait any longer now we're so close! And it's not that bad anyway. It'll be fine.' Cleo took a big step to demonstrate. 'Aghh,' she groaned, slumping against the wall.

'It's *not* fine at all, is it?' Ryan said. 'Come on. Let's go back up. You can lean on me.'

'No way!' Cleo snapped with all the ferocity of a cornered animal. 'We've come this far. We've got to find the tomb ourselves. If we go back up, Rachel and J.J. will get to come down here before us . . .'

Ryan couldn't deny he felt the same way. 'OK,' he said. 'What about you sit down here and wait and I'll check out each direction in turn? Then you'll only have to walk when we've got the right path.'

'Have you got any string?' Cleo asked. 'You could use it to mark your way. You know, like Theseus in the Minotaur's labyrinth.'

'Funnily enough, I don't happen to have a ball of string about my person, no!' Ryan snorted. 'We're not on a Boys Scouts' mission!' But then he paused. 'Hang on! Give me your scarf!'

Cleo unwound the frayed cotton scarf from her neck

and handed it over with a puzzled frown. Ryan pulled a thread from one end and gave the scarf back to her. 'Hold this.' Then he walked backwards. The thread continued to unravel. 'It works! As long as you don't mind your scarf being shredded?' he asked.

Cleo shook her head.

'Don't move from this spot,' Ryan told her. 'I'll come back as soon as I find something.'

Then he headed off into the tunnel again. He'd studied the snake map so often he could see it like a photograph in his mind's eye. He'd been so sure it showed the path through the maze. Perhaps they'd got the *wrong* snake? There'd been hundreds of Apeps in that tomb. He turned and looked back. The thread glowed like a pale worm in the torchlight for a few metres. Then it was swallowed up by the dark.

Suddenly it came to him.

Swallowed up!

Was it possible that Cleo had made a tiny mistake in translating the hieroglyphs of the Scorpion Papyrus?

What if they weren't meant to follow the path *of* Apep, as if crawling along behind him, but rather the path *through* Apep, as if being *swallowed* like prey . . . which meant they should read the map in reverse, travelling from jaws to tail as if they were being digested.

There was only one way to find out.

He made his way back to the entrance of the tunnel, then began to follow the new reverse route, accelerating with every twist and turn, spooling the thread out behind him like spider silk. *Yes, this was it! No more dead ends!*

At last he came to the final turn. The tunnel increased to a great height. He held up the torch. He was standing in front of a pair of huge, elaborately carved doors made of a wood so dark it had to be ebony. A huge sun disc of beaten gold was mounted at the top, long golden rods radiating downwards to represent the rays. It was just like the pictures he'd seen of the Aten, with each ray ending in a hand holding an ankh. Ryan gazed in awed silence for a long moment. Then he tied the scarf to one of the metal rays and plunged back into the labyrinth, running the thread through his fingers as he ran.

He couldn't wait to tell Cleo!

Meanwhile, Cleo had grown bored of waiting.

With nothing to distract her, the throbbing in her ankle was becoming unbearable. Ryan had been ages. *He's probably lost,* she thought. *He's always going on about me having a hopeless sense of direction, but he didn't seem to know his way through the labyrinth either . . .*

She took her phone from her pocket to check the time. There was no signal here, of course – they were deep underground – but the screen created a tiny pool of light in the impenetrable darkness so she left it on.

Perhaps she'd just go a little way into the tunnel and see if Ryan was coming. She left the scarf safely weighted down under a stone and set off. As long as she followed the thread that Ryan had left, she couldn't get lost. Feeling her way along the wall, she took a few more steps. She turned left, then right. She lowered the phone to the ground to check for the thread.

It had disappeared.

Her heart bolted into a wild hurtling gallop. It had been there a moment ago. Had it snapped? Had she taken a wrong turn? She backtracked and tried another branch. Then another.

Then the battery on her phone died and everything went black.

38

BENNU BIRD

RYAN STARED AT the spot where he'd left Cleo.

Cleo's scarf was still there, held down by a stone.

But no Cleo.

This isn't good, he thought. *Not good at all.*

Cleo might be a walking Wikipedia but she barely knew her left from her right. He'd often suspected she was even a bit hazy on up versus down.

Kaha's words played in his head once again: *take the wrong path and you will roam the labyrinth for eternity.*

Molten anger surged through his limbs. Which part of *don't move from this spot* had she not understood?

He yelled her name.

How could she have been so stupid?

Following the thread, he turned back into the tunnel. Surely even Cleo would have *started* off going the right way?

He shouted again. He held his breath and strained his ears. *Nothing.* He went a little further. What if she'd passed out? Her ankle was bad. He thought he heard a sound. It seemed to be moving, echoing, sometimes closer, sometimes farther away. Was he imagining it?

After what seemed like hours of wandering, Ryan was wondering how much longer his torch battery could last when his foot scuffed against something on the ground. He sprang back, his mind full of pits and spikes and other brutal Ancient Egyptian devices, but when he directed his torch downwards he saw a small brown bundle. *A dead animal?* He knelt and touched it. No, not an animal, it was beige *fabric.* Torchlight glinted on a metal zip. It was one of Cleo's detachable legs.! It looked as if she'd fashioned it into a rough arrow shape.

She'd been this way, and left it as a marker in case she looped back!

'Cleo!' he yelled, backing away from the arrow, hope flickering back into life. She couldn't be far away.

She wasn't!

'Ryan!' The screech came from right behind him. They bumped backs, whipped round and held each other by the elbows.

'Don't *ever*—' Ryan began.

'I won't,' Cleo gulped. 'Did you find—'

'Yes. This way!'

Ryan bowed with a flourish.

'Ta da! I present you with one long-lost secret tomb of Queen Nerfertiti!' He reached for the bronze lotus-shaped handles, all set for a dramatic throwing open of doors. He tried again. His hand dropped to his side. 'It's locked!' he groaned.

'Locked?' Cleo repeated the word as if she'd never encountered the concept before. Her energy reserves were so depleted by pain and fear that she had to bite back the urge to howl.

Ryan pointed up at a golden heron with outstretched wings carved into the door below the Aten sun disc. 'That must be the Bennu Bird in flight. It's Kaha's last clue. We have to do something with this heron to get the door open.'

Cleo hobbled closer. A row of symbols had been engraved inside the V of the heron's open beak, as if they were its words. *It's just like the creation myth,* she thought: *the Bennu Bird let out a cry of what would be and what would not be* . . . The symbols had to be the clue; they were the cry of the Bennu Bird! But what did they mean? They didn't look like hieroglyphs.

Cleo felt unsteady, as if on a boat in a stormy sea. *Those symbols must be a new code. But we've already solved one Phoenix Code. Is this the Bennu Code or the Heron Code?* Her thoughts were becoming more and more tangled. She slid down the door and sat with her head resting on her knees.

'The shapes look familiar,' Ryan murmured. 'I've seen them before. I can't think where . . .' He narrowed his eyes and tilted his head on one side. Suddenly he began flicking through the pages of his sketchbook. 'I thought so!' he said, crouching down next to Cleo. He directed his torch at the

278

page. Next to the Great Cat from Thutmosis's tomb he'd also copied the *wedjat* eye. 'Those symbols in the Bennu Bird's beak are all individual sections of this eye design,' he said. 'The eyebrow, the iris, the teardrop, that curling line underneath . . .' He clapped his sketchbook shut. 'Not that it helps much.'

'Yes! No! It does!' Cleo jumped up, hardly aware of the pain in her ankle. 'The Ancient Egyptians used the parts of the *wedjat* eye to represent fractions – a half, a quarter, an eighth and so on.'

Ryan stared at her in amazement. 'So these symbols could be telling us that there's a key or a dial somewhere . . .'

'. . . that we have to rotate by these amounts!' Cleo finished.

They both immediately began to pat and prod at the door, looking for any part that they could twist or turn. Cleo tried each of the twelve gold ankhs at the ends of the rays from the Aten. She twisted clockwise, then anti-clockwise, but none of them budged.

'This is hopeless,' she fumed. In her frustration she gripped the last ankh and gave it a shove. To her surprise it moved. She repeated the motion. The ankh wasn't turning, but it was sliding up the gold rod like a piece of meat on a kebab skewer. She showed Ryan. She tried the next ankh. It did the same.

Ryan peered at the door behind the sunrays. 'There are measurement markers carved into the wood!' he cried.

Cleo followed his gaze to a series of curved parallel lines. They looked like a decorative pattern, but when she counted them she saw that they divided the length of the rods into exactly sixty-four parts. Now she knew they were right! She looked back at the symbols in the heron's beak. 'The symbol closest to the left is the iris. That means a quarter,' she said.

Ryan slid the leftmost ankh a quarter of the way up the ray towards the sun. 'OK, next?'

'The eyebrow,' Cleo said. 'That's one eighth.'

Ryan pushed the next ankh into place.

'Then it's the teardrop and the curl together,' Cleo said. 'That's one sixty-fourth plus one thirty-second, so three sixty-fourths altogether.'

Ryan gave the third ankh a tiny nudge into position. And so they worked until eleven of the twelve ankhs were set.

The twelfth symbol was the left-hand part of the cornea. 'That's one sixteenth,' Cleo said.

Ryan pushed the final ankh into place. Nothing happened. 'Are you sure that's right?' he asked.

Cleo visualized the diagram of the eye. The left side of the cornea was the sixteenth, she was sure. Or was she? Maybe it was the other way round. Was the sixteenth the *right-hand* side, which meant the *left* was a half? 'Try a half!' she said at last.

Ryan didn't say a word. Slowly he pushed the ankh further up the ray. As soon as it hit the halfway point along the rod there was a sound of grinding and clicking from within the door.

Ryan tried the handle. It moved.

He grinned at Cleo and held his hand up for a high five. 'Team!' he said.

'Team!' she replied.

Together they pushed open the doors.

39

TREASURE

THE BURIAL CHAMBER was more magnificent than Cleo could possibly have imagined.

Every wall was richly embellished with painted scenes of Akhenaten and Nefertiti offering lotus flowers to the Aten, strolling in beautiful gardens or reclining on boats among lilies and rushes in the marshes. Instead of the usual star pattern, the ceiling was the vivid blue of the midday sky. An enormous solid gold sun disc was suspended from the centre with gold rays stretching out to every corner of the room. *The Great Aten!* Beneath it stood a glittering sarcophagus of rose quartz smothered with panels of fine gold carvings. At its side knelt a life-sized statue of Pharaoh

Akhenaten, his hooded eyes half-closed in inexpressible sadness.

As if in a dream, Cleo stepped closer to read the names in the cartouches on the sarcophagus. *'Neferneferuaten Nefertiti, Beautiful are the beauties of Aten, the beautiful one has come,'* she murmured.

Luxurious furnishings and objects filled the room: gold thrones and coffers and beds and shrines, each inlaid with ebony, bronze, ivory, lapis lazuli, red carnelian, turquoise and amethyst. Cleo's eyes could hardly take in the dizzying opulence. Exquisite jewelled collars, belts and crowns were piled next to elaborate wigs and robes. There were ivory senet boards, caskets of cosmetics and palettes for grinding pigments, delicate glass perfume jars, bowls and mirrors. To one side four alabaster canopic jars with lids fashioned from ivory and silver were guarded by an army of shabti figurines standing by to serve Nefertiti's every wish in the afterlife.

Cleo turned to Ryan. He was staring at a patterned tower topped with a flat platform. 'The Benben Stone,' he murmured, eyes wide with wonder. 'Mission accomplished.'

Cleo couldn't find any words. The gleaming black pyramid, its sides engraved with intricate symbols and patterns, its peak gilded with shining electrum, seemed almost plain amid the elaborate riches. And it was smaller than she'd expected – no bigger than a computer monitor. And yet it had a magnetic quality that made it hard to look away. While everything else in the tomb was thickly shrouded with the dust of time, the Benben alone shone as if newly polished. Light seemed to flow out from it. She noticed for the first time that Ryan's torch wasn't the only illumination in the chamber. She looked up. There was a slot in the roof just above the gold sun disc. Through it, a shaft of light struck the Benben Stone, real sunshine reflecting back from the stone's gilded peak to the artificial sun above it, and then back again from the gold disc and all its rays, in an infinite kaleidoscope of light. It was already halfway through the morning now. How much more dazzling it must be at sunrise, the moment when the first rays of the sun flooded in at the perfect angle!

Ryan sighed. 'I wish Rahotep could see this.'

Cleo smiled sadly and gave his hand a squeeze. 'Me, too.'

Ryan began to circle the chamber as if in a trance. He stopped next to the statue of Akhenaten and looked back across the sarcophagus at Cleo. 'There's something missing,' he said. 'Where are the ninety-nine servants who got locked in?'

Cleo glanced around. Ryan was right. If Kaha's account were true there should be skeletons everywhere. She turned to see Ryan pushing open a door at the other end of the chamber. It had been painted over with a hunting scene to blend into the wall. He stood with his back to her, leaning with his hand against the frame. 'I think,' he said weakly, 'I've just found them.'

Cleo hurried to the door and peeped under Ryan's arm. They were looking into a long narrow room with a row of high-backed chairs along each side. Everything was covered in a thick white layer of what looked like melting candle wax.

Cleo wished she still had her scarf to hold over her nose. The stench of ammonia burned her nostrils and pricked her eyes. 'Guano!' she muttered. 'Bat droppings.'

Ryan didn't reply. Cleo knew it was more than the smell that was getting to him. He'd taken the St Christopher from his pocket and curled his fingers tightly around it.

Some of the skeletons sat upright. Others slumped forward or listed to the side, their skulls resting on their neighbours' shoulders. Some clutched amulets in their bony fingers. Goblets lay on laps or on the floor where they'd fallen once their lethal contents had done their work.

Death's waiting room, Cleo thought.

'One hundred chairs,' Ryan announced, finishing a count. 'Ninety-nine bodies.' He pointed at the single empty chair near the end of the row. 'That must have been Kaha's place. How on earth did he find a way out of here?'

Cleo nodded. 'Maybe the same way the bats got in,' she said, pointing at the ceiling. Thousands and thousands of little black bodies clung to the rock. Suddenly, as if summoned to life by the mention of their name, the bats stirred. The air thickened with a maelstrom of pulsing wings.

Ryan flung his hands over his face and backed away.

'Let's get out of here!'

40

PINE

THE GROUP FILED out from the Royal Tomb.

They all flopped down near the entrance and glugged from bottles of water. It was now mid-afternoon, several hours since Cleo and Ryan had climbed the steps back up to Meketaten's chamber.

They'd attempted to tell Rachel Meadows about the treasures they had found beneath the trapdoor without J.J. overhearing, but it had proved impossible. He'd insisted on standing next to Rachel, studying his maps of the Royal Tomb, as if superglued to her right arm. Then Mohammed, the site guard, a skinny young man in a patched grey *galabaya*, with the biggest ears Cleo had ever seen sticking out from under the folds of his *shaal*, had started to gesture at his watch to indicate that they would have to leave the tomb and go back to the huts soon if they didn't find anything, and Cleo had realized that they had no choice but to reveal their discovery.

Disbelieving at first, Rachel, J.J., Mohammed and Rashid, the driver, had followed them through the labyrinth to the mighty doors and into the hidden tomb of Nefertiti. There were shouts of joy and triumph. Then they'd all wandered in a daze, examining one marvel after another.

Now Cleo leaned back against the sun-baked rock and closed her eyes. She had never felt so worn out. The buzz of Rachel's portable fan droned in her ear. Suddenly she felt someone shaking her arm. 'Don't fall asleep here, dear,' Rachel was saying. 'We need to get some ice on that ankle.' Then she clapped her hands. 'Let's get moving, people. We've got a lot to do before we head back to Luxor! Rashid, can you take Cleo back down to the huts? There'll be a first-aid kit in there. Ryan, you go with her and make sure she's OK.'

Ryan saluted. 'Yes, ma'am!'

Rachel smiled and ruffled his hair. 'You kids have done some great work this morning. I might just forgive you for stowing away!'

J.J. gave them a double thumbs-up. 'Yeah, awesome find, guys!'

'J.J. and I will stay up here and start photographing the main finds,' Rachel went on. She turned back to Cleo and Ryan. 'We'll join you at the huts in a couple of hours. See if you can rustle up some food and drinks for the journey back.'

'But we want to come back up and help—' Cleo began.

'No, dear!' Rachel's tone was firm. 'You need to rest. I promised your mum I'd look after you!'

Cleo couldn't deny that it would be good to sit down somewhere cool with her ankle up.

'Oh, and it's very important that we keep this find to ourselves for now,' Rachel added, as they walked towards the parked vehicles. 'No phone calls or texts. Even to your parents. You never know who might be listening in.' She smiled at Cleo. 'I'll call your mum and give her the good news once I'm sure I've got a secure line. If this story gets out the whole world will descend on us. We don't want anyone *undesirable* turning up . . . and certainly no press yet.'

Cleo couldn't help glancing at J.J. out of the corner of her eye. He winked at her. She slid her eyes away. She was sure he was up to something, but there was nothing she could do. *And, after all*, she told herself, *it isn't as if J.J. will be able to steal the Benben Stone out from under the noses of Rachel and the guard.*

When they reached the pick-up Rachel leaned into the cab and took out her massive shoulder bag. 'On second thoughts,' she said, pausing with her hand on the door. 'Rashid had better stay up here and help us secure the tomb.' She handed the keys of the pick-up to the site guard. 'Mohammed, would you mind running the kids down to the hut?'

Ryan propped his feet on the dashboard and enjoyed the icy blast from the air conditioner.

Mohammed was enjoying himself too. He hammered Rashid's truck down the straight, empty road, belting out an old Queen number at the top of his voice. Ryan joined in and they started competing to see who could sing the loudest.

Soon they were both laughing so much that Mohammed swerved off the road. The truck rattled along the rocky verge for a few seconds before fishtailing back onto the tarmac.

Ryan checked on Cleo, slumped on the seat next to him. She was leaning against the door of the cab and her perfect caramel skin had blanched to the shade of curdled milk. 'You feeling faint?' he asked, wafting cold air from the vent in her direction.

Cleo batted his hand away. She shot him a significant look and nodded her head at an air freshener in the shape of a bright green pine tree dangling from the rear-view mirror. 'That's *it*!' she hissed.

'That's *what*?' Ryan hissed back.

'The smell, of course!'

Ryan sniffed. Now he thought about it, that pine fragrance *was* pretty overpowering – sort of toilet-cleaner-meets-artificial-Christmas-tree-scented-candle. He wrinkled his nose. 'Ugh, that's chemical warfare!'

'Shhhh!' Cleo whispered, glancing across at Mohammed. But, in spite of those elephantine ears, Ryan was pretty sure the site guard wasn't listening in. He hardly understood a word of English and, anyway, why would he be interested in Rashid's choice of in-car air freshener?

'It's *Rashid* who's been following us!' Cleo said, still whispering. 'He drives this truck all the time. That air freshener's the mystery smell. It's so strong it sticks to him. The only reason we didn't smell it when he and Rachel got out of the cab when we first got here was because Rachel was half-suffocating us with that mosquito spray.'

'Lots of people have air fresheners like that,' Ryan pointed out.

Cleo reached into the glove compartment, which had popped open during their off-road excursion. 'But do lots of people have *these*?' She waved a pair of mirrored sunglasses at him.

Ryan was about to say *Sunglasses? Yes, they do, actually* when she pulled out a thick black false beard and held that up, too. 'Rashid was the tourist police officer who chased me at Karnak,' she said. 'This was his disguise.'

Ryan stared at Cleo as the terrible truth sank in. She was right. A pungent air freshener and mirrored sunglasses could be a coincidence, but you didn't carry a false beard around in your truck for no reason. 'Rashid's in on it with J.J.,' he said. 'He must be a member of the Eternal Sun too.'

Cleo nodded. 'Between them they could overpower Rachel and steal the Benben. We've got to go back to the tomb and stop them.'

'Mohammed, *stop*!' Cleo yelled in Arabic.

'Mohammed, *stop*!' Ryan shouted in English.

Mohammed snapped his mouth shut in the middle of a rousing chorus of *We Are the Champions*. He looked a bit crestfallen that they didn't like his singing.

'No, we meant stop the *truck*,' Ryan explained. He mimed slamming his foot on the brake and did a screeching sound.

'Please,' Cleo added, pointing back up to the Royal Valley.

Mohammed threw the pick-up truck into a three-point turn and gunned it back up the road. Within minutes they were pulling up next to J.J.'s white jeep outside the Royal Tomb. Mohammed leaned back in the driver's seat and patted the pockets of his *galabaya* for his cigarettes.

'We've got to try to get Rachel on her own to tell her,'

Cleo said as she threw open the door. 'Come on! We've got to hurry!'

If we're not already too late, Ryan thought, as he leaped down from the cab. *What if Rashid and J.J. have already turned on Rachel and tied her up?*

He sprinted after Cleo into the outer chamber of the tomb so fast that when she pulled up short he piled straight into her.

Cleo didn't seem to notice. She was staring into the corner. Ryan followed her gaze and could hardly believe their luck! There, in the shadows beneath a huge wall carving of the Aten, was Rachel Meadows. She *wasn't* tied up and there was no sign of J.J. or Rashid!

The two friends hurried towards her.

'Do you mind?' Rachel snapped. 'I'm getting changed!'

Ryan stopped, a hot blush creeping up his neck. He'd been so intent on telling Rachel about Rashid being a spy that he hadn't even noticed that she was in the process of pulling her flower-patterned tunic over her head.

'It's stifling down here,' Rachel said in a slightly friendlier tone, her voice muffled by the fabric as she hastily tried to tug the tunic back down over her large frame. 'I just needed to put on a fresh shirt.'

Ryan glanced down at Rachel's shoulder bag, which was lying near her feet, a plain white garment spilling from the open zip. *That doesn't look like her usual colourful style,* he thought.

'What are you two doing back here anyway?' Rachel demanded, still wrestling with the tunic. 'You really need to get your ankle seen to, dear,' she added.

'We've got something really important to tell you,' Cleo

said. 'It's OK. We won't look if you want to carry on getting changed.'

Ryan felt Cleo grab his elbow, trying to pull him round to give Rachel some privacy. But he didn't move.

'Ryan!' Cleo hissed. 'Stop it! You're staring.'

It was true. He *was* staring.

But it wasn't Rachel's large, white, half-naked body that drew his attention.

He was staring at a tiny tattoo on her left shoulder.

Rachel pulled down her tunic and it was hidden from view.

But it was too late. It had only been a glimpse, but Ryan knew what he'd seen.

Two ankhs side by side on a fiery sun.

41

RITUAL

RYAN WAS STILL staring at Rachel Meadows as if he were in some kind of trance.

Cleo couldn't understand why he was being so unbelievably embarrassing. But there was no time to worry about that now. Or about the fact that her ankle felt as if it might burst into flames at any moment. They had to warn Rachel that it wasn't just J.J. who was working for the Eternal Sun. Rashid was in on it, too. 'We came back to tell you that Rashid—'

But before Cleo could say another word, Ryan suddenly pushed in front of her. 'To tell you that Rashid's pick-up was about to run out of petrol,' he butted in.

'What?' Cleo spluttered. 'That's not—'

'That's not Rachel's problem,' Ryan cut across her again. 'You're right. And it's all under control. Mohammed has gone to get the spare petrol can from that storage shed outside. Sorry to barge in on you when you were getting changed like that,' he added, aiming a charming smile at Rachel. 'We just wanted to keep you in the loop!' He pulled Cleo back towards the tomb entrance and shot her a strange look she couldn't read. 'Come on! Mohammed will probably be ready to go again by now. He said it'd only take a minute to refuel the truck.'

Cleo had no choice but to smile weakly at Rachel and stumble out after Ryan. Her mind was in a whirl. Had Ryan lost his mind? That story about the truck running out of petrol was utter nonsense. Ever since he'd seen Rachel undressing he'd been acting like a total buffoon. *Could it be a boy thing?* she wondered. Was some surge of male hormones affecting his brain function?

'What on earth are you doing?' Cleo hissed as soon as they emerged into the bright desert light. 'Rashid or J.J. could come back at any second. We'll lose our only chance to warn Rachel while she's on her own.'

But Ryan dragged her further from the entrance until they were behind a wall of rock. He looked over his shoulder. 'Didn't you see it?' he whispered urgently.

'See what?'

'Shh!' Ryan put his finger to his lips. 'It was on Rachel's shoulder. Now I know why she always wears those long-sleeved tops.'

Cleo was getting more concerned about Ryan by the minute. Perhaps he was having hallucinations brought on by sleep deprivation . . .

293

'The double ankh,' he went on. 'The fiery sun.'

Cleo gaped at him. 'But that's the symbol of the Ancient Order of the Eternal Sun!' she gasped. 'Why would she have that?' Suddenly Cleo figured out what Ryan was telling her. 'You think *Rachel Meadows* is a member of the Eternal Sun? You're joking!'

Ryan didn't say a word but his amber-streaked eyes were rounder than she'd ever seen them. He wasn't joking.

Cleo shook her head. 'But Rachel is Mum's best friend. You must have made a mistake.'

'Two ankhs, side by side,' Ryan said flatly.

'Well, she is an Egyptologist. Ankhs are a good omen . . .'

Ryan swallowed. 'Two ankhs. In front of a fiery sun. In a circular border. I've seen it hundreds of times in Mum's notes. It's the Eternal Sun logo for sure!'

Cleo's head was spinning. 'We can't just make an accusation like that without proof. We're going to be in enough trouble when we get home as it is. If I start telling my parents that Mum's best friend is a member of the Eternal Sun who's planning to steal the Benben Stone and then it turns out we've got it wrong because of something you thought you saw in a split second . . .' Her voice tailed off. She couldn't even imagine how bad that would be.

Ryan replied with a grim nod. 'I suppose from that distance, in the shadows . . . *Could* I just have made a mistake?'

Cleo shaded her eyes against the sun and thought for a moment. There was only one way to be sure. 'We're going to have to follow her and see what she does next.'

Ryan took his phone out of his pocket and checked that it was still charged. 'OK. But the second we see any kind of proof that Rachel's involved, we get out of here and phone our parents and the police.'

Cleo agreed and without another word, Ryan took her arm to help her over the rocks and they crept back towards the entrance to the tomb. Very slowly, Ryan leaned in to look. 'All clear!' he said.

Ignoring the pain that jolted through her ankle with every step, Cleo followed him inside. There wasn't a sound. 'Rachel must have gone down to join Rashid and J.J. in Nefertiti's tomb,' she murmured.

Sticking close together, Cleo and Ryan tiptoed through Princess Meketaten's burial chamber, down the ramp and through the labyrinth, which was now illuminated with hanging lamps, the way marked with stick-on arrows. When they came to the huge doors to Nefertiti's hidden tomb, they found them ajar. A sliver of light escaped from within, painting a golden stripe across the stone floor.

Holding her breath, Cleo peeped through the crack between the doors. She closed her eyes for a moment, hardly able to take in what she was seeing, but when she opened them the incredible scene hadn't changed. The chamber was lit by three lanterns hanging from sconces on the walls and the sleek black sides of the Benben Stone seemed to quiver like the flanks of a racehorse in the flickering light. Clouds of heavily perfumed smoke from pots of incense hung in the air. Rashid and J.J. were kneeling before the Benben, their hands outstretched. Clad in white robes and chanting in Ancient Egyptian, their voices rose and fell and rose again, growing ever more urgent.

We bow to the Great Stone. We offer our allegiance. We are as nothing before the Benben . . .

'We were right about those two!' Ryan muttered, peering through the gap over Cleo's head.

'But where's Rachel?' Cleo whispered. 'I still can't believe she's got anything to do with this.'

Before Ryan could answer, Cleo turned back to the crack in the door and saw for herself. The two men had thrown themselves to the ground as a burly woman stepped forward from the shadows. She was swathed in a flowing white robe and a leopard skin, complete with teeth and claws, was draped over one shoulder.

So that was the fresh shirt *she was changing into!*

But it was her hair that struck Cleo most. Or, rather, the lack of it.

Rachel Meadows' shaved scalp glowed as pale as a mushroom in the lamplight.

All those bouncy brown curls were a wig!

'The High Priestess approaches!' J.J. and Rashid intoned.

Cleo knees were turning to water. She clung tight to Ryan. So it was true! Ryan *hadn't* been mistaken! Rachel bowed to the Benben Stone and Cleo saw that she had the double ankh symbol of the Eternal Sun tattooed on her scalp as well as on her shoulder, along with a single staring *wedjat* eye.

J.J. and Rashid were still kneeling at her feet.

Cleo knew there was no doubt now: Rachel wasn't just involved, she was clearly the leader. Rashid and J.J. were working for her . . .

A tide of nausea rose in Cleo's throat as the pieces began to thud into place, one by one. *It was Rachel who overheard us planning to go to Smenkhkare's tomb in the El-Masry Café. Coming over to buy us ice creams was just a way of getting closer to hear us better! She wanted to know if we would find the Benben Stone in Smenkhkare's tomb.* 'Rachel must have sent Rashid to follow us on our dawn raid,' she murmured. 'He must have heard us coming out of the fourth chamber and knocked the lid of the sarcophagus over in his hurry to get out before we saw him. That was the first time I smelled the mystery smell – the pine air freshener from his truck.'

Ryan leaned in closer and nodded. 'And then she must have ordered Rashid to follow us to the Theban Museum. He was the "woman" cloaked in black who came into the storeroom for computer paper.'

Of course, Cleo thought. *Rashid left his tell-tale pine fragrance behind him again then.* 'And J.J. never really had food poisoning at all!' she exclaimed – and then suddenly clamped her hand over her mouth, afraid that she'd be heard by the three people behind the doors. But Rachel, J.J. and Rashid were now chanting so loudly that there was little chance they'd hear anything other than their own voices. 'Rachel just pretended she'd visited J.J. in his room to provide him with an alibi while he was on the ferry trying to steal the writing tablets from us,' Cleo went on. 'And I bet Rashid was the accomplice in the rowing boat!'

'Yeah, it all makes sense now,' Ryan agreed. 'J.J. and Rashid followed us to Karnak as well, and chased us to try to get hold of the ankh.'

Cleo grimaced. 'Which is why I smelled Rashid's air freshener there, too. And it must have been J.J. and Rashid that Ali saw eavesdropping under my balcony when we were talking about the Scorpion Papyrus.' *Both acting on Rachel's orders all the while, of course,* she thought bitterly.

Ryan straightened up and pushed his hair out of his eyes.

'Remember when Rachel appeared with that plate of cakes at the banana grove?'

Cleo nodded. How could she forget Ryan jumping on her and pretending to kiss her?

'I guess she was listening to us trying to decipher the Phoenix Code on the ankh all the time,' Ryan said.

Cleo groaned as she remembered something else. 'And Rachel could easily have stolen my notes. She was always in and out of our flat: all she needed to do was pop into my room to fetch something when I wasn't there.' *And as for just being worried about us when she walked into our trap at Smenkhkare's tomb,* Cleo thought, *it was all rubbish. She wanted to see if we'd found another clue to the location of the Benben Stone. Our trap worked perfectly. We caught the Eternal Sun spy. We just didn't know it!*

Cleo ground her teeth. There was no denying it. Rachel Meadows had deceived everyone. She had been planning to steal the Benben Stone all along – no wonder she'd been so keen to come to Amarna!

Cleo put her eye back to the gap in the door as the chanting reached a crescendo then suddenly ceased. Rachel was raising one hand, holding out a golden cup. *What's next in this ridiculous ritual?* Cleo wondered. *Naked dancing? Sacrificial goats?* Now she was getting over the shock of Rachel's betrayal, Cleo was more angry than afraid. The Ancient Order of the Eternal Sun was all play-acting and fancy dress. Rachel had even shaved her head because that's what priests did in Ancient Egypt.

Ryan reached into his pocket for his phone. 'I'll see if I can get a photo through the door,' he whispered. 'Then we call the police.'

Cleo was about to agree when her mouth dropped open. That golden cup in Rachel's hand was carved in the shape of a grotesque skull and decorated with turquoise and silver. There could be no mistaking it! It was the Mayan ceremonial cup. The one that had gone missing from the dig in Peru last year. *Of course!* Cleo thought. *Rachel was there. Rachel stole it.* 'That's the Bloodthirsty Grail!' she gasped.

'Er, didn't you say that cup was used for the blood of human sacrifices?' Ryan gulped.

Cleo could hardly believe her eyes. Rachel was passing the cup to Rashid. Now she was handing him a small gold knife. Surely they weren't actually planning to *kill* one of their number? That was going too far! But, to her relief, Rashid slashed the blade across his palm and let the drops of blood fall into the cup. He passed the cup to J.J. and he repeated the action. Finally they presented the Bloodthirsty Grail to Rachel, who raised it to her lips, then thrust it towards the stone. She threw back her head and began to recite spells in Ancient Egyptian.

'What's she saying?' Ryan whispered.

'She's giving their blood as an offering, trying to dispel any curses that stop the stone being moved.' Cleo turned to Ryan. 'They're getting ready to take the Benben away to the secret Eternal Sun temple. I *knew* it!' She looked back through the gap. To her horror, J.J. and Rashid were climbing onto Nefertiti's sarcophagus and reaching up to remove the Benben Stone from its platform.

'They can't do that!' Ryan breathed. 'It's dangerous.'

Cleo nodded gravely. 'Very. They might break those delicate gold carvings and damage—'

'That's not quite the kind of *dangerous* I had in mind,' Ryan interrupted. 'I meant moving the Benben Stone is dangerous – you know, earthquakes, tidal waves, mass warfare, that kind of thing . . .'

'No!' Cleo couldn't hold back a scream as a gold panel splintered away from the sarcophagus under Rashid's weight. 'You're *damaging* it!'

Rachel, J.J. and Rashid all spun round at the sound of her cry.

'Run!' Ryan pulled Cleo away from the door.

But it was too late.

Cleo stumbled and, by the time Ryan had helped her up, Rashid and J.J. had already charged out of the chamber, grabbed them from behind and pinned them to the ground.

42

CAPTIVE

RYAN STRUGGLED BUT J.J. had him held firmly around the chest. Meanwhile Rashid had grasped hold of Cleo. They were both bundled in through the doors of the chamber.

'Rachel! How could you?' Cleo shouted. 'You're Mum's *friend*!'

Rachel Meadows walked slowly towards them. Ryan shuddered. With her head bald and lips stained with blood she looked like a gigantic evil doll. 'I wouldn't expect you to understand. Only very few are chosen to follow the path of the Eternal Sun and discover the hidden knowledge of ages past—'

301

'Rubbish!' Cleo seethed. 'You just want to steal the Benben Stone and take it to your stupid temple!'

Ryan had to hand it to Cleo. She seemed a lot less freaked out by all this than he was. That staring eye on Rachel's scalp had nearly given him a heart attack. And when the human sacrifice cup had come out he'd thought he was next on the menu! He'd nearly worn the pattern off his St Christopher!

Rashid clenched his fists at his sides, but Rachel waved a calm-down hand in his direction. 'We're merely *relocating* the Benben to its rightful place,' she said.

Ryan finally found his voice. 'But it should be in the visitor centre where everyone can see it.'

'The Benben belongs among those of us who understand its true powers.' Rachel's lips retracted into a cold smile. 'It *was* a bit of a blow when it wasn't in Smenkhkare's tomb. Thank you both for helping us to find it at last.'

'We didn't *help* you!' Cleo shot back. 'You lot sneaked around, spying on us.'

Rachel took a watch from within her robes and checked it. 'So sorry, but there's no time for chit-chat now. We have to get the Benben out of the country and to our temple in Arizona. We'll just be in time for the Return of the Phoenix. It's the spring equinox tomorrow. Danny Farr will be delighted.' She shrugged off her leopard skin, folded it carefully and stowed it in her shoulder bag which was lying on the floor. 'And it seems you kids aren't the only ones who've been poking their noses into our business. *Someone* back in Luxor has been asking too many questions.' She narrowed her eyes at Ryan. 'I'll have to get one of my people to deal with *that* little problem as well.'

Ryan's stomach clenched into a knot of fear. Rachel had to be talking about his mum.

'Lock these kids in that storage shed near the entrance for now,' Rachel ordered J.J. and Rashid. 'And tell Mohammed we've had a call from the guard down at the huts to say there's been a cave-in at one of the other tombs and he's needed over there – anything to get him out of the way for a while. I'm going to get changed. Then we'll start loading up.'

'Sorry about this, guys,' J.J. said as he and Rashid pushed Cleo and Ryan into the small concrete storeroom. 'Nothing personal.'

He didn't *sound* very sorry, Ryan thought.

J.J. held out a hand. 'I'll need your phones. Can't have you trying to make SOS calls, can we? Drop them into your backpack and pass it over.'

Reluctantly Ryan took his phone from his pocket and followed instructions.

J.J. pointed at Cleo's tool belt. 'And that.'

Cleo scowled as she took it off and added it to the backpack.

Rashid handed J.J. two coils of rope and together they bound Cleo and Ryan's hands behind their backs. J.J. made them sit down on the floor and lashed them back to back to the leg of a metal table. 'Don't go anywhere now!' he joked.

There was a slam of the door, the sound of a chain clanking and a key turning in a padlock and the two men had gone.

'We've *got* to get out of here! I have to warn Mum that Rachel's on to her.' Ryan wriggled his wrists but they were tied fast. 'We need something to cut these ropes.' He banged his head back against the table leg in frustration. The storeroom was completely empty apart from the table and a few plastic trays in the corner. 'If only J.J. hadn't taken your bum bag, we could have used the edge of your trowel.'

'It's not a *bum bag*!' Cleo said indignantly. 'It's a holster!'

Ryan sighed. *Who but Cleo could quibble over word choice at a time like this?*

'Anyway, I *have* got it! It's in the back of my waistband. I thought it might come in useful so I slipped it in there on the way from the tomb. I wasn't going to hand it over. It belonged to my grandmother.' Cleo leaned forward. 'You should be able to reach it.'

Ryan was so impressed he could have kissed her – if they hadn't been tied back-to-back. Instead he slid his hands under the hem of her T-shirt and groped around the back of her shorts for the trowel. 'Sorry about this,' he mumbled, realizing that in any other circumstances this would count as highly inappropriate behaviour.

'Just get on with it!' Cleo snapped.

At last he had hold of the worn wooden handle of the old trowel. With a few more contortions and a borderline dislocated shoulder he was able to hack at the ropes around Cleo's wrists. It seemed to take forever and his muscles burned but, eventually, the last strand popped. Cleo jumped up, grabbed the trowel and sawed at Ryan's ropes until he too was free.

Ryan ran to the door and rattled the handle. It was locked, of course. He cast around for another way out. There was nothing but a tiny air vent high in the wall. It was far too small to squeeze through but he hoisted Cleo up onto his shoulders to peep out and see what was happening.

'They're bringing stuff up and loading it onto the back of Rashid's pick-up truck,' she groaned after a few moments. 'Looks like they're helping themselves to a lot more than just the Benben Stone. Wait,' she whispered. 'Rachel and J.J. are right outside now. I can hear them talking.'

Ryan could hear their muffled voices too.

'What are we going to do with the kids?' J.J. asked.

'You take them in the jeep,' Rachel said. There was a pause. 'You know how *treacherous* the roads are round here. Road accidents happen *all the time*.'

Ryan lowered Cleo to the ground. 'If we get in that jeep we're dead,' he said flatly.

Cleo nodded. 'And, worse than that – *they* get the Benben. There's *got* to be a way to stop them!' She picked up the trowel from the table and twisted it round in her hands. 'I know! When J.J. comes to get us, I'll distract him and you attack him with this.'

'What? *Stab* him?'

Cleo thought for a moment. 'I meant hit him over the head, actually. Do you think stabbing would work better?'

Ryan took the trowel. Was it even hefty enough to deal a knock-out blow? He felt the end. The point was hard and sharp, but did he have it in him to trowel a man in the back?

There was no time to dwell on it. A key was turning in the padlock . . .

43

ESCAPE

CLEO AND RYAN dived back into position with their hands behind their backs as if still tied up.

'We're moving out, guys,' J.J. said in a friendly voice as he strolled over to untie them. 'I'll drive you back to Luxor.'

Cleo smiled up at him sweetly and fluttered her eyelashes. 'I *knew* you wouldn't hurt us, J.J. You're far too nice.'

But she spoke the words so softly, he had to lean over to hear them.

Ryan leaped to his feet. He'd never assaulted anyone before but he made himself think of his mum in danger, and brought the heel of the trowel down on the back of J.J.'s head as hard as he could.

It wasn't hard *enough*.

And he'd forgotten that J.J. had the lightning reactions of a basketball player. He whisked round and grabbed Ryan's arm. But Cleo was quick too. She swung her legs round and knocked J.J.'s feet out from under him. She yelped with pain as her ankle made contact with his shin, but she'd caught the tall man off balance and he toppled like a fallen tree. There was a thud as his forehead bounced off the corner of the table on his way down.

Cleo knelt and placed a finger on J.J.'s neck. 'It's OK,' she said. 'He's got a pulse.'

Ryan reached into J.J.'s jeans pocket and pulled out the keys to the jeep.

'Can you drive?' Cleo asked.

'Of course!' In truth, Ryan had only driven once or twice – and that had been in a go-kart round a track – but this was no time to worry about details. He raced to the door and looked out. Rachel and Rashid were heading back into the Royal Tomb, no doubt to fetch another load of plundered treasure.

'Now!' he said, pulling Cleo to his side. 'I'll start the jeep. You get the Benben Stone from the pick-up.'

Cleo tried to ignore her heart pounding out a frantic rhythm of *hurry up, hurry up, hurry up* as she searched the back of the pick-up truck. It was crammed with equipment cases, cardboard boxes and wooden crates stamped with *Best Egyptian Bananas* or *Formula Milk × 48 cans*.

Of course, she realized, *Rachel and Co. aren't going to advertise the fact that they're transporting stolen antiquities by labelling the boxes* Priceless Sacred Relics *or* Assorted Looted Treasures.

But which box contained the Benben Stone?

Cleo picked a banana crate at random and prised it open. It was stuffed with jewelled collars and necklaces. Her fingers clumsy with haste, she popped the clasp on a metal case. Inside were the canopic jars.

She heard the jeep engine start up behind her.

'Quick!' Ryan yelled through the window.

Cleo tore away at the lid of a box marked *Chickpeas*, and saw a gleam of black. *Yes! That was it!* She heaved the box over the side of the truck bed. It was heavy but, given that it was solid stone, not as heavy as she'd expected. She balanced it on her hip and began to stagger towards the jeep. Halfway there she remembered something she'd seen in the truck. She turned back.

'What are you doing?' Ryan shouted. 'I can hear them coming.'

Cleo reached into the back of the truck, grabbed what she had seen, and stumbled back to the jeep. Ryan put his foot down and they lurched forwards before she'd even shut the door. The tyres spun, flinging up a hailstorm of sand and gravel. There were kangaroo hops as Ryan grappled with the gears, but at last they shot onto the road and were away.

'With any luck they'll think this is J.J. driving us away for our *accident* and won't come after us,' Cleo said, clutching the box on her knees and trying to fasten her seat belt.

Ryan glanced up to the mirror. 'Or *not*!' he groaned.

Cleo looked over her shoulder. Rashid's pick-up was already in pursuit. 'Can't you go any faster?' she cried. 'They're gaining already.'

Ryan's knuckles turned even whiter on the steering wheel. 'Not without killing us! I'm not Lewis Hamilton, you know!'

Cleo closed her eyes. Their only hope was to reach one of the small villages clustered along the bank of the Nile. There they'd find people who could help them, and a boat or a car or a train back to Luxor. But first they had to make it all the way along the isolated road that followed the line of the cliffs. Suddenly Ryan was pulling the wheel round. She clung onto the door as they swerved off the road at high speed.

'Short cut!' Ryan panted. A barely visible track cut away from the tarmac and headed due west across the desert plain towards the hazy green band of date palms and wheat fields in the distance. The jeep jolted and bucked as the tyres battled over ridges and troughs. They drove for what seemed like hours, the track dwindling all the time, until finally it petered out altogether and they were crossing open desert. At least they'd gained a little on Rashid and Rachel. Twisting round to look back, Cleo could only just see the pick-up truck, a small dark blot surrounded by a cloud of dust.

Just when Cleo thought they would never reach civilization, she saw a line of dusty tamarisk trees up ahead. At last they were skidding onto a rutted farm road. They passed a rubbish dump and a pile of burned-out tyres and some field shelters made of rusted corrugated iron. Then a tiny roadside grocery shop and a petrol pump came into view.

Ryan rammed his foot on the brake.

'What are you stopping for?' Cleo cried as she shot forward against the dashboard. 'We don't need petrol!' She looked back again. She could already see the dust cloud through the trees and hear the whine of the pick-up engine. 'They'll catch us up in a minute!'

Ryan pointed at an old motorbike propped up against an oil drum. 'If we're on that, they won't know it's us.'

'You want to steal it?' Cleo asked in disbelief.

'Not steal, *swap*!' Ryan was already jumping down from the jeep and running towards two teenage boys sitting on a bench outside the shop.

Cleo hobbled after him, dodging the skinny black hens that pecked in the dust.

Ryan was motioning towards the bike and the jeep, waving his arms in a complicated charade. The boys were looking confused and laughing at him.

'We want to swap!' Cleo explained in Arabic.

The boys stared at her. One of them tapped his forehead in a *crazy* sign. She realized that offering a brand new Jeep Wrangler in exchange for a clapped-out Honda motorbike probably did seem a little nuts. She probably *looked* pretty strange too; she still had one leg of her zip-off trousers stuffed in her pocket after using it to make an arrow in the labyrinth, her ankle was swollen up like a balloon, and she was carrying a box that appeared to contain a lifetime supply of chickpeas.

One of the teenagers grinned and made a heart-beating gesture. The other laughed and mimed a smoochy kiss.

Oh, no! Cleo thought. *They think we're running away together! 'La!'* she spluttered, waving her hands in front of her. '*No,* nothing like that.'

'Yes!' Ryan shouted over her. 'They're obviously romantics,' he muttered. 'Play along!' He put his arm round Cleo's shoulder. 'Yes, we're madly in luuurve!'

Cleo forced what she hoped looked like a romantic smile.

One of the boys dug the motorbike key out of his pocket and exchanged it for the jeep key.

'Ask them to drive the jeep off in the other direction,' Ryan said. 'Rachel will think it's us.'

But the boys didn't need to be asked. They were already revving up and tearing off along the road. They clearly thought it was their lucky day!

Cleo hopped up on the bike behind Ryan. The vibrations from the engine sent shock waves of pain through her ankle. The box containing the Benben Stone was wedged between her front and Ryan's back and it was digging into her chest, but she gritted her teeth and clung on tight. The motorbike reared up in a wheelie and then they were roaring cross-country – veering past a little girl driving a herd of bony-haunched cattle, ploughing through a field of sugar cane, flying over an irrigation channel in a death-defying leap.

At last they were approaching the houses and markets and cafés of a small village.

Ryan took one hand off the handlebars to punch the air in triumph and almost swerved into a fruit stall.

Cleo looked back and, way off in the distance, she saw the pick-up truck barrelling away in the opposite direction in pursuit of the boys in the jeep.

Ryan steered the motorbike as best he could through the bikes and trucks and donkey carts. The village was strung along a single main road that ran parallel to the riverbank. Following the marshy smell, and a procession of children with fishing rods, he turned down an alley and, moments later, they were pulling up at a small jetty. Fishing boats, motor launches and sailing boats were moored up, along with rafts and barges of various sizes that were being loaded with goods to be ferried down the Nile.

Cleo and Ryan ran from boat to boat, asking anyone they came across to give them a lift. At last they struck lucky. An old man had just finished loading up his cargo barge and he agreed to give them a lift all the way to Luxor. Ryan left the motorbike in the care of the children who were fishing from the dock, with instructions for it to be returned to the boys at the petrol station. Then he climbed aboard the barge with Cleo.

It was only as they cast off from the jetty that they realized they were sharing their accommodation with hundreds of crates of live chickens.

But they were both too tired – and relieved – to care about their noisy, smelly neighbours. Cleo sank down with her back against a crate and smiled at Ryan over the chickpea box. 'We did it,' she said. 'We've got the Benben Stone!'

Ryan smiled back, but there was one more thing he had to do before they could celebrate. He had to warn Mum that Rachel was on to her and that she was in serious danger from the Ancient Order of the Eternal Sun.

Praying he wasn't too late, he reached into his shorts pocket for his phone.

But his pocket was empty. His heart sank as he remembered. *Of course, we handed our phones over to J.J. in my backpack!*

Ryan looked around in desperation. He *had* to find a phone, but the barge was now floating along in the middle of the Nile, miles from either shore. He was wondering whether the old skipper might have a phone he could use, when Cleo tapped him on the shoulder.

'Are you looking for this?'

Ryan watched in amazement as she slid his backpack off her shoulders and handed it to him. 'Where did you find it?' he gasped.

'What do you think I went back to the pick-up for?'

Ryan shook his head in admiration. He'd been so busy escaping he hadn't noticed Cleo carrying his backpack the whole time. He pulled out his phone and scrolled to his mum's number. He listened to it ring at the other end.

It rang and rang.

Ryan dropped his head onto his arms.

He was too late!

Rachel's henchmen must have got to her first!

Cleo held out her hand. 'Quick! Give me your phone. I'll call my parents and see if they know what's happened.'

Cleo held the phone away from her ear.

'What's the meaning of running off in the night like that?' Dad bellowed. 'You're lucky that Rachel agreed to look after you . . .'

'Dad. Stop! LISTEN!' Cleo yelled back.

Dad stopped. She'd never spoken to him like that before.

'This is important. Is Julie Flint there?'

'Yes,' Dad said. 'She turned up a while ago, ranting all sorts of nonsense about Rachel Meadows being a high priestess of the Ancient Order of the Eternal Sun, would you believe it!'

Oh, I believe it, all right, Cleo thought.

She gave Ryan a thumbs-up.

'I think she'd been out in the sun too long!' Dad was saying.

'Ryan needs to talk to her,' Cleo said. 'Can you give Julie the phone?'

There was a pause. 'Seems she just left,' Dad said. 'She looked so peaky Mum advised her to go to the clinic and get checked out by the doctor.'

Cleo clutched at her hair. She saw Ryan's eyes widen in horror at her expression. 'Go and fetch her back!' she shrieked. 'Now, Dad, *please*!'

She held her breath and listened to the sound of Dad running down the stairs to the front door and shouting, 'Julie! Wait!'

There was an agonizing pause.

'It's OK, I've got her,' Dad panted at last. 'One of the diggers was offering her a lift to Amarna to fetch Ryan back.'

'Don't let her go with him!' Cleo warned. 'He's one of Rachel's men.'

'Rachel's men?' Dad echoed. 'Would you mind telling me what all this is about?'

'I'll explain when we get back. Please, Dad, just call the police and tell them to look out for Rachel, J.J. and Rashid. They're in Rashid's pick-up truck. They'll be trying to leave the country to get to America – to their temple in Arizona, in fact.'

'They haven't got the Benben Stone, have they?' The worried voice belonged to Mum. Dad must have given her the phone. *Of course,* Cleo realized. *Rachel promised she'd phone Mum and tell her about the find as soon as she had a secure line, but that was just another of her lies.*

Cleo looked down at the chickpea box. 'No, it's safe.' She glanced at Ryan. 'And we're safe, too. We'll be home by . . .'

she looked around. The boat was crawling along at the pace of a water snail. '. . . by tomorrow morning.'

Ryan leaned back against a chicken cage.

Cleo's head was resting on his shoulder, her foot dangling in the water to cool her ankle.

'Pooh!' he groaned. The stench of thousands of chickens in a boat was almost as bad as the guano in the bat cave. 'I thought old Rashid's pine air freshener was a bit whiffy, but we could really do with it now.'

Cleo didn't reply.

She'd fallen asleep.

Ryan had pins and needles in his foot and he really needed to scratch his shoulder.

But it didn't matter, because they'd escaped!

J.J. hadn't left them as roadkill in the middle of the desert. They were heading home. Mum was safe. *And* they'd completed Rahotep's mission and rescued the Benben Stone!

He watched as a pair of ducks burst out from the reeds, paddled along the surface of the water and took off into a sky already tinged with gold as the sun began to set in the west.

He bit into the hunk of bread the old skipper had given them from his own supplies, along with a bottle of warm water and some dried dates.

If only he had a cold Coke and a strawberry Cornetto, life would be just about perfect right now.

44

FRIENDS

RYAN STOOD NEXT to Cleo and smiled for the camera.

Between them was a life-sized model of Rahotep. A team of artists had made the reconstruction based on his skeleton and skull in Tomb KV55. He looked exactly as Ryan had imagined him.

Reporters jostled for position with their microphones. Cameras flashed. The main gallery of the Theban Museum was full to capacity. Nathan Quirke from the *Mystical Times* hadn't even managed to get a ticket!

Ryan grinned at Cleo and pointed up to the banner above their heads that said *THE GREATEST LOVE TRIANGLE IN HISTORY*. 'It looks like it means us three – you, me and

Rahotep!'

'As if!' Cleo snapped back through bared teeth. She really didn't like having her photograph taken.

Ryan knew, of course, that the love triangle really referred to Akhenaten, Nefertiti and Smenkhkare. The event was the grand opening of the major new Benben Stone exhibition. Two months had passed since their narrow escape from the Royal Tomb at Amarna. Ryan and Julie Flint had flown back to Egypt from Manchester especially. Cleo and her parents had remained in Egypt all along, working with the magnificent finds from Nefertiti's tomb.

The new exhibition had everything – romance, theft, betrayal, gory death, a sacred relic, secret codes and scheming baddies! The Benben Stone itself was in pride of place in a special room, designed to let in the first rays of the sun at dawn. Rahotep's writing tablets and the Scorpion Papyrus were on display too, and there was even a reconstruction of Rahotep impaled on the spikes (which neither Cleo nor Ryan could bear to look at). There was also a section on Cleo and Ryan's part in solving the case over three thousand years later – complete with illustrations from Ryan's sketchbook, Cleo's translations and a model of the ankh with the two lines of verse that had proved to be the key to deciphering the Phoenix Code.

'Dr Badawi in the picture, please!' one of the photographers called.

Leila Badawi smiled and joined the group. The Benben Stone had saved the small Theban Museum from closure and she'd been promoted to Museum Director. Ryan waved to Dr Badawi's little granddaughter, Halima. He'd been pushing her round the gallery on the purple ride-on hippo all morning and now she wouldn't let him out of her sight.

Everyone had come to join the celebrations. Mr Mansour had brought Ali, who was sporting a shiny new Manchester United away strip for the occasion. 'I was James Bond spy,' he told anyone who would listen. 'And I saved Ryan from the crocodiles!'

Yusuf was there too, along with his brother and all the staff from the El-Masry Café. They were considering changing its name to the Benben Café in honour of the part they'd played in the story.

Even Sir Charles Peacocke had flown in from London. The director of the Department of Museums and Culture was the picture of elegance with his sweeping silver hair and his pinstriped suit. He provided sound bites for the media, shook hands with everyone and congratulated Lydia and Pete McNeil on their 'sterling contribution to British archaeology'.

'Looks like we're flavour of the month again,' Cleo's mum muttered rather darkly, although she smiled along with everyone else.

Later that evening the McNeils and the Flints met for a celebratory meal in the rooftop restaurant at the Golden Nile Hotel.

'I wonder how long a sentence Rachel will get,' Lydia McNeil said, looking up from her salad. 'I still can't get used to calling her Michelle.'

Cleo reached over and gave her arm a rub.

Rachel Meadows – or Michelle Symons, to use her real name – had been caught red-handed. The police had intercepted her, Rashid and J.J. as they attempted to drive across the border from Egypt to Libya. The looted treasures were all recovered safely – even the Mayan Bloodthirsty Grail, which had been returned to Peru.

Rachel's true story had gradually emerged, some of it from Julie Flint's research, the rest from police interviews. Michelle Symons had been an officer in the British Army during the war with Iraq, but she'd been court-martialled and thrown out of the military after she was caught stealing valuable artefacts from unguarded sites and museums in Iraq to sell on the black market. After a prison sentence, she changed her name to Rachel Meadows and started a new life. She'd dabbled with many different cults and sects, before ending up in the Ancient Order of the Eternal Sun. That's when she'd realized that she could use her influence in the group to set up an antiquities smuggling operation on a much larger scale.

'The reason it took me so long to track her down,' Julie explained, as she sipped her beer, 'is that she had so many contacts in high places, helping to protect her identity. Her qualifications as an archaeologist were all fake – as was her passport, her driving licence, everything. The Eternal Sun has members everywhere, but at least we've exposed some of the biggest players now.'

'Like Danny Farr,' Cleo put in.

Julie nodded. 'His foundation was a front for laundering the money they made from selling the stolen antiquities – not to mention a bit of drug smuggling on the side.'

'Well, at least Farr has done *some* good,' Pete McNeil said. 'All the funds that have been confiscated from the foundation will be used for the Theban Museum and for research projects to study the Amarna records and the treasures of Nefertiti's tomb.'

That was indeed a great result, Cleo thought. Rachel's two trusty accomplices had been caught too. They were both members of the Ancient Order of the Eternal Sun, of course. First, there was the American student, Josh Jennings – or J.J. – who'd only enrolled to study for an archaeology PhD with Professor McNeil so that he could gain access to valuable treasures. And, second, there was Rashid, who'd posed as a driver to help Rachel steal the Benben Stone. No wonder he hadn't wanted Ryan to sketch his portrait!

'It's funny,' Mum sighed, 'but even after everything she's done, I still can't get used to Rachel not being here with us.'

Cleo gazed out across the Nile. The city lights from the east bank shimmered on the dark water. She heard the blaring horn of a passing cruise ship, a prayer call and the haunting cry of a stone curlew. The warm air was full of the smoky smell of the barbecue. However much she studied, she thought, she'd never figure out why human relationships had to be so *complicated*. Mum still missed Rachel, even though she'd betrayed their friendship a hundred times over. Akhenaten had still loved Nefertiti, even though she'd tried to poison him and run off with his brother.

It's all totally irrational and inexplicable, Cleo thought.

But now she'd made friends with Ryan, she sort of understood.

She watched Ryan now, laughing with the waiters, who were trying to teach him to make napkins into peacocks and swans. She'd missed him while he'd been away, even though they'd texted and video-called most days. She even missed

Rahotep. She wished there was a way to keep in touch with him too!

Her thoughts were interrupted by a text buzzing on her phone. It was from Max Henderson in Colombia. He'd finally got to go on his hummingbird safari. *Congratulations on the exhibition!* the message said. He'd included a photograph of a black hummingbird with a green and purple throat with the caption *Spotted this beauty today!*

'Wow, that's a gorgeted puffleg,' Cleo said.

'*Gorgeted puffleg?*' Ryan laughed. 'You're *definitely* making that up!'

'I'm not,' Cleo insisted. 'They're really rare. I bet Max is in heaven!'

That reminded her of the postcard she'd received that morning from Alex Shawcross, who was on holiday in the Czech Republic. She took the card from her bag and showed it to Ryan. 'And *this* looks like Alex's idea of heaven!'

Ryan turned the postcard over to see a photo of a massive chandelier made of what looked like ivory.

'It's the Sedlec Ossuary,' Cleo explained. 'A whole church decorated with human bones.'

Ryan dropped the rib he was gnawing on and quickly changed the subject. 'You'll have to get even more glammed up than that for Mum's do next month,' he told Cleo, who'd been persuaded to change from her usual baggy T-shirt and zip-off shorts into a white summer dress for the evening. 'It's at the Ritz in London. Red carpet, speeches, the lot!'

At that, they all raised a glass in a toast to the journalism award that Julie had won for her investigative report into the Eternal Sun group.

'Actually, Julie,' Pete McNeil said. 'We wondered whether

you'd like to accompany us on our next dig. I can't say too much yet, but it's in China. It involves a tomb and some very suspicious ancient deaths, so I've been asked to go and have a look. I'm sure there'd be some interesting articles to write about it.'

Julie smiled. 'That does sound fascinating. I'll have to give it some thought.'

Cleo and Ryan finished their desserts and left the table to sit by the pool.

To her surprise, Ryan handed Cleo a present. She pulled off the tissue paper to find a beautiful long scarf of soft white cotton shot through with a silver thread so fine it was almost invisible.

'It's to replace the one I unravelled in the labyrinth,' Ryan said. 'And, anyway, I owed you something. You got me this.' He fished the plaster scarab beetle from under the neck of his T-shirt. He'd drilled a small hole and threaded it onto a leather lace along with his St. Christopher pendant.

'I'm glad the original one is still with Rahotep,' Cleo said.

Ryan leaned back to look up at the stars. He flinched. 'My back's aching from bending over to push little Halima round on her hippo.' Suddenly he laughed. 'It must be the final part of the curse from Smenkhkare's tomb. *He shall be devoured by the lion, the crocodile, the serpent, the scorpion and the hippo.* I've fought them all off now!'

'What *lion?*' Cleo objected.

'Snowball, of course! The little cat at the El-Masry Café.

She gave me a very threatening look when we first met her!'

'And the *crocodile* was a Nile perch!' Cleo laughed.

'But those weeds cut my legs to pieces!' Ryan argued. 'Then there was the snake on the donkey cart.'

'True, a saw-scaled viper bite would have been nasty,' Cleo admitted. 'But it didn't touch you.'

'And the scorpion!' Ryan added. 'Even you have to agree the deathstalker was a bit of a hairy moment.'

'It's lucky I was there to save you!' Cleo laughed.

Ryan grinned. 'That's what friends are for.'

Cleo looked down at the pool. Underwater lights flooded it a deep turquoise blue. 'So, are you coming to China with us?'

'I hope so.' Ryan dropped a fallen oleander flower onto the water and watched it float. 'I think Mum's just worried about me missing so much school.'

Cleo looked thoughtful for a moment. Then she smiled. 'You could study with me. I'll be doing an intensive Mandarin Chinese course *before* we go, of course, so I'll mostly be concentrating on early Chinese philosophy, as well as keeping up with all the usual algebra, neuroscience, inorganic chemistry and so on.'

'How could I refuse an offer like that?' Ryan laughed. 'I'll do my best to talk Mum into it. After all, there are probably a lot of holes in China.'

Cleo looked puzzled. 'What's that got to do with anything?'

Ryan grinned. '*Someone*'s got to be there to pull you out when you fall down them!'

Cleo glanced at the large sign that said *POOL CLOSED, NO SWIMMING*.

She wasn't the sort of girl who usually liked to break the rules.

But then, *she* wouldn't be the one doing the swimming!

It would only take one tiny push . . .

AUTHOR NOTE

The Phoenix Code is an entirely fictional story, although it takes place against the backdrop of some real places and real historical events. To try to avoid any confusion, the following notes outline some of the most important distinctions between the facts and the fiction.

All the modern-day characters, including Cleo and Ryan, exist only in my imagination. Neither Danny Farr, the retired rock star, nor his dubious foundation really exist. And, of course, the sinister secret society, the Ancient Order of the Eternal Sun, is entirely fictional and not meant to be based on any real group.

The Ancient Egyptian exploits of Rahotep and of Smenkhkare are also fictional, but I have woven certain real historical characters, artefacts and events into their stories.

The Valley of the Kings is a real – and truly remarkable – place. It lies on the west bank of the River Nile in Egypt, opposite the city of Luxor (formerly known as Thebes). It was the burial ground of New Kingdom pharaohs from about the sixteenth to eleventh centuries BC. Amarna, the site of Pharaoh Akhenaten's new city (originally called Akhetaten), is also a real place. It lies to the east of the Nile, hundreds of miles north of Luxor.

Many of the tombs that Cleo and Ryan visit in *The Phoenix Code* are real, including the tomb of Thutmoses III and Rameses I, KV55 and the Royal Tomb at Amarna.

The twelve-coiled snake in Rameses I's tomb, and the eye of Horus and the Great Cat, Mau, in Thutmoses III's tomb can really be seen there. The scenes of the family mourning the young Princess Meketaten in the Royal Tomb at Amarna are also genuine, although I invented the girl holding the cat and, of course, the trapdoor! I also made up the draughtsman's sketch of the animal stealing the duck from the table in Tomb KV55 and the hidden tunnel leading to the storage room and Rahotep's grisly end.

However, the tomb that Cleo discovers at the start of *The Phoenix Code* does not exist (as far as we know!). No such tomb of Smenkhkare has ever been found. Sadly, the labyrinth and the magnificent secret burial chamber of Nefertiti that Cleo and Ryan find beneath the Royal Tomb at Amarna at the end of the story are also entirely imaginary.

Smenkhkare, Akhenaten and Nefertiti themselves are all real historical figures. We know quite a lot about Akhenaten, the 'heretic pharaoh' who established the new religion of the sun disc – the Aten – and his beautiful queen, Nefertiti. They ruled together in their new city and had several daughters, including Meritaten and Meketaten. The sculpture of Nefertiti – the one that Cleo shows Ryan in the art book – is one of the most famous artworks in the world.

But, as Cleo explains in *The Phoenix Code,* Smenkhkare was a man of mystery.

Smenkhkare was almost certainly related to Akhenaten: perhaps he was a younger brother or his son with one of his minor wives. His name occurs in a royal double cartouche found on a vase in Tutankhamun's tomb, on a wine docket and on a few other items. His name also crops up, stamped onto the bricks of a large hall added to the Great Palace at Amarna, which may have been built for his coronation. These clues all suggest that he ruled as pharaoh for a short time – perhaps as co-regent, perhaps in his own right – but there is a great deal of confusion over names and dates and there are many fascinating theories about his true identity. It is even possible that one of the mummies found in Tomb KV55 was Smenkhkare, but this is open to debate.

There is no evidence that there was really a love triangle – that Smenkhkare and Nefertiti fell in love and plotted to poison Akhenaten and then ran away to Nubia. That part of the story is entirely my invention. But it does seem that Nefertiti mysteriously disappeared from all the records after about the twelfth year of Akhenaten's reign, and her tomb has never been found. Kaha's story is just one possible version of what might have happened to her. You never know – it could just be true!

All the other Ancient Egyptian characters in *The Phoenix Code* are fictional. As far as I know, there was no young priest called Rahotep, but I found out as much as I could about the life of a priest at the time to describe his duties at Karnak (and the exploits of the other fictional priests, such as Hori). Kaha, the old scorpion charmer, is also a made-up character, but the job of 'scorpion charmer' was a real one.

Karnak Temple Complex in Luxor is also a real place. You can visit and see the magnificent Hypostyle Hall, with the number of massive columns arranged just as Ryan describes. However, although there is at least one star-covered ceiling in the sanctuary, I invented the detail about the stars being in the same configuration as the columns in the hall, and about Thoth pointing an ankh at the third star in the third row.

Some of the Ancient Egyptian texts I refer to are real ones, including the *Book of the Dead*, the *Book of Amduat* and the *Instructions of Amenemope*. However, the other documents – most importantly, the Smenkhkare Confession, the Heliopolis Papyrus, the Bennu Bundle, the Scorpion Papyrus and the verse on the ankh that provides the key to the Phoenix Code – are all entirely fictional.

The information I have given about the nature of hieroglyphs is based on fact. They could be written in either direction and the convention was to start reading from the end that the characters are looking towards. In reality, Rahotep is more likely to have used the simpler 'hieratic' writing rather than hieroglyphs for everyday writing, but I decided to stick to hieroglyphs throughout to avoid confusion between the two systems. It is also true that the Ancient Egyptians used the sections of the *wedjat* eye design to represent fractions, in just the way that Cleo describes when she and Ryan are opening the door to Nefertiti's tomb.

Now for the most important question of all! Is the Benben Stone real? The story that it was a mound of rock that emerged from the primordial ocean is genuinely part of an Ancient Egyptian creation myth. It is also believed that the Benben was housed in the Temple of the Sun in Heliopolis (a real city which was destroyed in ancient times and now lies beneath a suburb of Cairo). No one knows what happened to the original Benben (if it really existed), but it is true that throughout history people have claimed that it has untold powers of all kinds and have searched for it in vain.

The story of the Bennu Bird swooping down to land on the Benben, with a cry of what would be and what would not be, comes from the same creation myth. In the fifth century BC the Greek historian, Herodotus, wrote about the Sun Temple at Heliopolis, describing how the Bennu Bird returned there every five hundred years with the body of its parent in a lump of myrrh. This gave rise to the Greek myth of the phoenix which was reborn from ashes.

The modern-day village of Gezira really does exist, on the west bank of the Nile, and you can take a ferry or motor launch across the Nile to Luxor, just as Cleo and Ryan do. Sadly, however, you won't find the El-Masry Café or the Golden Nile Hotel in Gezira (at least, not as far as I know), as I invented them for the book. However, you might come across other cafés called El-Masry in Egypt, as El-Masry means Egyptian!

The Theban Museum is also my invention, although it is inspired by the Luxor Museum which can be found near Karnak. However, the Mummification Museum that Alex Shawcross is so keen to visit is real and is in Luxor.

the
orion star